Praise for
The Magnolia Sisters

"A feel-good summer novel."   —BuzzFeed

The Magnolia Sisters

The Magnolia Sisters

ALYS MURRAY

FOREVER

New York   Boston

Forever
Hachette Book Group
1290 Avenue of the Americas, New York, NY 10104
read-forever.com
twitter.com/readforeverpub

Originally published in 2020 by Bookouture in London, England
First U.S. Edition: February 2022

Forever is an imprint of Grand Central Publishing. The Forever name and
logo are trademarks of Hachette Book Group, Inc.

The publisher is not responsible for websites (or their content)
that are not owned by the publisher.

Library of Congress Cataloging-in-Publication Data

Names: Murray, Alys, author.
Title: The Magnolia sisters / Alys Murray.
Description: First U.S. edition. | New York : Forever, 2022. |
    Originally published in 2020 by Bookouture in London, England.
Identifiers: LCCN 2021041289 | ISBN 9781538708415 (trade paperback)
    Subjects: LCSH: Sisters—Fiction. | Floriculture—Fiction. |
    LCGFT: Romance fiction. | Domestic fiction. | Novels.
Classification: LCC PS3613.U7567 M34 2022 | DDC 813/.6—dc23
LC record available at https://lccn.loc.gov/2021041289

ISBN: 9781538708415 (trade paperback)

Printed in the United States of America

LSC-C

Printing 1, 2021

To Elizabeth, Nia, and Lila.
My Sisters.

I tried to write something about how brilliant, how funny, how loving, how smart, how kind, how endearing, how clever, how creative, how warm, how passionate, how ambitious, how funny, how compassionate, how brave, and how loving you all are.
What came out was this series of books.

I can only hope I have done justice to three
of the world's most special people.

The Magnolia Sisters

Chapter One

Harper Anderson had one boot halfway on her foot and one exhausted eye on the peonies struggling to flower along the south bend of her family's property when her mother stormed into the kitchen from the sunroom, screaming with every step her slippered feet took across the hardwood floors.

"Family meeting! We are having a family meeting! Kitchen table! Two minutes!"

Muffled groans responded, but no one dared dispute her. Even Harper, whose alarm *somehow* kept getting snoozed, and whose to-do list ran longer than the Colorado River, slipped her boots back off—no muddy soles in the house—and joined the rest of the Anderson clan at the long-running dining table covered in twine, order invoices and water bills. Her mother fretted in the kitchen, practically falling over herself as she fumbled with the temperamental old coffee maker in the corner.

"What's going on?" Harper asked, as she leaned into her older sister, Rose, who'd wisely taken the farthest seat away from their mother's usual place at the head of the table.

"No idea," Rose muttered over the lid of her chipped mug, steam fogging up the teal cat-eye spectacles that perfectly complemented her loose red locks.

Joining them at the farthest end of the dining room with a *plop*, the youngest Anderson sister—May—leaned forward on her elbows, waving her eyebrows with a salacious flair.

"I've got a clue."

"What?"

"She just got off the phone with Elaine Bates."

"That's not a clue. That's a fact."

Today was Tuesday, and on Tuesdays their mother took her coffee into the sunroom and hung on to her telephone as if it were a lifeline instead of a landline. Instead of making calls like the *grande dame* she considered herself to be, Mrs. Annemarie Anderson, her short brown hair still in rollers, collected gossip from her friends in the comfort of her pajamas for hours, before emerging at lunchtime with a week's worth of news to share with the family. The family, of course, usually knew the news before she did—after all, May and Rose worked the family's shops in town and Harper and her father spent their days working with men and women *from* town—but they humored her anyway. The short, impossibly thin woman loved nothing more than sharing what she'd learned with her less-than-rapt daughters.

Today, though, was different. Gossip hour usually didn't end until well into the afternoon, and it never resulted in her calling a family meeting, despite the fact that there wasn't a human on planet Earth who called family meetings for less frivolous things. (Just last week, she'd called one to vote on whether the pictures she'd taken of a stray cat were cute enough to post on the company's Instagram page.) But while she hummed idly to herself and helped herself to a kiss on her husband's forehead as she made her way to her usual seat, something told Harper they weren't in for a repeat of the same.

"Good morning, girls." A small, nervous chorus of "*Morning, Ma*" from the assemblage of sisters answered her chipper greeting. She turned her gaze to her husband. "Good morning, Curtis."

Their father, for his part, didn't bother looking up from his copy of *The Hillsboro Gazette*.

"Morning, dear."

Below the table, Harper bounced her leg up and down in a twitching rhythm as she leaned forward and held her breath for the announcement. Unfortunately, for all of her rush and fuss, her mother didn't share her impatience. Shoulders curling up around her ears as she lifted her mug to her lips, she drank in a torturously long sip of her coffee before setting the drink down and folding her hands around the warm exterior.

"So, girls, did you sleep well?"

Harper's leg moved so fast she was sure it looked no more than a frustrated blur to the outside observer. "Mom!"

"What?"

"Family meeting. You rushed us all down here and now—"

"Who raised this impatient child?" She had the audacity to smirk as she brought her coffee cup back up for another sip. "I know I didn't."

Heat tugged at the skin beneath her collar and she bit down hard on her lower lip. In a month, she'd turn twenty-six. Maybe she wasn't financially solvent enough to move to an apartment of her own in town (but neither were May or Rose, as that was one of the pitfalls of working in a family business), but that did *not* mean she was a child. From her place across the table, Rose offered a fleeting smile of solidarity and a *you-know-how-she-can-be* shrug before picking up her peanut buttered toast. A flash of envy struck at Harper's spine. If there was one virtue her sister had that she did not possess, it was patience.

But there were thousands of flowers to be tended along the south ridge and her chores weren't going to do themselves. At worst, Rose and May would be ten minutes late to open stores no tourist wandered into until noon anyway.

"I had the most miserable night of sleep. Did I wake any of you up? I just kept tossing and turning and—"

"Ma," Rose said, perfect patience running out even as her voice ran cool as a September creek. "May and I have to get to work. Is something wrong?"

The soothing tones of the favorite child worked their magic. Harper bit back a flare of jealousy as their mother smiled and nodded, leaning into the table to deliver her news.

"I've just heard from Elaine Bates, we've got some new folks moving into town."

"Oh?" Rose asked, a tiny inward twitch of her eyebrow the only hint of her disappointment at this "breaking" news.

"Looks like Tom Riley is going to have some new company at that Barn Door Winery of his."

At this, everyone leaned in except for May, who buried her head in the discarded financials section of her father's paper. Harper didn't blame her. Back when they were in high school and had their heads full of world-traveling daydreams, Tom and May had everyone guessing they would run away together, a prediction that proved foolish on the night of their high school graduation, when May returned from the after-party in tears and refused to come out of her room for days. Even now, six years later, she'd never told anyone what caused the sudden breakup. All they knew was she had been single ever since, and refused to drink red wine.

Harper's mom continued with barely a break, "Well, he's getting married. And you'll never believe it, the girl's a big-time city slicker from Los Angeles and her brother owns some company down there, some tech firm or venture capitalist thing or something. Anyway, they're *moving here* until the wedding."

"What?"

"You'll never believe this."

Not if Elaine Bates told it to you.

"But apparently, she came here on a girls' weekend over Christmas, met him on a wine tasting tour, and they just fell *madly* in love. That love-at-first-sight you only see in the movies. That sort of sweeping love that—"

"That makes you marry someone when you've only known them for four months?"

December to April. Four months. Harper had a hard enough time imagining herself getting married *ever*, much less to someone she'd only known—long-distance, no less—for a few months. Scanning the faces of her siblings, she tried to get a read on them. Did they think this was even half as ridiculous as she did? Rose sipped her coffee while May's hands tightened desperately around her fork, clenching it like a weapon.

"Will you stop being so cynical? She's been coming down here *every weekend* to see him. That's real love if you ask me. Anyway, Elaine said that she told him she couldn't bear to be apart from him for another day, so she and her brother have rented out the Elsbury Estate until the wedding."

A million questions popped into her head, questions like: *How does Elaine Bates know the details of this apparently private conversation* and *Why are you telling us any of this*, but the one question that *didn't* pop into her head was the one May asked.

"And when's that going to be?"

Unable to help herself, Harper chuckled. If these people were as rich and powerful as the gossips claimed, they weren't going to be anywhere near the venue. "Why? It's not like we'll be invited."

"You don't know that."

The muttered reply knocked sense back into Harper's thick skull. Of course she was curious about the wedding. Her high school love was the groom. A moment of tense silence followed, only to be broken by Rose's desperate optimism.

"It would be nice to do the arrangements for a big wedding."

"Exactly." Ma nodded knowingly, beaming around the table. "Lots of money to be made on an internet star's wedding."

"What is she? Insta-famous?" May asked, a painful pull in her teasing tone.

Ma snapped her fingers. "*Insta-famous*. That's what Elaine was saying. I couldn't for the life of me understand what—"

A dark misery ashened May's cheeks. Harper swooped in to save her from any more of their mother's fawning.

"So, we're going to try and get a big floral contract. Great. Can we go now?"

The woman either didn't hear her or didn't care to. Instead, she barreled forward with breathless glee. "And the man's handsome.

And young. And single. Her older brother, I mean. Apparently, he went to Religious last night and dropped almost a thousand dollars on dinner, and that was *before* a tip."

The conflation of looks and wealth broke whatever control she had over her snark.

"I'm sure his wallet makes him look *very* handsome." Pushing away from the table, Harper moved towards the doorway and her sturdy work boots. Today, she'd be grateful for the simple pleasure of the outdoors. Out there, she didn't have to listen to mothers extolling the virtues of rich men. Out in the fields upon fields of flowers, nothing disturbed her but the conversations between the winds and the birds. Desperation pulled her towards the freedom. "Now, I've got chores to do—"

"I just worry about you girls." An exasperated sigh forced its way up her throat, but she pushed it back. Ma often went into these moods, these half-joking but more than half-serious lectures about her *poor daughters* and their distinct lack of lives outside of their work. Usually, it happened when one of them wore too-loose jeans into town or refused her pleas for them to join dating apps. Today, it was over a very real man none of them had even met. "Cooped up in this house all the time. You never go out. You never see anyone." By *anyone*, she meant *any one man*, but Harper decided not to interrupt the sermon. She usually ran out of steam faster when she was allowed to wear herself out. "I just worry. I want you girls to be happy."

"We are happy, Ma." Reaching for the coverall she'd draped over her chair, she tossed her mother a reassuring glance. Just because the woman tugged at her nerves didn't mean she wanted her to suffer.

"Don't worry. If I see the rich man, I'll go right up to him and ask if he and his wallet will take me out on a date."

"Harper Anderson! I don't know what I'm going to do with you."

She turned to her husband, still hidden behind the newspaper, and pressed him to help her, but Harper tuned the conversation out, turning instead to her sisters with a glance at the ever-quickening hands of her wristwatch. If there was ever a time their mother was going to let them escape, it was now.

"Rose, May, are you going to open the stores today?"

"Yeah. We'd better get going. Love you guys!" Rose practically bolted for the old wooden farmhouse door with May quick at her heels as they slipped into their shoes, collected keys and raincoats, and struggled to make it out of the door fast enough. "See you at supper!"

None of them waited for a reply to their farewells before shutting the house door behind them and walking away from the cozy warmth of home and down the steep driveway towards the ancient Jeep waiting patiently for them like an old, reliable hunting dog. It was spring in Northern California, but no one had told the weather yet. Though the sun blazed in a clear, blue sky over the rolling fields of blooming flowers that was the Anderson family's way of life, the wind occasionally sliced through them with the sharp edge of a wicked cold snap. Not that Harper cared. There may have been heat in the house, but her mother and her mother's opinion about her daughters' lack of romantic interests were *also* in the house. She'd take the company of the flowers and a cold wind over that any day.

"Harper."

Rose's voice, now stern and maternal out of the presence of Ma, cut through Harper like a pair of freshly sharpened shearing scissors.

"What?"

"It's okay to let her have a little bit of fun. You know she gets excited. It wouldn't kill you to humor her a bit."

"She shouldn't get excited over some rich jerks who're going to throw their money around town and look down on us poor country cousins."

The deepest part of her knew her sister was right, as she usually was. The oh-so-perfect Rose knew and saw their mother's excitement as harmless fun, a release for a woman who spent her days counting flowers and keeping perfect accounting logs. Where Harper saw a woman's desperation to control her daughters' lives, Rose saw a woman who truly wanted to see her precious children loved by good, honest, and true men. She wanted them to be happy.

The problem was Harper *also* wanted to be happy. She also wanted to be loved. But small-town living meant she knew every eligible person from the time they were children. Now, at almost twenty-six, she hadn't fallen in love with any of them. With every passing day, love became a more and more remote possibility, a hope she couldn't afford to pin her heart on. She hadn't sworn off of love or anything, but she'd long ago become pretty comfortable with the prospect that she would be a happy old maid, surrounded by a sea of flowers and friends, growing into her gray hair and comfortable walking shoes with dignity. She wouldn't let her mother tempt her into silly daydreams and delusions of grandeur when she could have a practical, joyful life on her own.

"You don't even know these people," Rose tutted.

"No, but I know their type."

"The type who could save the farm with internet fame and a big fat check for some flowers."

"Yeah, but they're also the same rich jerks who overran the town square with so many of their high-end shabby-chic condos and San Francisco high-concept restaurants that we can barely afford our storefronts there."

As they arrived at the Jeep, a ringing silence followed and Harper knew her blow struck true. In the last few years, tourists from across California and the Pacific Northwest had turned their once sleepy wine-and-flower town into a weekend escape for big-city dwellers desperate for a piece of the country. The new business meant they could raise the prices on the flowers they grew on the farm and the bouquets Rose created at her store and the perfumes, soaps, and candy May crafted at hers. But it also meant they *had* to raise prices. If they didn't, they'd be bankrupt tomorrow.

Ever the peacemaker, Rose shrugged into the silence and did her best to defuse the tension tightening the air.

"I'm just saying we don't know them. And we should reserve judgment until we do. We're all pretty good judges of character."

May kicked a pebble. "Not me, apparently."

"Oh...I didn't even think..." *You idiot, Harper. How on earth did you not ask her how she's doing?* The obvious answer was that Ma drove her to the edges of her patience and clouded her best judgment, but the true answer was that perhaps she didn't want to know. Her youngest sister was a tightly kept secret of a woman. To see her heartbreak at learning her once-love was getting married was too much. "Are you okay?"

"Yeah. Whatever." Slinging the Jeep's door back, May helped herself to the passenger seat, plucking the keys from behind the rearview mirror to turn the radio on. "We need to get going."

The two elder sisters shared an uneasy look, but when neither of them could figure out what to say, they silently and mutually agreed to wait until May opened up to them. Prying at her wouldn't do them any favors.

"See you both. Have a good day at work," she said, patting Rose on the shoulder. A slender smile stretched across her face as she slipped into the driver's seat and waved goodbye.

"See you. And don't scare off any magnates while we're gone!"

With that, the Jeep peeled off in a cloud of dust, leaving Harper alone. Alone with her flowers and her wide-open sky. Just the way she liked it.

Chapter Two

Luke Martin loved his sister. He adored her. He relished her friend-ship. He relied on her counsel. He appreciated her insights. But there was something about his beloved sister that bothered him. Well, two things.

One, he didn't care for her taste in men. And two—

"Stop here. Stop the car right now!"

He found her impulsive. And this entire exercise with their sudden upheaval to this provincial wine town only proved it more and more with each passing day. When Annie first told him about her intentions to run away with this *Tom Riley* character, he'd scoffed and asked her if April Fool's had come early this year. But when he caught her with a suitcase and their mother's wedding veil waiting at a Los Angeles bus stop one random night in March—a stunt for attention, of course, considering she had her own car—he decided intervention was necessary.

He was *sure* acceptance would suffocate the flame of love between her and this winemaker. *Sure, let's decamp to a town in the middle of nowhere, where we, the two heads of a data compression company, barely have internet or phone access. Sure, you can marry the man. In fact, let's go live close to him and see how much you* really *like each other when you're not sneaking around all the time. Sure, if you want a wedding so badly, why don't you let me help you plan the wedding?* He thought sunlight would be the disinfectant that killed this silly love affair.

That theory had not proven itself out. And in the wake of the fallout, he resigned himself to her happiness. If she thought this quiet, smiley winemaker would make her happy, he'd have to suck it up and help make this the most beautiful wedding wine country ever saw.

That didn't mean he had to like it though. Or the whiplash the sudden demand to stop the car as they were driving back from lunch caused.

"What? What's wrong?" he asked, checking her for injuries or the lost look of a woman who realized she was making a mistake by marrying a veritable stranger. He found neither. Instead, he found a pair of wide, awed blue eyes gazing up at something he couldn't quite see through the slanted front of his slick black Italian car.

"We *have* to go up there."

"Go up where?"

A small hand slapped his shoulder, dragging him down until he looked up under the lip of the windshield in the same direction as she was. And he had to admit . . . the slack-jawed expression on his sister's face—the one that looked as if she'd caught sight of a passing angel—was completely warranted. Because there, just beyond a crooked fence of wires and single wooden posts, was a sea—no, an ocean . . . no, a sky of flowers, streaming up the side of a hill straight up into the heavens. Like the painting of an old master of Impressionism, the rich petals and stems of the flowers mixed and swirled together until their texture—so far away from him—felt so real and tangible that just the slightest outreach of his hand would let him touch the softness of their petals. And the colors. They were like none he'd ever seen, a hypnotizing array of pinks and oranges, in too many varying shades to count or name. Even now, inside of his car, parked on the opposite side of the road, the perfume of the flowers reached him, a dizzying cocktail of sweets and spices that conjured up memories of his mother's shampoo and her favorite candle, memories of a childhood he thought he'd long forgotten.

"Luke? Luke? Earth to Luke?"

He snapped out of his reverie to see his sister with one leg out of the car and her oversized sunglasses settled firmly on the bridge of her nose.

"Huh?"

"Are you coming?"

"Coming where?"

She pointed just a bit further down the road, where a dirt path cut through the fence line. A rickety wooden sign that read—in an unpracticed, unprofessional hand—"Full Bloom Farms." For the life of him, Luke couldn't quite figure out why she'd want to hike all the way up that hill to see some flowers clearly visible from the comfort of their car. Neither of them were *hiking* or *walking* people. They were Angelinos. If car rides weren't involved, they weren't interested.

If she wanted flowers, there were florists in town. Or they could order flowers to their house online. Or any number of secretaries and personal assistants could make sure she had more flowers than she knew what to do with. A skeptical glance between the curving arc of the farm and his sister's excited smile forced a nod out of him.

"Okay, if you want. But let's drive. That hill looks pretty steep."

Steep was an understatement. For all of the suped-up gadgets and gizmos in his car, the poor thing barely made it up the practically sheer side of the hill. As Luke finally drew the brakes on a flat plateau between the road and the large wood and stone homestead a little farther afield, he made a mental note to have a few serious words with his mechanic. Superior engineering his foot.

"What are we doing here?" he finally asked, turning the ignition before flipping the sun visor back into place.

"I just want to see something. Do you think we should go up to the house or is there an office?"

An answer to her question came quicker than either of them anticipated.

"Can I help you?"

There, at the small patch of land where the road met the fields of blooms stretching out into the distance, from behind a curtain of tall flowers, emerged a woman. Luke had absolutely no idea how to name the flowers she stood beside, given that they weren't roses or tulips, but they had bold, blossoming petals of pink and white that brushed the woman's cheeks as she appeared in the view of his spotless windshield. Beautiful as they were, though, in all of their fragile strength as they held their own against the chilled wind and the warm sun, it wasn't the flowers that held his interest.

It was her. His entire world focused in that moment onto the sight of the woman who, with all the grace of a conjured spirit, parted the wall of color to greet them. She was tall. He noticed that first. Taller than the arcing stalks crawling towards the sun and certainly taller than any woman he'd ever dated before. But her long, strong limbs were clothed in a rugged marriage of denim and work-fabric. Loose pockets exploded with rags and shears, stray leaves and water bottles, while her hand, stained by green plant filament and soil, stretched out in something of a greeting. Her body was curvy and alluring, reminding him of the carved marble goddesses of bounty he'd seen in museums. With her eyes squinted towards the sun, he couldn't exactly make out her expression or their color, but her wide stance told him she wasn't to be messed with. Brown locks tumbled out of a messy half-bun, but the disarray didn't make her any less beautiful. If anything, she was perfect in imperfection.

He was entranced. And he wasn't sure he'd ever been entranced before. The unfamiliar sensation tightened his throat and straightened his shoulders. Nervous energy tensed his every muscle. Thankfully, his sister spoke first, opening her car door to call to the one-woman welcome party.

"Hi, there!"

For his part, Luke made no movement to get out of the car. He took pride in his body, stretching it to its limits every morning at six a.m., but all of that careful training amounted to nothing when he stared at the woman through his windshield. And anyway, what would even happen if he moved? Would he speak to her? What would they have to say to one another? Would he manage to speak at all? At the moment, he could barely so much as twitch an eyelid. Speech seemed impossible.

In general, he wasn't a people person. He let his sister do the outreach and hobnobbing for their business ventures. Since childhood, he often worried about what people thought about him. Fear about how others saw him tied him in knots he found too difficult to untangle. Beautiful women only made it worse.

"Are you lost?" the figure called, moving from the edge of the shoulder-high flowers towards the dirt road that swirled through the center of the expansive fields. Now that he was in the midst of it, a brief glance around of him awarded him a better understanding of his surroundings. Unlike the view from the road, which showed the hill as one, sweeping homogeneous space, he now saw the farm as just that: a farm. Above them, a series of farmhouses, each bedecked with kitschy charms like tin can chimes and white steps covered in muddy boot prints, lined the rim of the hill. The fields of flowers populating this farm grew neatly in plots as far as the eye could see, divided by green thoroughfares trod down almost to the dirt by working feet. Out in the distance, sky-sweeping green fir trees struggled to contain everything, like the walls of an overflowing bathtub.

It was like standing in the rough draft of a colorful Impressionist painting. Beautiful. Consuming. Dizzying.

"Not at all. We saw your flowers from the road and I just knew we had to stop. My name's Annie. Annie Martin."

His sister extended a perfect, manicured hand out towards the stranger, who stared at it for a moment, her eyes flickering between the painted nails and the car behind. Try as he might and though she no longer squinted, Luke still couldn't get a read on her. She guarded her expression carefully, even as she wiped her hand on her dungarees and shook a greeting.

"Nice to meet you."

"And your name?"

Another pause. Hesitation. Her chin furrowed as she withdrew her hand and shoved it in her pocket defensively.

"Harper Anderson."

Harper Anderson. The name repeated itself in his brain like an unfamiliar but catchy refrain, one that repeated through the silence. An awkward, unspoken tension pervaded the air, cutting even through the steel of his car. *Oh*, he thought, *she doesn't want us here.* Which naturally begged the question: *Why?* And: *How can I make sure Annie doesn't annoy her and burn the goodwill this town has towards us?* As good as she was with people, her enthusiasm sometimes ran away with her and trampled everyone in her path.

"So..." Annie rocked back on her hips, a sure sign she felt that same awkward weight of Harper's stare. "Nice place you have here."

"Ma'am." A polite strain flickered in Harper's tone. "Is there something I can help you with? If you're looking for flowers, I'm sorry, but we don't sell them here. You can go down into town and get some from our—"

"Oh, no! No, no, no! I mean, I'll want some flowers eventually, but I've just gotten engaged."

A diamond big enough to crush a medium-sized bird flashed as Annie waved her hand. If this Harper Anderson was impressed, she didn't show it. If anything, her smile thinned.

"Congratulations."

"Thank you! You know, you would not believe how hard it has been finding a venue. I've had the worst time with it. But I just think this will be perfect."

"What?"

"*What?*"

The mention of a wedding venue shocked motion back into his body, beautiful woman be damned, and before he knew it, he was out of the car and standing near his sister, creating the final point of this triangle. Despite his thundering voice, Annie beamed, glancing back and forth between them for introductions. Introductions Luke didn't care to make.

"Harper, this is my brother, Luke. Luke, this is—"

He placed a hand on his sister's shoulder, guiding her away from this discussion. "Would you excuse us for a second?"

"Sure." Harper shrugged, nonplussed. The move tossed her hair into a beam of sunlight and even though he knew he needed to focus on his sister's tendency towards impulsiveness, at the moment he couldn't prevent the squeeze of his stomach at the stray sight of beauty. He pulled his sister away to stop himself from gawking at Harper's looks. As he spun on her, he channeled his anger, funneling it straight at her impulsive skull.

"What on earth are you doing? I thought we agreed you'd get married at the vineyard?"

"Oh, the stupid vineyard where there aren't any grapes? Hm? It'll be late summer. Everything is harvested. How will the pictures look then?" She turned down the sass, took a deep breath, and gazed at the beauty all around her. Even the most ignorant of men could see how much she was captured by the place. "Please, Luke?"

Another plan changed. Another hundred emails he'd have to send to the caterer and the photographer and the calligrapher writing out the invitations. His jaw clenched, but no matter how hard he tried to fight it, he knew that if she wanted this, he'd move heaven and earth to make it happen for her. "Do you really want this?"

"Yes." She broke into a face-breaking smile. The blue from a nearby patch of flowers swam in the blue of her eyes. "It's gorgeous. Just look at it."

But when Luke's eyes scanned the horizon and they latched onto the only other human being in sight, he knew he wasn't just talking about the flowers. "Yeah. I guess it is."

They returned to the bargaining conversation, but somewhere during their departure, the frosty woman in the oversized dungarees had bent over a large plant and took out a pair of shears. She tugged and grunted at something; to Luke's untrained eye, she seemed to be pulling out weeds, though he couldn't be certain.

"Sorry about that." Annie flashed one of her winning *everything-is-fine-don't-pay-attention-to-my-brother's-inability-to-smile-just-focus-on-my-perfect-white-teeth* smiles and clapped her hands together the way she did when rallying her friends to put their drink orders in before the end of happy hour. "Anyway, is there somewhere we can sit down and discuss something? An office or a place like that?"

"I'm sorry," Harper muttered into the ground, her ungloved hands tearing at a knot of roots poking out of the earth. She blew a stray strand of hair from her face. "I really need to get back to work. If you need directions into town, there's a map at the bottom of Runner's Mountain. Just take this—"

"Of course! You're busy! I'm so sorry. Now, do you have the number of your events coordinator?"

"Events coordinator?"

"For the wedding. I'd love to have the ceremony just there on the hill in the middle of the blooms."

As understanding dawned, the guarded eyes of the farmhand dropped their shields. All at once, a negotiation of politeness turned into a thinly veiled warning, one his sister blatantly ignored. After joining the ranks of Los Angeles elites, his sister had a habit of driving forward with a smile as she plowed over any obstacles in her path. Like a slightly shady car salesman, she knew exactly how to answer every protestation until she got precisely what she wanted. Unfortunately, it seemed she had found her match in this Harper Anderson, and Luke had to grudgingly admire her for it.

"We don't have weddings here, ma'am."

"First time for everything."

"No, I'm not sure you understand."

"I understand it'll be different, yes—"

"We don't have events here. This is a working farm."

"Which is exactly what I want! A working farm is perfect for—"

"We can't cut harvest short for—"

"And we're willing to pay anything you'll ask for. Think of the fortune we'll spend on bouquets!"

"Ma'am!" For the first time, perhaps in his life, someone snapped his sister into silence. Her harsh tone, combined with a single, halting hand motion and a sternly furrowed brow, knocked Annie back a step. He would have been more impressed if his brotherly instincts hadn't kicked in. "We don't do weddings. At any price."

"But—"

This time, Harper didn't even offer a dismissive glance. She turned back to her flowers, sending them away with her refusal to pay attention. "I'm sorry but I'm going to have to ask you to leave."

A knot curled the center of Luke's stomach as he spotted the defeat in his sister's eyes—a look he didn't see in them often. He'd sworn he would give her the wedding of her dreams. And he wouldn't let some proud small-town lady farmer keep him from that promise, no matter how beautiful she was.

Clearing his throat, he sent up a quick prayer that his words wouldn't fail him. And, if they did, that his checkbook would make up for it. "Ma'am?"

"Yes?" she asked tersely, picking up a basket of some sort and resting it on her hip, preparing herself to return to the busy fields in the distance.

"Can we have a moment?"

"My answer won't change."

"Just a moment?"

As if to signal *your loss,* she gave a shrug of indifferent shoulders and waited for him to catch up. "Fine."

Determination pushed him forward and drew his lips into a tight line as he muttered to his sister.

"Wait for me in the car."

"Luke—"

"I'll be back in a second."

With nothing more to say to her, he followed the marching Harper into the rows upon rows of upward-reaching buds. He could only imagine how this field would look when they finally opened up and spread out into the sun.

"Harper—"

She halted in step and turned to him, a nonviolent action that still somehow yanked at his vocal cords. Her eyes were green, he noticed.

The traitor muscle in his chest tightened at the realization, giving power to the conflict raging in the back of his mind: How could he want to ask this woman on a million dates when he also thought she was being selfish and stubborn, just like all of the other small-town folk he'd met since arriving? In a rushing hurry, Luke scribbled his signature on a check and thrust it at her, fighting the urge to look her in the eye again.

"Here."

"What's this?"

"It's a check." When she didn't show any signs of recognition and made no move to take the piece of paper from his outstretched hand, he shook it and reiterated: "A blank check."

"Yeah, I have eyes." Eyes which she then brazenly rolled at him. "But I've already told you—"

"Write a number. Any number and it's yours. I'm sure you could use it at a place like this."

Before the sentence was even out of his mouth, he knew it was the wrong thing to say. Her slouched, earthy exterior shot up into tightly coiled walls of muscle as she straightened defensively against the slight. Or, rather, the perceived slight. He didn't see any harm in talking business with a fellow business person.

"Excuse me?"

"Listen," he said, trying to level with her. "I understand how businesses like this work."

"Oh, you do, do you?"

An eyebrow raised in a challenge. Her arms dropped the basket and folded across her chest. Dropping his voice to a more conspiratorial mutter, he tried to get her to see this for what it was: a bargain between two like-minded people of business.

"You don't have to be proud. Just let my sister have the location and the money is all yours."

He couldn't see the harm in it. After all, if she was as worried about the harvest as she said she was, she could just write herself a check for the summer's worth of work and call it a day. An entire year's worth of cash for one day's work. There were no downsides as he saw it, and when she rubbed her eyes and released a lengthy sigh, he assumed triumphantly that they saw eye to eye.

"Do you have a pen?" Harper asked sweetly.

"Here."

Carefully, he avoided her fingers to keep them from brushing his as he withdrew the pen from his breast pocket and offered it to her. For a brief moment, she teetered in the mud as she struggled to prop one leg up as a desk for her check-writing. She needn't have bothered with the charade. When he saw the single large zero she was adding to the "payment of" line, he knew he'd been fooled. Then, with a rough crumple, she threw the ball of paper right at his face.

"You wouldn't know what this business is like if it knocked you over the head, you L.A. jerk. Now, will you get off my property before I call Officer Peters."

And then, she was gone. Like a punch in a bar fight or a car wreck, one minute she was there, colliding with him and leaving him breathless, and the next, it was all over, and he was watching her get smaller and smaller in the distance. When he returned to the car, the humiliation didn't end.

"That looks like it went well." Annie's voice was brimming with suppressed humor.

Harper's words rang in his head. *You wouldn't know what this business is like if it knocked you over the head, you L.A. jerk.* His very being bristled at the accusation that he was nothing more than his car and his address, his nice jeans and sunglasses. A plan, the outline of one, but a plan nonetheless, formed in his mind.

"Don't worry, Annie. I'll take care of it."

Hours later, he found himself alone in his office, thinking about the woman at the farm. Harper Anderson. Every time his mind wandered to her sparkling green eyes or the way long tendrils of her brown hair would escape from her bun or the curves his hands itched to touch, he tried to remind himself that she was the enemy. She was a distraction standing in the way of what he wanted, and, in business, there could be no distractions.

Desperate to shake her from his thoughts, he picked up the phone and dialed his business manager. A moment later, the familiar voice of his aging advisor picked up.

"Mulvey and Associates. This is Seth speaking."

"Seth, it's Luke. There's a farm out here I want you to take a look at."

"Financials?"

Luke considered the question for a moment. If he was going to convince Harper Anderson to give him what he wanted, that was a battle he'd want to go into with a full arsenal.

"Everything."

Chapter Three

By the next morning, Harper's rage hadn't subsided. Every time she'd thought she'd put Luke Martin and his arrogant assumptions away for good—after all, when was she *ever* going to see him again?—a new wave of frustration welled up in her as a hundred new arguments against him formulated in her mind. She played out their encounter over and over again, re-imagining ways to utterly destroy him with words, to lay him as low as he seemed to think she was. The gentler parts of her conscience—parts that sounded remarkably like her oldest sister—reminded her it wasn't sensible to hate someone after having a single conversation with them. But the memory of the way he oh-so-casually handed her a blank check, as if money were the only important thing to a poor provincial like her, burned her from the inside out. Even if she never saw him again, something she hoped for with all of her might, she suspected she'd still hate him.

Sure, he was handsome. Like, undercover James Bond handsome. He was dressed totally impractically for the country in that infuriatingly bougie suit, but he was handsome. And that was the thing that bothered her. Every time she thought she'd shoved him out of her mind, her hormones resurrected him, inspecting every memory of his sweeping dark hair and his mysterious brown eyes, his tall, imposing form and his chin carved out of stone.

So, by the time Harper sat down to family breakfast that morning, she was thoroughly annoyed and not in any kind of mood to entertain foolishness. Especially not her mother's.

"Harper, darling, do you need to borrow any concealer?"

That was her mother's brutally unsubtle way of suggesting she hadn't gotten enough sleep last night, and it was enough to make Harper regret coming to breakfast at all. A morning of work on an empty stomach was better than suffering this.

"No, thanks, Mom."

"Are you sure? You're looking a little worse for wear this morning."

Over her plate of eggs, she shot Rose a pleading look. When their mother got into one of these moods, there was rarely any stopping them; the best anyone could do was provide a distraction.

Thankfully, Rose took pity on her. "Mom, I was thinking about heading to Windsor to do some clothes shopping this weekend. Do you want to come?"

"I do. I want to come." May joined in the game, as she always did. Riling up their mother was one of her favorite pastimes. "Maybe you could help me find something for the festival?"

"The festival's two months away."

"Yeah, and if we wait, everything good will be gone."

"Well, when you put it that way—"

That was all the cover Harper needed. Saying a silent prayer of thanks for good sisters as her mother's attention turned to her two precious daughters, she crept to the door, slipping outside with her boots in hand before anyone had any bright ideas about her joining them on this little shopping excursion. Out in the distance, the sun was just rising up over the rim of the hill, flooding the fields with silent, golden light, a welcome reprieve from the crowded, loud kitchen table inside.

She loved her mother. Really, she did. Her mother was a good woman who'd loved her husband and kept their business afloat while raising three daughters, who all were pretty fantastic, if Harper did say so herself. Despite droughts and poor crops, she'd always balanced the books so her entire family was clothed and fed and, when they were old enough, the proud owners of a stocked wine cellar. But no matter how much love and respect she carried for the woman, Harper always felt that she stood in this nagging shadow, one that cast a dark shade over their relationship. She'd never be good enough for her mom. Or, at least, it felt that way. Harper couldn't count the times she'd bemoaned her dateless daughters and then, as if by coincidence, suggested they go on a family diet or ever-so-subtly fawned over a wedding invitation for someone they knew in town. Whenever she pulled a stunt like that, Harper repeated the refrain that carried her through years of dateless proms and lonely Saturday nights: *She just wants us to be happy. She just wants us to be happy.* After all, her marriage made them extremely happy. Why wouldn't she want her daughters to feel the same happiness she'd enjoyed for years?

But just because she understood it didn't mean she liked it. Or wanted it, for that matter. There were other ways to be happy. She didn't need love to give her joy. Even if sometimes attending weddings they'd provided flowers for made her chest ache with a longing she could never quite name or fully shake.

Harper looked out onto the fields, where the flowers were rising up to greet the sun. Irrational jealousy filled her as their petals whispered sweet scents in her direction. Their colors were so vibrant, their purpose and their place so clear. She could only wish that someday, someone could see her in the same way she saw those flowers.

No, she thought, leaning against the house to slide into her sturdy, work-worn boots, there was no use entertaining her mother or her whims for her life, even if meant being a perpetual disappointment. Better to escape into her work, bear the shame, and let her tire herself out on her sisters. She could be content with this life of hers. She didn't need to be a beautiful flower. She already had her hands full making a whole field of them grow.

"Morning, Harper."

"Morning, Joe."

Joe, the slouch-shouldered man who'd worked on the farm as long as she'd been alive, greeted her with his usual gruff grimace firmly in place, his brown skin catching the warm glow of the morning sun. He approached Harper where she was walking along the path to the potting shed to the left of the main farmhouse at a quick pace, his head bent at a concerned tilt that sent immediate warning flags up in the back of her mind.

"Everything alright?" she probed, hesitant.

"Well, it was until Stella stole the new guy's lunch."

That was all? Stealing sandwiches was one of Stella's many hobbies. Her lips tugged at the ends, but she bit down to hide her amusement. Joe didn't seem like he was in the mood for her to laugh. When that didn't work, she turned away from him, out towards the wilder corners of the property.

"...that dog," she managed, before shouting to the distance. "Stella! Stella!"

She never had to call the fluffy, white Maremma more than twice. No matter where she was on the property, Stella heard her voice and came running as if she was the starting gun for a dog race. Sure enough, no sooner had she gotten the final syllable out than a flash of white fur sprang out from behind a distant line of trees in the west, disturbing pine needles and grass until she stood at the ready in front of Harper, panting all the way.

But one look up in Joe's direction was all it took for the proud pup to lay low, pressing her belly into the stone patio beneath her and her head onto massive paws.

"Stella," Harper growled, finding it difficult to put on a show for Joe when all she wanted to do was rub the dog behind the ears and feed her out of her own lunch pail. "What did you do?"

The Maremma didn't answer. After all, she wasn't a Disney character. But she didn't have to answer. Because a heaving-chested, huffing and puffing, red-faced figure staggered up the hill in the large dog's footsteps.

"*He-stole-my-lunch.*"

Even bent over to pull a barb out of Stella's soft ears, she stiffened. That voice. It had played in her memory, in last night's dreams, all night until it wrote itself into her very muscle memory. She prayed she was wrong. Hoped for it. And yet, she knew she wasn't, and a brief glance in the voice's direction confirmed the dread boiling in her stomach.

Luke. Luke Martin. Her enemy. The guy who she'd assumed she'd never see again.

"What are you doing here?"

"That dog's a menace!"

He took a step closer to her, but Harper knew something Luke didn't. In the absence of a herd—she was a sheepdog, after all—Stella had adopted the family as her own. And instinct took over any time she felt her family was threatened. Once, she'd almost lost an eye trying to defend Rose against a particularly nasty snake slithering near the truck. Another time, she'd slept at the foot of May's bed—something she *never* did, as the position by the house's front door was much better, defensively speaking—when she had contracted pneumonia. And now, that one step Luke took towards Harper was enough to spur her into action. She popped up from the patio floor and set herself in a defensive crouch between them, a fearsome growl rumbling in her chest.

Joe took that as his cue to leave, while Luke sprang backward. Harper tried to control her smirk. Yesterday, he'd been so high and mighty, but now, she had control. And a guard dog.

"See! He's a menace!"

"You're afraid of a little puppy like Stella? She's harmless."

"Puppy?" Luke choked, incredulous eyes widening. She hadn't noticed yesterday that the brown had flecks of green within them. She tried not to notice now. "A horse puppy, maybe. That thing almost took my hand off!"

In all of his flailing, he'd stepped forward again, earning him a fierce warning bark. Again, he stumbled back.

This time, Harper didn't hide her laughter, but she did grab Stella by the back of her bright red collar, too. The last thing she needed was a wrongful injury suit from a rich L.A. jerk.

"Took your hand off?"

"Your dog came up behind me and snapped!"

"I'm sure she was just trying to play with you."

Playfully maul you, maybe. Not that I'd object.

"Well, I don't like her kind of playing."

"She just doesn't like intruders, that's all."

"I'm not an intruder."

He blinked, his words blunt and dull, but just sharp enough to cut through her fog. Joe said Stella stole a worker's sandwich. Luke claimed he wasn't an intruder. And, since she'd seen him last, he'd exchanged his suit for a pair of jeans and a too-tailored plaid shirt. A pair of boots, without a scuff or sign of wear on them, replaced his mirror-shine wingtips. Everything about him was too put together, as if Armani or Prada or a high-end perfume line hired him for a farmhand-themed spread in *GQ*. But he still looked like he was at least trying to fit in here.

And she did not want him to.

"What do you mean, you're not an intruder? I remember telling you to get lost."

"If I keep my hand, I'm going to be working here for a while."

Oh, no. No, no, no. It had to be a joke. A joke, so she laughed. After all, if she showed up at one of his fancy Los Angeles parties in her Walmart best, he'd laugh in her face, too.

"Work *here?*" she asked, incredulous. The image was too hilarious. She'd had seasoned workers quit and return to comparatively easier jobs on vineyards after a week working on the farm. He had no chance.

"What's so funny about that?"

But he wasn't joking. Or, if he was, he had an incredible poker face. As he lorded over her, Harper was suddenly aware of just how big he was. He dominated her field of vision, obscuring from her the sight of her beloved flowers in the distance. She hated what his great, imposing presence represented almost as much as she hated the way her body reacted to him.

"You're serious?" she asked.

"Yes. I'm working here. I started this morning."

"No, you're not."

"I don't really think it's up to you."

Her stomach churned. There was only one person on the entire farm who could make hiring decisions over her head.

"My father hired you?"

"He told me you'd enjoy a new hand."

"I'm going to talk to him."

"What? Don't leave me here with that thing."

She wasn't leaving Stella near him because he'd be leaving soon, but she obliged his fear anyway.

"Stella." She snapped her fingers and Stella came to heel. "Come."

And just like that, she left him behind, strutting around past the main house and higher and higher up the hill. Years ago, her father built himself an office on the highest point of their property, all the better to look out over the fields. It made for a beautiful view out from over his desk, but the steep incline was always a struggle. Now, though, she relished the effort. With every step, she could imagine she was pushing out a little bit of her rage and confusion. Her *father* hired that infuriating man? Even after she *told him* yesterday how rude he'd been? And he had sympathized!

Okay. Okay. You can fix this. She'd produced a full crop during a drought and saved seedlings from wildfires. Once she'd run a pack of wolves off of the land with nothing but Stella and a flashlight. Getting rid of one out-of-towner who didn't belong here in the first place wouldn't be so hard, right? Her father was many things. Eccentric. Devoted to his work. But he wasn't unreasonable.

She walked through the open door of his office without knocking or announcing herself.

"Dad, I—"

"So, you've met our new hand, then."

Her father was a stately gentleman, but he'd been aged by the sun and a lifetime of manual labor and worrying about things out of his control, like rain and sunshine. Though he stood at a tall six-foot-four, he relaxed deep into his chair, his salt and pepper hair leaning well below the headrest of his chair. Sitting at his desk, he faced away from her, but she spotted his smile in the reflection of a family picture on his desk. A mischievous smile was his face's most constant companion, but today, it ignited a new heat wave of rage.

"You *hired* him? What in the world are you thinking?"

"I'm thinking I like him."

She scoffed, "You don't like him."

"Harper, I've been me for forty-seven years. I think I know when I like a guy."

"You once told me you didn't like Bear Grylls because he seemed phony." She crossed to the window, forcing him to look up at her, not bothering to lower her voice even though the open screen door meant just about anyone could hear her. "How can you look at *that*," she pointed further down the hill at the employee in question, who was currently engaged in a struggle to bend over and pick up a bale of hay for the barn because his jeans were too tight to allow him any freedom of movement. "And like it?"

It. That. How easy it was to hate him when she thought of him as a dangerous object instead of a person. Definitely easier to think that way than acknowledge how the ripple in his exposed forearms hinted at a strength that made her heart flutter. Oblivious to her silent struggle—or maybe just amused by it, she could never tell, that man's face was perfect for poker—her father shrugged.

"He's working for free. I'm still a businessman, aren't I? If he washes out, then I still got a day of labor for free."

"Well, if you're not paying him, there's no paperwork. It'll be easy to fire him. Now."

For the first time since she walked in, her father betrayed surprise.

"Fire him?"

"I don't know why you're doing this, but it's been very funny and now it's time to go back to work." When her father glanced up at her with blank eyes, the air caught in her chest. He had no intention of firing Luke or listening to her advice. "You don't think I'm going to keep *that* on my staff, do you?"

He nodded, once, and went back to flipping through the *Home and Garden* magazine splayed out on his desk.

"It'll be good for you."

"You're kidding me."

"A good test of your managerial skills."

No, a good test of her managerial skills was when she kept the growers from going on strike by lowering her own salary to give them a better wage. A good test of her managerial skills was when she hired a Spanish tutor so she could help her staff file for health insurance. Turning a lazy, know-nothing city drone into a good farmhand was not a good test. It was a waste of her time.

"We're about to come up on harvest season. I can't have any dead weight."

"Harper, who's the head of this company?"

A groan practically begged to rumble to the surface, but she swallowed it. According to her parents, presumption was her greatest flaw. Because she'd been in the family business since she was fourteen (first as her father's occasional assistant, then as a delivery driver, then as an assistant foreman before finally rising to her current position three years ago when her father entered pseudo-retirement after a fall from a horse that ruined his back and hobbled his walk for good), she sometimes carried herself like she owned the place. And, as her father never tired of reminding her whenever they disagreed, the loans and the mortgages were in his name. Her head dropped as defeat sunk heavily beneath her skin.

"You, of course, but—"

"Work with him. You might learn something. Besides, Mateo quit yesterday. He's moved down to San Jose to live with that girlfriend of his. We need a replacement and the good news is, we got one."

He gave no room for debate or argument.

"Fine."

As with her mother, just because she understood it didn't mean she had to like it. Or accept it. With every angry step back towards her blooms and the struggling man waiting for her—to gloat, no doubt—a plan formulated in her head. He couldn't be fired. Fine. She'd just have to make him quit.

The prospect of running him out of the place was so sweet, she almost managed to smile.

Chapter Four

He'd only been here five hours and already he was ninety-eight percent sure he hated her.

"Put your back into it, Martin!"

Nope. Ninety-nine percent. The only thing keeping it from one hundred was the way the warm—too warm—afternoon sun hit the amused light in her eyes, but as soon as the sun ducked behind the clouds, it would be over for any flicker of affection he still held for her.

Well, that wasn't entirely honest, was it? Those green eyes of hers were important, sure, but there was something undeniably alluring about her curves. He did his best not to stare—she didn't give him much time to take in her looks, what with the back-breaking labor and all—but he couldn't help but be slightly entranced by the way her hips moved when she marched up the hill or her gloved hand rested on the grabbable dip of her waist whenever she gave him an order.

From the moment she emerged from her father's office at the top of the hill, those piercing eyes were full of steely determination: determination to see him run away from this place. She'd first started him on weeding, where he walked through the rows and rows of fields one by one and tugged the offensive bulbs out by hand. Even with the gloves Joe offered him, some of the barbs cut through the thinning material straight to his palms almost as painfully as the effort of bending over time and time again cut through his spine. Then, when he'd gotten almost halfway done with that task, Harper pulled him into the barn, where they were now carrying fertilizer from one end to the other, though for what purpose, he couldn't begin to guess. To her credit, Harper didn't assign him a day of back-breaking labor just to sit up in a tree somewhere and eat an apple as she watched him suffer, as he'd half expected her to. Instead, when she threw him a pitchfork, she picked up one of her own and joined him in the task. Despite how much his body hated her for what she was putting him through, he couldn't deny the well of respect he felt for her.

"You should be able to carry twice what you're carrying. Lift with your knees!"

He could tell every single command and word was meant to push him away, but he wouldn't give in, no matter how many taunts and menial tasks she threw his way. She thought he was a stuck-up pretty boy who couldn't stand the sight of dirt under his fingernails? He'd show her just how tough he could be.

At least, that's what he had told himself. Before he'd actually had to bend over flowers and carry fertilizer bags for an entire morning. When he approached her father last night, it all seemed so simple. Put in a few hours of manual labor, earn her respect, and before either of them knew it, she'd offer Annie the farm for her wedding and everything would be resolved. Annie would have her dream wedding and soon, he'd return to the city with nothing but pretty pictures to remember this place.

But now that he was actually *executing* his perfect plan, he realized there *might* have been some *slight* flaws. He made a mental note to kill his trainer back in L.A. The man swore that his diet regime and exercise regimen of throwing around tires and ropes would make him strong as an actor in one of those superhero movies, but clearly he'd been lying. He doubted Harper went to interval training four times a week, but she was running circles around him, moving effortlessly from task to task without so much as breaking a sweat.

Harper Anderson. She'd been a constant figure in his thoughts since yesterday, an inescapable presence who had invaded and taken up space in his mind without an invitation. She was as much of a contradiction as he'd ever seen: utterly beautiful and utterly infuriating. A threat to his pride that he couldn't stop thinking about. He wanted to ask her a million questions, to better understand her, but at the same time, he wanted to forget ever having met her. She'd insulted him and tried to crush him with work, yet his mind kept forming the words *would you join me for dinner* over and over again, a reality that annoyed him no end.

"Did you hear me? Put your back into it!"

Knocked out of his daydreaming, Luke glanced over at his companion in the flesh. Much to his dismay, despite the ache already accumulating in his joints, his muscles followed her command, scooping up a bag onto each of his shoulders.

"Yes, ma'am."

The *only* good part about renewing his efforts with a smile was the sight of her disappointment. Every time she issued a new order, he tried to oblige as gleefully as possible, just to see the space between her eyebrows furrow in apparent confusion that he didn't throw his tools down and storm away in a huff.

It would have been cute if his aching body didn't hate her.

"So," he began, struggling to keep his voice light and breezy when all he wanted to do was groan from the repeated effort of moving fifty-pound bags of fertilizer from one end of the barn to the other. If he wanted her to like him enough to give him the farm for a day, then working in stony silence wouldn't be to his advantage. He needed to befriend her, even if doing so meant glancing more often than necessary in her direction or getting tongue-tied all over again. "Do you like working here?"

No sooner were the words out of his mouth than he internally cringed at them. It was times like these he thanked heaven for Annie. When she was around, he never had to make small talk or open his awkward mouth. Focusing intently on the task at hand, he bit back a groan. He didn't need to look at her face to confirm she thought he was an idiot.

"Do I like working on a farm when I could be doing literally anything else in the world?" she asked, raising one sardonic eyebrow.

"I just didn't know if you *had* to work here. Family business, and all that." As soon as he got home, he'd invest in one of those two-way spy earpieces, that way Annie could just feed him lines all day. Not even four sentences in and he'd already messed up. His sweaty hands slipped on the slick plastic packaging separating him from the fertilizer. "I mean, your family is obviously important to you."

"My family is everything, but that's not why I do this job."

"Why, then?"

There was no way he'd tell her he found this work absolutely miserable, that he couldn't imagine ever doing something like this when his idea of roughing it in the office was when the coffee maker was on the fritz. His stupid mouth may have made *some* mistakes, but he wouldn't give her any more reason to think he was the human embodiment of everything she so clearly hated.

"I do this job because I love it."

"Why *do* you do all of this, anyway? I wouldn't love hauling fifty-pound bags around all day. Surely there's got to be some machine that could move these or pull up the weeds."

Finally, she graced him with a smile, but it wasn't the smile he'd been wondering if he would ever see. Far from genuine, this was a bitter smile, like she'd taken a sip of terrible coffee but had to tell the barista it was the best cup she'd ever tasted.

"There he is."

"What do you mean?"

"All morning, I've been wondering where the lazy tech genius went, but you've just been hiding him."

Genius? She thought he was a genius? No, he couldn't harp on that now. He'd lose himself if he thought about the compliment over the insult. *Lazy.* He'd built a company from scratch and given his sister a better life and she had the audacity to call him *lazy*? Muscles burning, his efforts at hauling doubled.

"I'm not lazy—"

"For your information," she cut him off, her own efforts at her work quickening to meet his, as if they were in silent competition, as if she couldn't bear to be outdone by someone she hated as much as she apparently hated him. "We do things the old-fashioned way here because sometimes the old-fashioned ways are the best."

In his opinion, old-fashioned was best for roadside diners and movies with lots of kissing in them, not for a business. Purposefully choosing to deal with heavy lifting by hand instead of letting a machine do the work seemed unbelievable to him when in his world apps did everything for him from ordering dinner to scheduling dentists' appointments. He shrugged, unconvinced.

"You're the expert."

With an almost lazy, flippant shake of her arms, she dropped the last of her fertilizer bags on the barn house floor, the rattling sound disturbing an owl hiding up in the loft. "Follow me."

"But I'm not done—"

"Just come on."

She didn't seem angry, but something in the tightness of her shoulders, the way they crept up towards her ears, told him she was desperate to keep him from creeping under her skin, a novel idea considering she currently held all of the power. As he set aside his work and followed her as she walked towards the closed barn doors, he couldn't decide if he liked that little insight. Getting under her skin was appealing in a revenge-for-the-manual-labor way, but not nearly as appealing as seeing what she would look like if she smiled at him. After half a day under her scowls and verbal jabs, he craved something nice from her. Anything. A kind word or secret curve of her lips would have been enough. He tried to tell himself it was because he wasn't used to not being liked. Most everyone he knew either liked him or were indifferent to him, usually thanks to his money or Annie's interference. But he knew a lie when he heard it, even when it was a lie he told himself.

The creaking, slightly rusted barn doors slid open, flooding the darkened space with golden light. One thing he'd be sure to put in his online reviews after this trip ended was the strange quality of light in Hillsboro. When it wasn't raining, the sun always shone with the rich luster of precious stones at the bottom of a shallow creek, the sort of treasure a miner in 1849 would have killed for. The sun cast their shadows long behind them, not that Luke paid them much attention. Harper had his full, undivided attention.

"What do you see?" she asked, her long, slightly dirty fingers grazing the horizon.

"Is this a trick question?"

"Tell me. What do you see?"

"It's flowers," he answered, praying that was the right answer. "Lots and lots of flowers."

In his line of sight also stood some trees and horse pastures, a few trucks for the workers and, of course, Stella eating potato chips out of someone's lunch bag, but he figured he'd just start with the basics.

Arms crossing over her chest, uncaring of the mud she was tracking across the blue denim button-up carelessly thrown over a white T-shirt, she leaned back against the barn door and took in her kingdom. Not prone to hyperbole, Luke decided kingdom was the only word for it. He'd never seen a woman look more like a queen than she did just then, hair dirty and unraveling from her braid, face and hands tracked with mud, eyes flickering with passion. And, for once, she didn't train the passion on him. She reserved it for the blooms before her.

"Flowers are one of the oldest, simplest pleasures. People have been giving each other flowers as gifts and signs of affection for thousands upon thousands of years. It's an ancient pastime, a tradition we've kept going through wars and famines and droughts and…" A distant smile tugged at her lips and an almost dreamlike quality took hold of her eyes. For a brief, fantastic moment, it was as if she'd forgotten he was there or that they were enemies. "There isn't enough happiness in this world, but these flowers… they can make people happy, can make them feel loved or respected or seen just by the very virtue of existing. We…"

She trailed off, as if she remembered she wasn't talking to just *anyone*, but someone she saw as an enemy. He considered dropping it, letting it go, but like a story that got good just before bedtime, he needed to hear the end.

"You what?"

The pose she held—of her arms crossed and her back against the wall—no longer held any power. She went defensive, her arms now hugging herself instead of defiant. "We do things the old-fashioned way around here because that's the best way we know how to keep that tradition alive. And if it means picking weeds and hauling fertilizer with our own hands, then so be it. And if you don't like it, then I guess you'll just have to quit."

Maybe she'd never smile at him, but he couldn't hold to the same rules. Not when the sunlight illuminated the lighter flecks in her eyes. And not when she'd gone from defender of her lands and her ways to haughty challenger in a fraction of a second.

"I think manual labor is growing on me, actually."

"I'll wear you down eventually," she said, a tiny lilt in her voice the only hint she found his quip amusing.

"I don't doubt it."

You already are. For as much as she hated him, insulted him, worked him like a dog, he couldn't hold the same feelings for her. Sure, her refusal to let them rent the farm annoyed him, but he'd spent the better half of the night before replaying the moment he first saw her. The thrill of that moment combined with the respect she'd earned today was enough to at least temper his hatred for her. It wasn't gone, not by any stretch, but there was at least something a little sweet and cool lingering in with the intense, fiery burning that captured him whenever she glanced in his direction. She must have felt his stare, because she turned away from him, returning to her work with little more than a shrug of her shoulders.

"Break time's over. Let's get back to work."

The command was enough for him. But ten minutes of silent work later, he couldn't help but speak again.

"What's on the docket for the rest of the day?"

Shoving glass under my fingernails? Plucking out my eyelashes? Forcing me to listen to "Never Gonna Give You Up" on repeat until sunset?

"I was thinking I'd give you something easier for the rest of the afternoon, actually. You've been working pretty hard this morning," she said with grudging respect.

His ears perked up. *Easier* wasn't quite as good as *easy*, but it was a start. A start towards something. Maybe something like respect. Had he really managed to wear her down that fast? Pride ballooned in his chest.

"Great. What do you want me to do?"

"Catch Bermondsey and bring her home."

"Who?"

"Bermondsey. She's our cat. She's a mouser, but we need to bring her in and get some flea treatment and shots."

He could have cried with relief. Last year he'd run a marathon that zigzagged up and down the Marin County hills. Catching a cat would be a piece of cake. And maybe he'd finally earn that elusive Harper Anderson smile.

Catch a cat, you said, it'll be fun, you said.

Famous last words. Time on the flower farm was dictated by the sun and its position over the growing petals, and if the darkness surrounding him was any indication, work had been officially finished over an hour ago.

But he wasn't going to be bested by an orange furball.

He'd been tracking the creature for hours now and had only caught glimpses of it through the trees, but he was *certain* he'd find it eventually. He had to. He couldn't fail. Not when she must have put this task in front of him because she *knew* he'd fail.

"Here, Bermondsey . . . here, kitty, kitty, kitty . . ."

A little voice in the back of his head said it was pointless. Stupid, even. He should just quit now and forget the whole thing. But then, he spotted her. There, in a patch of darkly shadowed greenery near the fence, the little fuzzball nestled itself in the light of a moonbeam.

"Gotcha," he muttered.

He'd gotten her cornered. Cornered! The corner of the fence created two walls of a triangle and his body created the third. A sort of giddy energy, propelled by the physical exhaustion coursing through his body from a day of back-breaking labor, no doubt, coursed through him. His mind conjured images of Harper's beautiful face lighting up in surprise as he handed the cat over to her. Would she say thank you? Would *this* earn her respect, the one task she didn't believe anyone could finish?

Alright. Slowly. Slowly. Moving forward inch-by-inch, he leaned into the cat, ready to trap it in the warmth of his arms. *Easy. Easy. Easy.* With its eyes closed in sleep, it couldn't see him until it was too late. His fingers buried themselves in the scruff of her neck and he pulled her into the warm embrace of his arms. Triumph warmed his blood. He'd done it. He'd actually done it!

And then, the scratching started. Claws sunk into his skin, somehow ripping through his long sleeves. For such a small animal, it rebelled energetically against his strong grip, swiping at everything its little paws could reach. But Luke held fast. No way would he let this animal run off after he'd been chasing it all afternoon. Every step from the farm's northernmost point offered him new tortures from the small animal, until about halfway home, when the poor thing tuckered itself out, giving up the fight, a fact for which Luke was eternally grateful. He could have cried when he finally saw the warm lights of the Anderson house, a sign he was almost home. Just a few more minutes and formalities—he would be gracious in his triumph—and he'd be in his car, on the way to his house for a bath and a beer and a couple of hours of sleep before turning around and doing it all over again tomorrow.

His pulse, which had relaxed with the cat in his arms, suddenly quickened when he realized the front porch wasn't empty. Teacup balanced in one hand and book open on the arm of the white porch swing upon which she curled up, Harper waited for him. Or, maybe she wasn't waiting for him, because when he cracked a branch a few yards away on his path towards her, her head snapped up, eyes widening in shock.

"You...you actually did it."

"What? You didn't expect me to?"

"She's just..."

Oh. This all made sense now. She'd sent him on an impossible mission to torture him. After he'd spied a little bit of her true self this morning, she'd done all of this to push him away, to force him to quit. He wasn't supposed to find the cat at all; it was a fool's errand. He felt the earlier softening of his feelings slipping away and in that moment he hated her with every fiber of his being.

All of the commotion woke Bermondsey, because she wriggled in his arms until Harper finally reached out to take custody of the fearsome animal. Luke tried his luck, pushing his supposed ignorance a little further than he probably should have.

"Because I'm sure you'd never give someone a task they had no hope of completing just to see them suffer, right?"

Guilt whitened Harper's face; not even the orange glow of the porch lights could save her complexion. It gave her away.

"Thank you for bringing her home," she almost whispered, moving towards the door in an apparent retreat.

"You know, I'm not so bad," he called after her, the terse anger in his voice stopping her before she could disappear entirely.

"If Bermondsey likes you, you must be alright."

The words were so quiet, he could have easily been convinced he'd made them up in his head.

Chapter Five

"And *then* he just shows up at the house and hands her to me like it's no big deal! I've *never* seen someone just carry Bermondsey up like that! I've still got scars from the first time I ever tried to pick her up!"

"Mm-hm."

Rose didn't look up from her knitting as she hummed an acknowledgment, not that Harper expected her to. In the five long days since their dad hired Luke, she must have heard this story at least half a dozen times, one for each member of their family *and* several of the people who worked the land with them. Harper had even recounted the story to Nayeli, the woman who'd delivered pizzas to their house since they were twelve years old. By now, Rose could probably recite the story herself. But that didn't stop Harper from repeating it. Every time she opened her mouth it was like she couldn't stop the stories and thoughts she had to keep bottled up, work day after infuriating work day, from tumbling out, snowballing until they consumed her. Even now, as she was juggling a bucket full of candy and the nail polish she was attempting to paint onto her toes, he was at the forefront of her thoughts.

Stupid, arrogant, sexy Luke Martin.

"And *then*," Harper chewed the words through a handful of jelly beans, a staple at their sister movie nights, "I didn't even tell you what he did today—!"

"Stop it!"

"May!" Rose shouted, mouth agape at the interruption of the rant.

"This is ridiculous! You work with him all day and then you come home and complain about him all night! I'm sick of it! If I have to hear about how he managed to figure out how to get through the deer fence without cutting himself one more time, I swear I'm walking out of this house and never coming back!"

"Wow. Sorry for telling you how I feel."

"You can tell us how you feel without knocking us over the head with it!"

"You guys are my friends. You're who I tell about this kind of stuff."

"Right. And as a *friend*, I'm telling you that it's absolutely ridiculous to talk about how much you hate a guy *nonstop*. If you really hated him, you'd work with him all day and then forget about him at night. This is *your* time. If you didn't *want* to be thinking about him, you wouldn't be."

Jelly beans long forgotten, Harper slackened the tight muscles in her jaw. Tension drained from her face. May couldn't possibly be implying what she *thought* she was implying.

"What are you saying?"

"I'm saying that you like him."

"Oh, *please*."

With a roll of her eyes, Harper turned her attention out towards the great window overlooking the fields. Moonlight caught the soft droplets of water upon a sea of petals and stems, giving the great field an otherworldly glow. If only she could be as soft and content as her beautiful flowers. Flowers didn't worry about what her sisters thought. Flowers didn't have to deal with hired hands who'd never worked a day's manual labor in their lives. Flowers didn't have to deal with a strange cocktail of feelings about a rude man and his rock-hard abs.

"I've seen him walking around here. You like him, but you *hate* that you like him. You just can't stand it, so you're trying to run him off before you can feel something for real. Not that I blame you, because he *is* the worst, but I'm sick of hearing about it."

"That's..."

True? Well, it's possibly true. Harper didn't finish the sentence aloud, but that's how she finished it in her head, all of her pent-up anger deflating. Warmth rose in her cheeks as she felt the weight of her sisters' collective stare upon her, waiting for her to defend herself, to deny it.

Her gut said *yes*. But her pride wanted to deny it. *Was* she starting to warm up to him? Was it even possible?

"He's the worst. He insulted me the first time we met. I could never feel anything for him," she finally replied, though she kept her eyes firmly trained on her drying red toenails instead of meeting either of their gazes.

"Hatred is a feeling," May countered.

Smart aleck.

"I could never feel anything like you're suggesting. That's what I mean."

"...I don't know about that."

It was Rose who spoke this time, her voice thoughtful and careful as it always was. How had *both* of her sisters decided to conspire against and gang up on her?

"What do you mean, you don't know?"

"It just seems to me that you're harboring something very strong for him. There's no denying that."

"Exactly."

"But I think time will tell if that feeling is hatred or—" Harper shot her a death glare that stopped that sentence in its track. The mere hint of Luke and *liking him* in the same thought was enough to bring her to the edge of barfing. Rose caught herself, smoothing a strand of hair back behind her ear with a shrug. "Something else."

"Great. So you both think I am a big puppy with a crush who's projecting my fears about romance onto a total stranger."

"I didn't say that," Rose corrected with a grin. "Only that you *might* be."

"Alright, geniuses. What do you want me to do, then?"

Rose spoke again, splaying her hands out as she made her dry pitch. "You could just try being nice to him."

"He wasn't nice to me!"

"Yeah, but if you're always yelling at him, you're never going to know how you really feel. Have the two of you had a real conversation since that first day on the farm?"

Sort of. In her stories about the last week, she'd neglected to mention the small talk they'd made while working together. No one needed to know that the way he looked at her made her feel as if no one had ever seen her before. No one needed to see her shiver, like she did every time she replayed the memory of his handsome half-smile in her mind.

"Not really, no."

"That's your problem, then. You can't tell how you feel because you don't *let* yourself feel."

"Exactly." May nodded. "I mean, she's not giving the advice I would give, but she is right."

"What advice would you give, then?"

"I don't know." May folded her arms tightly against her chest and slumped down deeper into the couch. "Shoot him into space? At least then I wouldn't have to hear about him anymore."

One of the problems with being a sister was that living with someone their entire life meant you had a stockpile of ammunition against them. More often than not this proved useful, for example when she could tell their boyfriends embarrassing stories about times they puked at state fairs or Rose's disastrous seventh birthday party. Any time she got in trouble, she could pull out a story about something bad Rose or May had done just to keep her parents' anger from focusing squarely on her. The stories and secrets that they knew as sisters helped them all through life, not just in those silly ways, but in knowing that they weren't alone, that they had a lifetime of shared experiences and stories to commiserate and laugh over.

But now, that knowledge was a boot upon her throat, pressing down until she almost choked. Every part of her wanted to make some snappy retort about how May looked ready to cry every time someone mentioned the name *Tom Riley*, and yet she didn't seem ready to face her own feelings about that. Harper bit her tongue before she could hurt anyone.

"Why don't you just try to be..." Rose trailed off, a sure sign she was trying to find some way of putting her thoughts nicely. "A *little* kinder to him? Not even for a whole day, if you don't want to. Just one nice thing and see how it makes you feel."

"Just one thing?"

"Yeah. And if it makes you miserable, then you don't have to ever talk to him again. Work him to the bone and complain about him whenever you want. Just please...not to May."

Harper didn't ask what she should do if she found out she *didn't* hate him. Frankly, she didn't want to know.

After their movie night, Harper decided she did *not* need to be watching any more romcoms. Every time the handsome leading man delivered a quip, Luke's face flashed in her mind, adding more credence to her sisters' theories about her *feelings*. Even worse, after their movie night, she couldn't stop thinking about what they'd said. They couldn't be right, of course. He'd done nothing but insult her and invade her life without her permission, hovering around like an annoyingly buzzing fly; even if she didn't hate him—which she was pretty sure she did—there certainly weren't any feelings of warmth or affection there, like they said.

And to prove it, she resolved to follow their advice. Just one day of being nice to him. Putting in one work day of kindness wouldn't kill her, and when it was all over, she could gloat that she'd been right all along and then her sisters would *have* to listen to her complaining about his presence. A foolproof plan.

Or, so she thought. After going easy on him all day—giving him light shifts, jobs in the shade, easier assignments—she'd noticed his car was still parked at the bottom of the hill, so she went off in search to remind him that they didn't really work this late. She'd even tucked his time card into her back pocket so she could sign it and send him to her father's office to turn it in, something she never would have done without the constant refrain of *be nice* in the back of her head. In fact, on the first day he'd shown up to work, she'd hidden the time card in a tree and it took him three days to find it, so as far as she was concerned, actually bringing it to him was as kind a move as any.

But when Harper peered into the barn, where Luke had been cleaning and dividing dahlia tubers for the better part of the afternoon, she stopped short. Technically, she was spying on him, but she preferred the word *observing*. Yeah, she was just observing.

Observing the way his hair fell in choppy waves across his forehead. The way the strong muscles in his jaw tightened. The way his shirt rode slightly up as he worked, revealing a muscled torso beneath.

Harper bit her lip. This was the problem with growing up in a small town. If you aren't paired off by the time you're grown up, you'll swoon at the sight of any halfway decent man who rolls into the city limits. It had nothing to do with *who* the man was. At least, that's what she told herself. The truth about the way she followed a single drop of sweat as it disappeared down his chest…that was more complicated.

Judging by the piles of work done around him, and the buckets of tubers filled to the brim, Luke must have finished recently. He carried himself in a way she'd never seen before, a way he'd never allowed her to see him. His shoulders slumped. His chin dipped. His eyes opened and closed at a weary pace. Meandering from his post, he leaned against the nearest stall door before sliding down it. From her current distance, she couldn't be sure if the collapse was a conscious choice or a failure of his knees. For a moment, he just sat there, staring at the ceiling and breathing in the spore-filled air.

He looked so tired. And she'd pushed him there.

But her pride bristled at any mental suggestion that he hadn't deserved it. He'd barged into her life and insulted her and tried to throw his weight around because she was some stupid hick and he was a big shot. She'd been right to take a few small vengeances where she could...right?

All of the armor she'd built around herself where he was concerned, though, cracked down the middle when he moved to take off his boots and socks. Of course, she'd noticed their newness on the first day. They hadn't been broken in and she had the sneaking suspicion he'd bought them that morning. The idea he'd get blisters from walking around in them all day had actually brought her pleasure that first day and fanned her hopes that a little discomfort would see him quit.

She'd been right. He *had* gotten blisters. But she didn't get any pleasure from seeing them. Luke's feet were a mess of painful-looking wounds, each of them caused by the too-tight, too-new boots.

"Hey!"

Calling out to him surprised even her, and she'd been the one to do it. He glanced up at her, chest pumping in shock. In a mad scramble, he tried to leap to his feet, but the pain locked him down on the ground.

"No you don't," she warned, closing the gap between them with a few long strides of her own well-worn boots, slamming her foot on top of one of his shoes before he could reach for them. Her stomach turned when she realized even his socks were sticky with blood.

"I was just napping on the job."

In any other scenario, she might have laughed at the obvious lie, but today, she wasn't in the mood. She settled for rolling her eyes.

"Don't lie to me. Your feet are a mess. You can't work like this." The closet in the barn didn't have much by way of footwear, but there were some plastic clogs for rainy days somewhere. She dug around until she found them and tossed them in his direction. "Here."

He sniffed. "What are those?"

"Some temporary shoes until I can get you a pair of boots someone's actually worn in. You can't keep wearing those, you'll get an infection or something. Put these on."

Despite the fact they both knew she was right, he had the audacity to look affronted at the bright green plastic clogs—an ugly relic of the mid 2000s her mother had tossed out for barn shoes when she realized how hideous they were—but it all melted away when he slipped them on and the insulted glare turned into relief.

"Better?"

"I don't know," he muttered, clearly not ready to thank her yet. Of all the things he'd done over the course of their acquaintance, this, she actually understood. She'd intruded on a private, vulnerable moment for him. Had the roles been reversed, she wouldn't want to thank him either, even if he was trying to help. "I haven't tried walking in them yet."

"Why don't you try them out?"

"I was just going to sit here for a little longer, if you don't mind."

"I do mind." An idea popped into her head, which meant she couldn't just leave him here. Shoving her hands into the pockets of her tattered overalls, to keep her tingling fingers from reaching out to him, she waited for him to move. He stared at her warily, a look that would have wounded her coming from anyone else. But coming from him, after the way she'd treated him all week, skepticism made perfect sense. She breathed a laugh, unable to help herself. "C'mon."

After a moment of contemplation, he struggled to stand. Harper hadn't known him long and, to be totally fair, there wasn't much she *wanted* to know about him, but she had to hand it to him. He wasn't the kind who showed weakness. It must have taken a lot of guts to stand up on two busted feet and hobble towards her. Whether his pride was a good thing or a bad thing, she wasn't sure, but it was definitely *some*thing that he let his guard down in front of her. "Where are we going?"

"I know a place."

For the first ten minutes of the painfully slow walk, they moved in silence, guided only by the flashlight on her phone and the light of the full moon bleeding through the woods behind the farmhouse. Having walked this path a million times since she was a kid, Harper could have made it blindfolded and sprinting, but she held back her pace and added the extra light for him. The night air was warm around them as they made the trek, and the carefully cultivated rows of flowers gave way to towering magnolia trees and wildflowers.

"I don't mean to complain, but how much farther? I could have just walked home at this rate."

"It's right around this bend."

"What is?"

Before she could even answer, they broke through the woods and reached their destination, a flowing creek bed bathed in moonlight cut through the center of the woods rimming their property. If you followed the creek down another hundred yards, you'd find the pond where she and her sisters spent so many summers, but this little spot had always been her favorite. Everything was quiet there. Not that the farm was particularly loud, of course, but there were always people, always someone wanting something from her. In a house with two sisters, two ever-snarking parents, a host of workers who looked to her for leadership, scores of buyers constantly calling her and dogs and kittens and horses and chickens always squawking for food and attention, she relished the days when she could dip her toes in the water and soak in the silence.

Over the years of visiting, Harper managed to give the place her own personal flair. Some things, like airtight, bear-proof tins of Girl Scout cookies and waterproof bags full of her favorite books and sunblock tucked into tree openings, were simple, products of lazy Sunday afternoons spent out here snacking and unwinding. Others, like the lighting system she'd rigged into the network of magnolia trees around this bend in the creek and ran on their own generator, were more complex, but no less important. Leaving her guest on the bank, she found the control panel for the lights and turned them on, filling the area with the glow from the tiny lanterns threaded through the branches around them.

"What is this place?"

She tried not to let the quiet appreciation in his voice affect her too much.

"We call it Sae's Place. She was my…" As she returned to his side and situated herself on a rock, she trailed off, counting back on her fingers. "Great-great-grandmother. Apparently she used to come out here and fish."

"Are there any fish in there?"

"Only minnows."

Stiff shoulders and a pair of pursed lips communicated his hesitation without him ever having to say a word. She could almost hear his internal monologue as he wondered if this was a trap or not, some kind of trick that would end with him humiliated and her sides splitting from laughter. In a sign of good faith, she moved down the cool face of her favorite rock and, after tossing aside her shoes and socks, rolled up the frayed legs of her overalls and pressed her bare feet into the water. All around them, the heavy magnolia flowers dipped low on their branches, carrying their sweet scent on the breeze that wrapped its lazy, loose arms around them both. The cool water reflected the lights and the blooms and the stars and the moon back at them until everything was light and beauty.

The tension in her shoulders dissolved almost the second her toes slipped beneath the surface, even though Luke seemed less than sure about all of this.

"Why'd you bring me out here?"

"Well, the real reason we call it that is because Sae had a bum leg from a swimming accident when she was a kid, and everyone said standing here to fish cured her. This water is magical. Legend has it that it can cure anything."

"We have things that can cure anything back home. They're called hospitals."

Nope. Her sisters were wrong. He was a garbage person and she hated him. Smarmy, smug, arrogant—

"Fine. Forget it."

"No. I'm sorry."

Sorry? She couldn't imagine that was true. But when she looked up, she saw something in his face she hadn't ever seen there before: actual regret. He ran a hand through his hair, tugging on the ends uncomfortably. Okay...so, maybe her judgment had been a *tad* hasty. Leaning back against her rock, she let the cool current of the cold rock and the icy water and the cool disappointment in his eye calm her temper.

"I'm not very good at this."

"At what? Talking?"

"Yes."

"Oh."

"Every time I think I'm getting somewhere with you, I say the wrong thing and I mess everything up."

Pressing back the urge to ask him *where* he was trying to get with her, she instead took a moment of the still silence of the woods to examine what he'd just said. In a way, it made sense. Partial sense, at least. When they'd first met, he'd not stammered or stumbled over his words, but he *had* managed to say precisely the wrong things at every turn. Even when they were working together, it only took a handful of syllables muttered from his strong mouth for her to feel thoroughly eviscerated.

"Why don't you let me do the talking, then?" She patted the rock at her side in a gesture similar to one she'd seen her mother do thousands of times when close friends came to call. Besides her sisters, she had no experience with *close friends* but, at least for the moment, she could forget about all of the hatred she'd felt for Luke and instead pretend they were something like friends. This was, after all, only temporary. Once she'd done her good deed, she'd be able to run away and tell her sisters how wrong they were and go back to tormenting him. "Take a seat. Stay awhile."

Maybe it was the warmth she'd injected into her voice or maybe it was that the rocks near the edge of the water were digging uncomfortably into his plastic shoes, but he obliged her, slipping down the boulder she also leaned against until they sat almost close enough to touch on the edge, their feet dangling into the water. Thinking about how close he was—close enough to touch—sent a shiver down her spine, one she hoped he attributed to the water.

She'd always chosen this as her reading rock because she could sit on a smoothed-out lip of the thing and still feel the cool water under her toes. Apparently, Luke also appreciated the sensation.

"Wow."

"What did I tell you?" she teased. "It's like magic."

"It's amazing. What's in it?"

"Nothing. Nothing that I know of, at least. Just cool, natural spring water."

He said nothing in reply at first, but after a moment of disturbing the water with his feet, he muttered, mostly to himself, "I've got to get something like this for my house."

Against her wishes, a tide of sadness broke the shores of her chest. He was sitting right here, right now, with her, and he was already thinking about how he wanted to buy it? She'd resented his blatant consumption earlier, but now...She had to wonder how shallow a life like that was, that he couldn't just sit beside her and enjoy the moment they were sharing.

"Not that I want to encourage you to stay any longer," she started, gentler than she'd ever spoken to him before. "But it's free right here, you know. You don't have to buy it."

"Yeah." He ducked his head. "Of course."

No matter how she tried, she couldn't decide if the silence that stretched between them was awkward or not. Desperate to end the silence, she picked the first topic of conversation she could think of.

"So, I don't know anything about you. Except that you're infuriating," she teased, not quite letting the joke lift her smile beyond a polite quirk of her cheeks.

"I thought you were going to do the talking."

Sure, she'd *said* that, but that was the kind of thing you said because you wanted to make someone feel comfortable, not because you wanted to talk about yourself.

"You don't want to hear about me."

"Yeah. I do."

Her breath caught, but she recovered quickly, splashing up some of the water beneath her toes in an attempt to keep him from so much as looking at her face. With the cold wind, she couldn't tell if she was blushing.

"Really? There's not much to know."

"Just start at the beginning, then."

Maybe all of this was stupid. Maybe she should have left him in the barn and forgotten about her promise to do something nice for him. Maybe she should have run him off of their property the moment she saw him driving up in his battery-powered sports car. But those were just *maybes*, not certainties. And, in that moment, the only certain thing she could hold on to was the knowledge that she couldn't remember the last time someone asked her about herself. No one wanted to know her any deeper than they already did. So, she started talking. She talked about her family's history in the region and how they'd bought the land, about the generations that came before her to build this business, sprinkling a few of her father's funnier anecdotes from before her time. She even told him about her sisters, who he hadn't even met yet.

"...And they used to call us the Magnolia Sisters instead of the Andersons."

"Why'd they call you that?"

"Well, when May was just starting school, she was so scared. She didn't want to go to school and leave home, so Rose and I came out here and picked the magnolias off of the trees up there and gave them to her, so she would feel like she'd brought a little piece of home with her. But, of course, she didn't want us to feel left out, so on the first day of school, we all walked in with flower crowns made out of magnolias."

The nickname had bothered her when she was a kid, but the way that Luke looked at her when she finished that particular story was so warm and kind, she couldn't help but dive into another story. And another. And another.

"They sound nice," he said, when she finished telling him about the year they donated an entire crop of flowers to a nearby high school for their prom, which happened just a week after a terrible wildfire raged through their town.

"They are." She shrugged. "But I guess I'm biased."

"I worry about my sister."

It was the first thing of substance he'd said since she offered to do the talking, and it caught her off guard. During her rambling, she'd not gotten vulnerable. Most of the things she'd told him was the sort of practiced, rehearsed stuff about her family and her home she often gave when they put up their stalls at farmers' markets or town festivals. But this vulnerability...was it a product of his *bad-at-talking* thing?

"I think she's lonely out here."

"She's just got to find her crowd. Hillsboro is full of good people. It shouldn't be too hard."

"Yeah." He looked at her meaningfully, though, for the life of her, she couldn't figure out what meaning he was getting at. The light from her overhead tree lanterns got caught in some branches and cast a shadow over his eyes, leaving her to guess his thoughts. "I guess you're right."

"And what about you? L.A. is a pretty big place. Are you lonely out here?"

Another meaningful look. Another meaning she couldn't decipher. And then, he smiled. The first real smile she'd seen since she met him. And it was beautiful.

"No. I don't think so."

She could only hope he thought her shiver was from the chill in the wind.

Eventually, they made their way back to the bottom of the hill where his car was parked, careful to avoid any parts of the woods that would disturb the fresh, tender wounds on his feet.

"I guess, for liability purposes, I should let you know that that water isn't really magic. You should definitely see a doctor."

He opened his mouth to protest, but she cut him off with a wave of her hand.

"We've done perfectly fine without your help for years, I don't think you missing work tomorrow for a little check-up is going to sink our operation."

"If you say so. And thank you. This was nice."

Before she could make some joke or defuse the tension or curse the warmth his smile kindled within her, he was already in his car, leaving her alone on the long, dirt driveway. All of her sisters' assurances that she'd know where she stood with him once she'd been nice to him were for nothing. She'd been nice to him all evening and yet, there she was, waving at him as he drove away into the night, less sure of her feelings than ever before.

Chapter Six

"Someone got in late last night."

The last thing Luke needed this morning was his sister's sing-song voice prying details from him about his night, but no sooner had he tiptoed into the kitchen than she made her presence known. Their house—a former ranch converted into a stately, modern manor on the outskirts of Hillsboro township—was too big for the two of them. Six bedrooms, seven and a half baths, a tennis court *and* swimming pool should have given them enough space to avoid one another. Considering how much Annie's followers simply adored her constant posting about her retreat from the big city and the plans she had to turn her new house in Hillsboro into a social media-perfect palace, he expected that by now she'd be snapchatting about sunrise yoga in front of the mountains or comparing tile samples for the bathroom renovation she asked him about pursuing, but no. She'd blown off her duties to her followers to berate him about missing his imagined curfew last night.

"Just another long day at work."

"A very, *very* long day. You didn't get home until ten. I was about to call the sheriff on you."

Ignoring the way she delighted in small-town culture like calling the sheriff when someone stayed out past curfew, he padded further into the kitchen and set about putting together some breakfast for himself. Of everything his sister was good at, and there were a lot of things she excelled in, cooking and baking were not her strong suits, so he stayed away from the muffins cooling on the counter and dove straight for the bread and toaster. His phone was a mess of notifications from headquarters back in L.A., but he ignored them all for the moment. Now that he owned his own company, he spent most of his time checking code and glad-handing with investors and venture capitalists. The day-to-day running was done by some of his most trusted developers, meaning he was free to work on his own schedule and time. He'd save these emails and messages for the evenings, when he allowed himself to unwind from a long day on the farm by checking someone else's code or working through a development issue. Last night, he'd skipped that particular ritual to spend time with Harper, meaning he'd have twice the work tonight. But somehow, he didn't mind. He wouldn't have traded last night with her for anything.

"Farmers, you know. They're always…" He reached for a pot of coffee and poured himself a large cup, hoping that the two-second distraction would help him find a coherent way to end the sentence. It didn't. "Farming."

"And are farmhands always making eyes at pretty forewomen?" Annie asked, wiggling her eyebrows as though she'd just said something *very* scandalous.

"I'm not having this conversation with you right now."

"Just hear me out—"

"I've heard you out every time you try and give me one of these pep talks."

"It's not a pep talk! It's a prophecy!"

That prophecy was probably about as magical as Sae's Place, but he couldn't tell her so without revealing his whereabouts from the night before. His shoulders were still warm from the place where Harper leaned against him.

"I don't need any love spells, thank you. I'm working there for one reason and one reason only: to get you that wedding venue. That's all."

"Yes, I know. And I'm very grateful." She finished the last of her coffee as her perfectly manicured fingers scrolled the screen of her phone. Her stare was unseeing, though, her mind clearly wandering elsewhere. "It's just..."

"Just what?" he asked, shoving the toaster's depressor with more force than necessary.

"I just think it would be sort of like...fate, right? I come to Hillsboro and find romance, then you follow me to Hillsboro and find romance...it's just..." she sighed "...too perfect for words. I should do a post about this town. There's got to be something in the water."

A more cynical man would have rolled his eyes and told her to stop watching so many Hallmark movies, but he didn't have the heart. His sister believed in love, and he wouldn't be the one to tell her it was all bunk. It was bad enough he'd been the one to tell her about Santa Claus when they were kids.

"You're right. It would be." He offered her a smile. "But it's not going to happen."

"Why not? Why won't you even open yourself up to the *possibility*? She was lovely when we met her that first time—"

"She was *not* lovely."

"Fine, she didn't have great manners, but there was something there! A spark or something, you know?"

Last night, he'd said so many things he shouldn't have. He shouldn't have told her he didn't feel lonely here. He shouldn't have told her he agreed Hillsboro was full of good people. Now, for fear of making yet another mistake, he remained silent.

"And if there *is* a spark, then why shouldn't you pursue it—"

"Because that's not what I'm here for. I'm here to make sure my little sister has the happiest wedding ever, and then I'm going back home." Then, to divert her attention from the forceful way he buttered the too-burnt toast he'd made, he lied, "I don't need any reason to stay here for longer than I have to. These small towns give me the creeps."

"Really? I think they're wonderful. Yesterday, I tried seventeen different kinds of pie, and that was at just one restaurant."

She said it like a light-hearted joke, but he saw the weakness in her normally brilliant, camera-ready smile.

"And where is your fiancé during all of this?" he asked, looking into his coffee cup to keep her from feeling attacked by the question.

"He's working. Not everyone in the world can just take off like we can. Some people have to work."

"I don't need a lecture about work when I've been pitching manure and cleaning out tubers for the last week, *while* maintaining a business remotely."

"You're right. I'm sorry." She paused, and he waited for her inevitable rebuttal, the same one she pulled out every time he brought up the farm. "Though, in my defense, I *did* tell you not to go chasing after that place."

"Yeah, and then you spent the entire night scrolling through their website looking at every picture."

Annie had no defense for that, and they both knew it. When she had her heart set on something, it was almost impossible to tear her away from it. One of the many quirks of her personality that made her near-constant distance from Tom a point of contention in this house. He didn't like to see his headstrong sister suddenly changing her personality because some guy was too busy for her.

"Stop changing the subject. Your fiancé. Where is he?"

"Working."

"When he's not working?"

"We've been out! Don't get touchy. We don't need to be together every minute of every day. That's not healthy."

Right, but it wasn't healthy for them to be apart all of the time, either. Biting his tongue, he held his hands up in surrender.

"I just think you'll adapt better to life out here if you make some friends. They can show you around, give you a lay of the land."

"*We* could have done that if you didn't run off to work with your farm woman."

Farm woman. She obviously picked that particular nickname to get a rise out of him, to remind him Harper wasn't like the other women he'd dated in Los Angeles.

"You know her name," he snapped through a bite of burnt toast.

"Of course I know her name." With a swipe of her finger, she began furiously searching for something on her phone. When she found it, she offered the device to him. "I know her name, birthday, favorite movies—"

"Annie! Stop internet stalking my boss!"

"If she's going to be my sister-in-law one day, I'll need to know all of this stuff."

That was the last straw. He had to get out of here. And fast. His visit with the doctor wouldn't be for another hour yet, but waiting in a stuffy office would be infinitely better than listening to his sister daydream about his wedding to the *farm woman*.

"Find a friend, little sister. Maybe they'll be able to keep you out of my business."

"But—"

Giving her a goodbye ruffle of her perfectly coiffed hair, he began his retreat.

"I'm late for an appointment. I'll see you for dinner tonight. I love you! I want to see real progress made on the friend front when I get home tonight!"

"Fine! I love you too!" She waved him off, but then stopped herself. "Make sure you call back your business manager! He called the house a few times!"

It was Luke's turn to wave *her* off. He'd been so busy with the work on the farm, he'd completely forgotten about his business manager and their talk about the Andersons' financials. Promising to call him soon, Luke retreated into his car. But before he could close the door behind him, he could have sworn he heard her mumble something about *stupid brothers*.

The town doctor, a surprisingly young man named Jake Forester, made fairly quick work of the gnarly-looking blisters, prescribed him an antibiotic, and sent him on his way without much small talk or any probing questions, something for which Luke couldn't have been more grateful. No less than an hour after he'd eaten at Religious—where he had had dinner his first week in Hillsboro—he walked into a drugstore halfway across town only to be greeted by the old man behind the counter with a hearty, "So, how were the spicy yuzu drumsticks? I heard they're pretty spectacular." News traveled fast in a town as small as this one, where everyone knew everyone and didn't mind sharing gossip, and while he hoped a doctor would abide by patient confidentiality, he couldn't be sure in a place like this. He didn't want half the town—or, more likely, the *entire* town—to know that he'd gotten such terrible, nearly infected blisters, or how. The work he did on the flower farm was no one else's business or concern.

Unless... he hadn't considered it before. Did everyone in town already know? Harper had any number of reasons to blab to the entire Hillsboro phone book about the rich out-of-towner demanding a job on her land. His stomach twisted at the humiliation of it all. Not for himself, of course, but for Annie. She probably wouldn't want her fiancé thinking her brother had to pick up extra shifts on a farm just to cover the cost of their wedding.

Doctor Forester gave him a firm word of warning against pushing his luck—boots were definitely out for the rest of the week, meaning he couldn't go anywhere near working a full day at the farm—but with every turn of the gears in his mind, his fear at the thought of ruining Annie's reputation here agitated him further. Heat rose under the collar of his fitted T-shirt. His hands gripped the steering wheel tight. The sound of rushing blood filled his ears.

...And before he knew it, he found himself driving up the front road of Harper's farm. The decision wasn't a conscious one, but once he realized he'd steered the car all the way there, miles across town from his home and conscious destination, he didn't regret it. Once, he'd bought an entire bar because one of the bartenders groped his sister without her permission, and the proper legal channels for discipline weren't working fast enough. If Harper—if *anyone*—even accidentally hurt Annie's reputation while trying to harm him, he had to know.

But the closer he got to the house, the stranger he realized the sight in front of him was. The house's usual assortment of pickups and terrain-ready vehicles were increased by one this afternoon, a sleek, silver Tesla with a Los Angeles Dodgers sticker proudly stamped on the back.

His sister's car.

He didn't even have time to question its presence. Instead, he slammed the car into park, stormed straight up the front steps, and knocked on the white-painted frame of the screened front door with all of his might.

"Hello? Anybody home?"

He'd scanned the fields and hadn't seen Annie or Harper anywhere out there; they *had* to be inside.

"Coming! Coming! Hold your horses—"

Harper's face appeared behind the screen door, and if her expression was any indication, she definitely hadn't been expecting his sudden, unannounced presence. Quickly, she composed her face, but her voice still wavered in surprise. She made no move to open the door.

"Luke! What are you . . . what are you doing here?"

"Where's my sister?"

He'd never seen her this knocked off her axis, so thoroughly unsettled. It only raised his levels of confusion and worry to new heights.

"She's—"

"I'm right here! Geez."

He heard her before she materialized, but when Annie finally came into full view, literally none of his questions were answered. In fact, approximately three thousand new ones popped up in their place. Not only was his sister *not* being held hostage in this house or even appearing mildly uncomfortable about being there, she seemed to have made herself very much at home in a pair of pajamas and a loose—but clearly carefully constructed—ponytail. In one hand, she carried what appeared to be one of those white plastic jars she kept on her bathroom sink, and the sudden smell of jasmine and avocado told him it contained one of her favorite face masks.

"Are you having a...slumber party?" he asked, unable to think of any other explanation. Pajamas, home spa treatments... this had all of the hallmarks of his sister's favorite activity. Sometimes, she even convinced him to partake in the festivities with her. He recognized the signs, but she scoffed at his suggestion.

"Don't be ridiculous, Luke. It's barely noon."

"But—"

"We're getting ready for the slumber party."

"What?"

"Well, you can't just show up and have a slumber party. Have *you* ever been to a slumber party without cookies?"

No. Because the only slumber parties he'd ever been to were the ones she threw to show off on social media, and those were always packed to the gills with everything from home-baked cookies to funny matching flannel onesies…not that he'd tell Harper that. He turned his attention to her.

"What did you do to her?"

"I didn't do anything. She just showed up and—"

Annie? He'd never known her to be so blatantly rude. They *always* called before they went somewhere, always asked permission before doing something like this.

"You just *showed up*?"

"You told me to find friends!"

"Yeah, with literally *anyone else in town*!"

Harper apparently didn't care for that. She snapped to him, her eyes blazing. Separated from the pair of women by the screen door, he felt as if he'd suddenly been tossed into a thunderdome, where three would enter, but only one would win. With the two opponents he'd been given, the odds were totally stacked against him.

"What? I'm not a good enough friend?"

"Don't put words in my mouth. I just meant—"

The tension rose incrementally with every word, until brother's and sister's voices were nearly at shouting level.

"I don't know anyone else in town apart from Tom! Harper seemed as good a place to start as any! And I like her!"

"She told me you threatened her," the *new friend* in question interjected.

"I did not!"

"She told me she *had* to have progress in the friendship department by the time you got home."

They had him there. He *had* said that. And now, he saw that he should have been more specific in his requests.

"...I did say that, yes. But—"

"And see?" Annie gloated. "I made a friend."

For a moment, no one said anything. Luke glanced between the two women, the two poles at opposite ends of his life. For her part, Annie beamed as she held on to her pot of face goop, barely fazed by his sudden intrusion into her "pre-slumber-party party." Harper, on the other hand, backed away a few steps, uncertain how the battle between siblings would play out. He pushed on the screen door, ushering his sister outside.

"Come here."

"But we were just going to put the masks in the fridge," she protested, eyes widening. He noticed Harper didn't protest his demand either, whether out of fear of him or unwillingness to get involved, he couldn't tell. "Her sisters...well, not both of her sisters. The younger one said she has something to do tonight and is busy all day, poor thing, but the older one is coming home during her lunch break to help us make—"

"Now."

After that low command, she didn't hesitate to follow him. It wasn't often he used his "dad" voice on her—after all, he wasn't their father, and their deadbeat parents could never have given them the life he did—but when it happened, she usually acquiesced. She did it this time, but she clearly wasn't happy about it, slamming both the house door and the screen door behind her.

"What is your problem?"

"*My* problem?" he asked, incredulous. His problem should have been clear as day.

"I found a friend!"

"My *boss* cannot be your friend!"

That should have gone without saying, especially when she convinced herself that one day he and said boss would run off together. Shoving his hands in his pocket, he clenched them into fists and fought to keep his jaw loose when all he wanted was to throw a grown-up temper tantrum at this turn of events.

"She isn't really your boss. You're not even being paid."

"Still."

Instead of losing her cool any further, Annie took three long, stretching breaths between her teeth, a calming technique she'd learned from some meditation instructor on the internet. Her use of the technique *never* meant good news for him. While he thought these "mind recalibration tactics" or whatever this guru spouted were absolute gibberish, the placebo effect was enough that it always refocused Annie's energy to dangerous effect. When she turned on him again, he took a defensive step back.

"Why does this worry you so much?" she asked, her narrowed eyes probing him.

"Because it's—"

"You're afraid we're all going to have to spend more time together, aren't you? If we're friends, you're going to be seeing her and you're afraid you'll start to like her. You're afraid I'll be right."

"Is that why you did this?"

"Hey." All airs of fake questioning disappeared. "I was at the wedding of a girl I met in line at Taco Bell on Beverly Boulevard. I can make a friend *anywhere*. I didn't need to come to a farmhouse on the other side of town to do it."

"So, you're—"

"I'm doing this for your own good. And for mine." A dismissal. She was *dismissing* him. With little more than a goodbye wave in his direction, she let herself back into the house, separating them once more by the rickety old screen door. Waving the pot of green glop, she completed her taunt in a sing-song voice. "Now, go home and rest. Unless you want to stay for face masks?"

Stupid, meddling sisters. He had to hand it to her: Annie knew how to meddle. She loved orchestrating and conducting other people's lives, something he hadn't minded until she left Los Angeles and realized that, without her hosts of friends around her, *he* was the only project she had left.

Which, if her track record could be trusted, meant he was probably doomed to fall for Harper Anderson. When his sister put her mind to something, she rarely failed.

But this . . . this, he had to fight. After all, he still kind of hated her.

"Can I talk to Harper for a moment?"

"Why?" she asked, clearly caught between suspicion that he wanted to talk to her and thrill that he wanted to talk to her *alone*.

"I want to make sure she knows your curfew."

The joke earned him a huff and a roll of her eyes, but she did what he asked all the same.

"Harper? My brother wants to talk to you."

A moment later, she appeared on the porch, a vision in dirty jeans. She hadn't yet slipped out of her work clothes and into pajamas, a small comfort. He didn't think he could talk to her in such casual attire. At least in her work clothes, she felt a bit distant from him, a bit superior. He saw her glance down towards his feet, clearly remembering last night.

"What happened?" he asked before she could pry about his doctor's appointment.

"I don't know. She showed up here and told me she needed help, so I agreed."

"You gave up an entire day of work just to hang out with my sister?"

"She seems like the kind of person who would help me if I needed it."

Tugging at the base of her loose braid, Harper shrugged. Generally, he found her pretty easy to read. Most of her emotional range focused on making his life miserable, a fairly blatant set of expressions and quirks to spot. But now, he couldn't even guess at what she was thinking. And the not-knowing drove him to the edge of frustration. When it came to Annie, he *needed* to know. He'd never let anyone hurt her.

"Are you messing with her?" he probed, folding his arms over his chest.

"You really think I would do that?"

"I don't know. You worked me until I bled. I have no idea what you're capable of."

With that one flash of cruelty, that one misspoken sentence, everything they'd built up between them vanished. All of the small kindnesses he'd collected from her over the last few days disappeared from her eyes. Any hint of the warmth she'd shown him by the creek last night was gone, and he knew he'd said the wrong thing.

"Go home, Luke."

"But—"

He tried to apologize, to explain he'd only been trying to protect his sister, but that screen door slammed in his face, obscuring her and dividing them once more.

"You're ruining our sleepover. Go home."

Chapter Seven

So...apparently, she was friends with Annie Martin now. It was a development she wasn't entirely sure she hated. Or, at the very least, she couldn't decide how she felt about her.

"Are you more of a mango and sage girl or an avocado and jasmine girl? I prefer the avocado myself because of the moisturizing properties, but I was reading a post on this blog—BeautyBaberina, have you ever heard of it?—about how the avocado can actually block your pores, and so now I'm thinking I might go with the sage. Sage, of course, smells terrible, but that's partially what the mango is there for—"

Harper's first opinions of Annie, the ones she'd made the first day she and Luke had driven up to the farm in their sports car and she'd invited herself to have her wedding on the property, didn't change much. In fact, the longer Annie stayed, using the food processor in their kitchen to blend face masks and brown sugar skin scrubs while talking faster and with more enthusiasm than she'd ever heard another human being speak in her entire life, the more firm her opinions became. Annie *was* every bit the social media obsessed, conspicuous consumption princess Harper first pegged her as. She took pictures of *everything* she did, even asking Harper if she would sign a release for pictures of them to be posted on all of her handles, a proposition to which she hesitantly agreed. She'd even brought along her own baking equipment, having the grace to cringe a bit as she mentioned her brother calling their farm "old-fashioned."

She was a human Pinterest page. A stereotype of everything Harper believed about Angelinos.

And she was also wonderful. Harper couldn't help but like her. When she first appeared next to her in the fields, as if by some sort of teleportation magic, she held her high-heeled black suede booties in her hand and, instead of making a traditional greeting, asked if she could help at all. No one *ever* asked Harper if she needed help unless she'd paid them first, and even then, it was hit or miss. After that, despite her best efforts to keep some emotional distance between them, she found herself actually enjoying her time with Annie. Besides movie nights with her sisters, she couldn't remember the last time she'd unwound like this, just chatting and drinking tea without guilt on a Tuesday afternoon.

She couldn't get Luke's words out of her head. Not his mean and totally true words about her working him until he bled, but the ones he said yesterday by the creek. *I'm worried about my sister. I think she's lonely out here.* She wanted to hate him, but she couldn't help but feel for him when he said that. She knew what it meant to worry about a sister. Both of her sisters lived with her and worked with her, but she still worried when they left for a long weekend or suffered a particularly bad date. And even so many years on after what happened between May and Tom Riley, she couldn't help but worry about *that*, too.

"How's Tom?"

"Hmm?"

"Tom Riley. Aren't you two…"

"Oh. Yeah. Right. Sorry. My mind was totally somewhere else. He's great. We're great. Everything's great," she said, her smile too bright and too still to be honest.

Since the announcement of their engagement, the town had literally buzzed with questions about them. After all, Tom Riley was one of Hillsboro's favorite sons. For him to suddenly get engaged to a stranger from so far away, one he'd only met a handful of times as far as anyone knew…nothing could be more certain to set the town tongues wagging. All of those questions bubbled to the surface now. *How did you two meet? No, really, how did you two meet? Why are you getting married so soon? Are you pregnant? Is this just for your Instagram fame? Do you really love him?* None of the answers to those questions really mattered. Tom broke May's heart with whatever he did to her years ago, and that was all Harper needed to know to despise him. But her morbid curiosity still itched to know something no one else knew about the mysterious couple.

"Have you guys found a place for the ceremony? The clock is ticking on that, I guess."

"Oh. Luke hasn't…?" Annie's hands froze over her immersion blender, which stopped its furious work in the homemade ice cream base she'd started working on. Harper frowned in reply.

"Hasn't what?"

Annie's lips tightened, tugging in discomfort. Such an odd expression for someone who lived in a perpetual state of sunshiney smiles. "Err, I guess my brother hasn't told you why he took the job on the farm?"

After tons of thinking on just this very question, she answered it easily. "To torment me because I wouldn't let you ruin our farm for your wedding."

"...Not exactly."

Harper's mind flipped through possibilities. What was Luke hiding from her? She instantly feared the worst and her mind snowballed from there: He was going to try and buy the farm from her father, just to spite them. Her father wouldn't sell, but then he'd up and up and up the offer until he *couldn't* refuse, and Luke would take everything her family worked for generations and...

"Why, then?"

Annie held up her hands in pre-emptive surrender. "Promise you won't freak out."

"...Sure."

Sure couldn't be classified as a promise, and internally, she swore she *would* freak out if she had a reason to. Annie's gaze shifted from Harper's face out through the window where the flowers were doing their swaying dances in the evening wind, her face a complex array of uncertain emotions.

"Luke is working here because he thinks you'll let us have the wedding here."

"*What?*"

"You promised you wouldn't freak out!"

She didn't have time to explain to her the technicalities of the word *promise*, not when she was so busy freaking out.

"He knows all the work in the world won't change the fact that a wedding could ruin the flowers in the middle of harvest, right?"

"I don't think either of us really realized that until Luke saw all the work that goes into the farm. And...do you want my honest opinion?"

Greedily leaning across the kitchen counter and nodding her head, she waited with bated breath. No one understood Luke's mind like his sister did. That man was an enigma. She'd take all the help she could get cracking his code.

"I think he likes you."

Not this again. Sisters were the *worst.* Even sisters who weren't her own sisters were trying to shove them together. Sucking in a sharp, annoyed breath, she fought to control her temper. Had it been May or Rose who'd said something like that, she would have given them a piece of her mind. But Annie was a guest. A guest who needed a friend. A guest with a powerful brother who'd probably buy the farm and burn it to the ground if Harper so much as hurt a hair on her head or looked at her the wrong way. She couldn't afford to lose her cool.

"...Come again?"

"I think he likes you. He's done some pretty amazing things for me in my life, but he's never done so much manual labor his body started to break down. Not for anybody."

"I didn't mean for him to get the blisters!" she replied, all-too aware how her voice raised in a tone too high to be anything but defensive. "I even got him a pair of worn-in boots upstairs from my dad's closet. He can borrow them."

"Oh, so you like him too!"

Not a question, but Harper answered it anyway.

"No. I don't like him."

And, to be completely honest, at this moment in time, that answer was an honest one. She'd tried to be nice to him, brought him to her favorite spot in the world to heal his blisters and taken in his highly strung sister when no one else in town probably would, and instead of thanking her or even being a little bit kind, he insulted her and assumed the worst. Any confusion she had last night about her feelings settled themselves firmly. Annie shrugged at the declaration.

"They say people who pick on you really like you."

"They say that about boys and it's a reassertion of toxic masculinity."

"That's true, but that doesn't mean you don't like him." She practically whistled the words as she shook a cocktail straw in Harper's direction. Finding no exit from this conversation, she resorted to threats. Not the best to escape, but the only one she could think of for the time being.

"Annie."

"Yes?"

"Do you want to have this sleepover?"

"Yeah." She released a heavy, relieved sigh, blowing a stray strand of hair from her face. "I'm getting cabin fever locked up in that house all the time."

"Great." She helped herself to one of the garnishing maraschino cherries waiting in a jar to be plopped into a homemade cherry lemonade they had cooling in the fridge. "Then, let's agree your brother is an off-limits topic."

"But—"

"Or you can go home."

"I think the lady doth protest too much, but fine." Annie grinned and waved her hands, dismissing their boy talk, but even though she'd won the battle, she could sense from the Martin sister's demeanor that she wasn't poised to win the war. "Now, where are your sisters? I can't wait to meet them! I hope they'll like me. Do you think they'll like me? What are they like?"

Any fears she had about her family disliking her proved thoroughly unfounded. Rose, as usual, could be trusted to put on a dazzling show of kindness even for the worst of her enemies, which Annie certainly wasn't. May called earlier to say she'd already planned on going over to a friend's house, which Harper knew was a lie, but didn't try to fight her on it. Even their mother invited herself to the party when she saw the girls relaxing in the warm evening at the edge of the pool with their beauty masks smeared across their faces. Harper tried to stop her, but the determined woman slapped on a cleansing mask of her own and joined them anyway.

"And what about you, Annie?" Mom asked in a lull in the quickfire conversation, her voice too excited. Harper's stomach dropped. She had given her mother *one* instruction when they came out here, and she was going to break it. *Don't embarrass them.* "How do you like Hillsboro?"

"I love it here. Everyone's been so nice and the food is amazing and—"

"And your brother? How does he like it?"

She hesitated, taking the opportunity to drink a long sip out of the too-cute-by-half glass of cereal milk she'd made during her one-woman cooking show earlier in the night. For the first time since she arrived in her Mary Poppins–like whirlwind, she seemed to actually consider her words before she spoke them, instead of her usual practice of letting loose whatever rampaged around in her head.

"I think he likes it very much."

"He's been spending quite a lot of time here at the farm."

Harper interjected, reminded of the revelation she'd been given about his motives earlier in the evening. "Funny thing about that, actually—"

"Funny thing about that is that he's not usually much of a small-town guy. He really prefers the big city."

"Oh. Really?"

"He really just came for me, I think. Like I said, I love it out here."

"Right. I see. And his work? What about that? I hear he's…" Harper shot her mother a look across the corner of the pool, a look Annie absolutely spotted but generously didn't call any attention to "…doing very well for himself."

"Yeah, for a high school drop-out, he's done pretty well for himself."

Harper's soft focus snapped to crystal-clear attention at the words *high school drop-out*. "What?"

"You've never heard the story?"

"No."

"It's all over the internet."

"We're not really into the whole online stalking people thing."

"Not even when he's working on your farm?" Annie asked, her confusion and the furrow in her brow only deepening.

"Well…" Rose hummed. "When you put it that way—"

"Don't sound so worried. I'm sure your father did a background check. Besides"—her mother patted her new, young friend's hand—"your brother's reputation is impeccable. Everyone in town says so."

"Really?"

"It's sterling."

Stop it! Stop distracting her! Harper wanted to scream at her mother, something she hadn't even attempted since she was nine years old. But the information Annie just dangled in front of their noses was too precious, too exciting to let go of. A high school drop-out who became a multi-millionaire? She'd known he'd had something to do with some kind of tech company, but she'd assumed he skated through life on their parents' money or was some kind of kid genius who'd gotten several college degrees by the time most people managed one. And, in fairness, a lifetime of burying his head in books and in computer code or a youth insulated by obnoxious wealth was the best explanation she had for his lack of manners or social grace. A lack of an education didn't matter to her. He was obviously smart enough without it if she'd thought he had several degrees instead of the zero he held, but it *did* surprise her. Even worse, she knew someone like that would need a whole lot of grit and a work ethic for days, two things her first perceptions of him assured her he could never have possessed. The image of him she'd conjured in her mind changed slightly, chafing against all of the suspicions and prejudices she'd built up since working with him on the farm.

When she resurfaced from her mental loop of questions without answers, her mother had gone into full humiliation mode. She didn't break the rule against embarrassing them; she shattered it. Jumping up out of the water and splashing them all—earning a hearty groan from Rose and Harper, but a beaming smile from Annie, who laughed as if she'd never had this much fun in her entire life—she slapped her hands together and raised her voice to new heights.

"There was an article! I can't believe I forgot all about this! Shannon Park—she writes the society column for the *Gazette*— wrote just the nicest article about you and your brother coming to town. Come on up to the house with me and I'll show you—"

"Mom! She doesn't want to see that—"

Nothing for it. Her mother was already leading Annie back up the steps to the house, leaving the two sisters alone by the edge of the water. For a while, things between them were still and unmoving, peaceful. But there was a confused riot breaking out in Harper's chest. Not only about everything she'd learned about Luke, but about . . . well, everything else in her life, too.

"Rose?" she asked after a minute of companionable silence, pulling her legs up out of the warm water. Her sister didn't budge, choosing instead to cast her gaze up towards the stars. Her pale skin, which had been protected by years of working indoors, almost glowed.

"Hmm?"

"Do you think this is a good idea?"

"Is what a good idea?"

"Having Annie here, being her friend." She shrugged. Indecision washed over her in a fresh new tidal wave. May's voice ricocheted in her mind, that small, quiet voice telling her she wouldn't be home tonight, that she had made other plans. "I don't know."

"You're worried about May."

"Yeah. I mean, when Annie showed up here all miserable...she just looked so lonely. It was a no-brainer to invite her in. What else could I have done? And I know May is still broken up about Tom Riley, but..."

Ever the even-headed one of the family, Rose pulled herself up out of the pool, biting her lip the whole way. She took her time, considering the question before shrugging and moving towards the path leading to the house. "It's complicated, to be sure. I *think* you did the right thing. What kind of people are we if we aren't going to help someone who needs it?" The warmth of affirmation tickled the back of Harper's neck, only to harden to ice at the follow-up. "But if you are going to be friends with Annie, and I think you should because she's great, then just make sure you don't forget about May, alright? She needs us, now more than ever. It's not every day the love of your life marries someone else."

"He wasn't the love of her life," Harper scoffed. No, May would be fine. Better than fine. She'd find the perfect person someday. And when she did, Harper would know for certain she'd done the right thing by befriending the lonely Angelino who showed up on her doorstep today. But her confidence in that belief wavered when her sister placed her hands on her hips and raised her shoulders in something resembling a shrug.

"I don't know. They always seemed perfect to me."

"Well, maybe this will help her get past it. If May meets Annie and likes her, she'll realize she's not some horrible monster trying to ruin her life, and she'll realize she can move past all of this."

"I'm not sure life works quite like that, but maybe."

Quiet followed, broken up by Stella's barking in the distance and the occasional chirp of a cricket or two. About halfway up the stone steps leading to the open back door of home, Rose gave Harper a nudge.

"You're sure all of this Annie stuff doesn't have anything to do with who her brother is?"

Luke. She'd almost managed to go five minutes without thinking about him directly. A surge of new rage rose up inside of her, a fresh streak of confusion. On the one hand, if Annie's account of him was true, he'd worked himself up from nothing and given her an amazing life. Also, he protected her, even from imagined threats. But, on the other hand, he'd been cruel and callous. He was using Harper to get to her farm, trying to manipulate her into offering something she couldn't give. And, even worse, for everything he gave Annie, she didn't see him trying to be her friend. She didn't see him driving her around town or taking her and her fiancé out to dinner. He was substituting his closeness with things he could buy. It reminded her of the moment when he said he'd have to buy a creek for himself. Did he think he could buy people's affection?

If he did, she didn't want any part of him, no matter how Annie claimed he felt about her. The walls around her heart calcified.

"Yeah. I'm sure."

Chapter Eight

Okay. He'd made a slight mistake. A *slight* error in judgment when he thoughtlessly accused Harper of being a witch who would somehow hurt his sister just to spite him without, really, any evidence to speak of. At first, when he'd left the scene of their argument, he tried to maintain an air of dignified indignation, a state that wore off as soon as he remembered the way she recoiled from him, as if he'd flung a knife in her direction instead of an insult. His best efforts at convincing himself he was in the right failed, and by the time he arrived back at the empty house he shared with his sister, he resolved to make things right. He wasn't exactly sure how just yet, but he'd think of something.

After several pots of coffee and most of a sleepless night, he'd mapped out a plan of attack. All he needed to do was execute it. Around six o'clock, fresh from a shower and pouring a cup of coffee into a travel mug meant to fit the famed trenta-sized pour from Starbucks, he readied himself to meet the day, only to be disturbed by the opening of the front door. Annie arrived back home with heavy, sleepy steps and a big, dopey smile on her face, the likes of which he hadn't seen in a while, dragging her bags behind her for a few paces before dramatically throwing herself onto the nearest blindingly white couch. He couldn't help but smirk at the way her exhausted body still managed to avoid getting her shoes on the pristine, unblemished fabric.

"So..." He trailed off, raising one eyebrow in her direction, careful not to seem *too* interested. "How did it go?"

"Can't talk." Despite the sunglasses firmly over her eyes, she threw an additional arm across her face to block out the sun's light. He wasn't the gloating type, but if he was, he'd absolutely remind her of the hundreds of times she demanded "floods of natural light" during their Hillsboro house hunt. "Too tired."

"Why?"

Stupid question. He hadn't been to a slumber party since he was eight, but television assured him they were basically all-night affairs. He only asked because probing questions like that would be the only way to get any information out of her. He couldn't just come right out and ask everything he wanted to know. She'd suspect in a heartbeat any interest in her night was actually interest in her host, and he couldn't have that.

"Stayed up until four this morning watching a marathon of *Fresh Prince of Bel-Air* episodes."

"And then?"

"We got one-dollar tacos from a twenty-four-hour food truck in Santa Rosa."

"Isn't that, like, forty-five minutes away?" He'd seen too many television ads about how driving tired was worse than driving drunk and his heart clenched at the thought of her eyes drooping as she struggled to steer the car down the highway. "You drove there this tired?"

"Don't be silly. Of course I didn't."

A sigh of relief. "Good."

"I took the Tesla. It drove itself most of the way."

"Annie!"

She snorted. Exhaustion hadn't robbed her of her sense of humor, thankfully. "I'm just kidding. We used one of those ride-share apps. It was so much fun."

Was Harper nice? What did you talk about? Did she say anything about me? Anything at all? Did she rant and rave about how rude I was to her or did she keep the secret? Nothing his sister said answered any of his questions, but he busied himself by replying to a few work emails on his phone to distract him from asking them out loud.

Another email from his business manager about the farm. Guilt gnawed at him for having asked for their financials in the first place. He archived the email, not responding to it.

"You had a good time, then?"

"The best. They're really great people. I can't remember the last time I had so much fun."

Ouch. Surely she couldn't have meant that as a dig at him. With the exception of a few normal brother-sister fights, she'd never purposefully tried to hurt him. Yet, the sentence still stung. She'd had more fun in one night with the Anderson family than with her own?

"Not even in L.A.?" he asked, trying to balm some of the pain coagulating in his chest.

"Nope. Not even in L.A."

Work emails didn't interest him, but he kept his gaze on the screen, not wanting her to see the hurt. When she yawned, he took the opportunity to get away from her altogether.

"You should get some sleep."

"Yep. On it." She stumbled to her feet and grabbed the bags again. "Where are you going this early? I thought you couldn't go back to work until you healed up?"

"I've got some errands to run in town."

"Okay. Thanks for the suggestion, by the way."

"I didn't suggest you go to Harper's," he snapped, harder than he intended, knowing his pain was petty and beneath them both. He'd told her to find a friend precisely for this reason. He wanted her to have a good time. He just didn't know then that he'd feel this cavernously empty imagining his sister and Harper hanging out without him.

"Maybe not, but I wouldn't have gone if you didn't like her."

"I don't like her," he retorted, mostly truthful.

"Sure." Sunglasses hid her eyes. He somehow knew she was rolling them anyway. "Whatever you say."

He put the talk with his sister behind him. The plan. He needed to think about the plan. He needed to *remember* the plan. Not just the plan for today, but the plan for the rest of his time here in this small town. *Make nice with Harper and her family. Get their permission to use the farm. Give Annie the perfect wedding. Get the heck out of this place before their Main Street USA vibes start rubbing off on me.*

Problem was, every time he started to think about "the plan," the louder that little voice in the back of his head got... the one that told him this was a poor excuse for a plan. That there were easier ways to spend time on the farm.

And that he wasn't just doing this for altruistic brotherly reasons. He was doing this because the farm was the only place on earth he could reliably see Harper Anderson.

As he drove up to the farm, ready to begin his grand apology—something he'd cooked up on four pots of coffee and romcom reruns playing on TV at three in the morning—he wondered if it was really necessary at all. When first devising his Flower Farm Wedding Master Scheme, he'd always envisioned he'd be the one to convince the Andersons to let them use the property. But with Annie being such a big hit, perhaps it wasn't necessary any longer. Perhaps he could give up this entire charade and leave her to do the schmoozing and convincing. They all seemed to like her way more than any of them ever liked him. No doubt she'd have better luck, too.

Temptation gripped him. He could spend his days back at the house doing *actual* work for his *actual* company instead of hauling around dirt and water. Colleagues and columnists described him as a hands-off CEO, but ever since he moved to Hillsboro, he'd become more of an absent CEO, deferring to his co-developer for most of the big decisions that needed making since he set his status on the company's cloud software to "Working From Home."

And maybe he would. Maybe he'd quit the day job he'd taken up, tell Harper she was right about him being too weak, and run back home to his computers and his tech. But he couldn't run away without apologizing to Harper first. Even if he gave Annie the reins on winning the farm, he needed Harper to forgive him. He didn't want her thinking he was the world's *biggest* jerk. He'd settle for third or fourth, but he couldn't live with having the ultimate title resting on his shoulders.

Hours later, Luke had to admit that he'd gone all out with the grand gesture. He could only hope it was good enough.

For a grand gesture, the idea and execution were simple really. He'd started that morning by meeting a man he'd met on Craigslist and exchanging $150 for two hours with his pickup truck. Then, he drove to every flower farm, grocery store and florists' shop that were open in a twenty-mile radius and bought every flower he could get his hands on, filling the bed of the truck with them, packing them so tightly only a few petals had the space to move when he drove quickly down the roads towards the Andersons' farm. After all of Harper's training, he could reliably name every flower he saw, and the sight of the towering pink hollyhocks in the light of the sun distracted him, for a moment, from his goal.

All he had to do was park the car near the patch where Harper was working, get her attention, give her the world's biggest bouquet of flowers and apologize like his life depended on it.

Unfortunately...Harper didn't seem exactly thrilled when he showed up. He should have known. She never acted the way he thought she would. Unpredictable as the wind.

"What is this?" she asked, wiping her chin with the back of her sleeve. He could tell she didn't anticipate this conversation lasting long, because she didn't bother to take off her gloves.

"It's..." Wasn't it obvious? "It's an apology."

"Yeah. I can see that. For what?"

"I was a jerk. Annie had an amazing time last night. You were a real friend to her and I was..." He faltered, but then cleared his throat and finished his prepared speech, "a total jerk."

How many times had she called him that since they'd met? If he had a dollar for each one, he'd probably be close to doubling his personal wealth by now. And yet, his admission didn't move any of the tense, frowning muscles surrounding her downturned lips, nor did they loosen the tight arms that wrapped across her chest.

"So..." The ground crunched beneath her boots as she sunk in deeper. Of all the reactions he'd expected, this was the most surprising. Most women he knew would swoon at this kind of gesture. He'd thought Harper would maybe laugh and make a few jokes at his expense, but thank him sincerely for thinking of her. Instead...she frowned and raised an eyebrow in his general direction. "You went and paid for someone else's flowers in an attempt to apologize to me. Me. Harper Anderson. Of Anderson Family Flowers. You know, the people who grow and sell flowers?"

His stomach dropped. *This is what happens when you make a plan at stupid o'clock in the morning, you moron.*

"I just..." His brain made the noise his computer used to make when Annie picked up the phone while he was trying to connect to the fledgling internet. "I know you like flowers."

"Because it's my job to like flowers."

"Sure, but—"

"Just forget about it, alright? I hung out with Annie because I like her. It didn't have anything to do with you."

Of *course* she hadn't acted like all of the other women he knew. She wasn't like any woman he'd ever met before. In an attempt to end the conversation, she stormed off down the nearest row of rising stalks. But he couldn't let her get away that easily, catching up with her in a few long strides.

"You know, I could have made a better apology if you'd let me get to know you. And if you'd get to know me."

"I don't need to get to know you. This—" She wheeled around on a dime, pointing emphatically at the overflowing truck. The sudden movement brought them closer than they'd ever been before. He could count her eyelashes and the freckles crossing her nose. "Tells me everything I need to know."

"And what's that?"

Instinct drove him in an inch closer to her, and to his surprise, she didn't back down.

"That you're stuck-up, selfish, thoughtless, and you like to wave your money around instead of actually caring about things."

"That's not true."

"Oh, yeah? Then why is Annie so lonely? You give her a big house and great clothes and a fancy car but you're never around, are you?"

He staggered back. The accusation slapped him right across the cheeks, leaving burning red in its wake. Everything he'd done in his life, all he'd accomplished had been for his sister, to give her a better life. Sure, it meant he couldn't be with her as much as he liked, but...

"Did she tell you that?"

"She didn't have to. You've shown me who you are. And I'd never want to *get to know* someone like you." Throwing his own words sarcastically back at him, she bent down and ripped a basket up from the ground. "If you want to break your back trying to get this farm for her wedding, fine. Go ahead. It's your funeral. But don't try and get close to me. Don't try to be cute. Don't bring me flowers. Don't pull any of your rich guy tricks because I don't need or want anything from you. Are we clear?"

Running naked through Times Square would have felt less revealing. He wanted to explain, to defend himself. But his sister's excited voice from this morning ran through his head. *They're really great people. I can't remember the last time I had so much fun.* Fighting with Harper wouldn't end well. Pride begged him to rise in his own defense, but he quieted it. If they fought and it ended worse than it was now, maybe she'd decide being friends with Annie wasn't worth it. His pride mattered so much to him, true. But he wouldn't risk Annie's one friendship here for a chance to soothe it.

"Crystal. I'm sorry I bothered you."

When he left, he donated the flowers to a nearby nursing home. At least someone would appreciate them. And he had to admit, the smile on the nurse's face when he delivered them made getting kicked in the teeth by a beautiful, intriguing, infuriating and fascinating woman almost worth it.

But even as the small gesture filled him with warmth, he couldn't help but face the knowledge that Harper was right. She was right about everything. And he felt an irrational anger against her for it.

For the next few days, every time he even approached the farm, whether to do a few hours of work or see his sister, who'd taken to bringing picnics for picturesque lunches with her new best friend, the air between them remained almost painfully tense. They both did their best to ignore one another, a task she pulled off with greater aplomb than he did. In fact, she made ignoring him look easy. And maybe it was for her. But pretending she didn't exist didn't come easily to him. The more he tried to tell himself not to think of her or pay her any attention, the more time he spent swatting away daydreams and mental images of her.

But even as they somehow occupied two distant worlds while standing directly next to each other, he couldn't stop thinking about what she'd said to him, the opinions of him she made quickly and held on to for dear life. He considered asking his sister if there was any truth to Harper's snapping judgments, but whenever he tried, his mouth dried up and air circled uselessly around the base of his lungs. Maybe he didn't want to know.

He replayed this mental debate once again when he arrived late one night to pick Annie up. She was having what she called an "Italian Vineyard Night" with Harper and knew they'd be drinking red wine, so before she left the house that afternoon, she asked him to drive her home when the evening ended. Admiration at her responsible decision-making warred with anger when he realized he'd have an entire evening alone to think about Harper, and then he'd have to see her face-to-face after all his stewing. Now, getting out of the car, he dragged his feet with every step up the hill towards the small building where he'd met Mr. Anderson on his first day of work, where Annie told him they'd be dining. He didn't intend to eavesdrop, but as soon as he reached earshot, his attention was caught by the conversation floating on the wind.

"Dad, what's wrong? Annie's here and—"

Built into the side of the hill, the building was angled such that he could stand under the window without being seen. There wasn't much to it, just Mr. Anderson's office overlooking the working fields, a bathroom and a small back patio that looked out into the forest beyond, meaning Harper's voice had to be coming from the privacy of his workspace.

"We need to talk."

From his tone, which sounded approximately like what someone delivering a body bag would use, they weren't going to discuss when would be the best day to see the new *Star Wars* movie. Heart racing at the fear of being caught, Luke tried to control his breathing and keep it low enough that no one would hear. He settled himself between two bushes and leaned casually against the red siding, hoping for plausible deniability if anyone downhill happened to spot him.

"Now? Can't it wait?"

"No."

Harper's protestations ceased. A small miracle. Luke never heard someone so effectively quiet the spirited woman before. He couldn't see her father's face, but it must have been fairly grave to accomplish that feat.

"I'm going to shoot straight with you. We may lose the farm. And we only have a few days to make something happen if we want to save it."

Silence punctuated the bullet of a sentence. And then: "That *snake*—"

"Who?"

"Luke Martin." Hair on the back of his neck stood on end at the way she spit the syllables of his name. The old saying *eavesdroppers never hear good of themselves* popped into his head. "He's trying to run us out of business so he can turn this place into his family's personal wedding chapel, isn't he?"

"No, Harper, I wish it was that simple. Our bills are piling up. And if we don't have something big happen soon, we won't be able to pay for the medication and the mortgage. I've even had someone calling and making inquiries about...about selling the old place, but I was too stubborn to even listen."

Out of the corner of his eye, a white dot of fur appeared at the edge of the tree line. *Oh, no. The dog is going to expose me.* His thoughts torn between the heartbreak in Mr. Anderson's voice and the terror he felt as the dog stalked forward, Luke held as still as possible and tried to catch every bit of conversation he could.

"Stop paying my salary," Harper demanded, shattering Luke's heart with her sincerity.

"You have to eat."

The dog got closer.

"No, stop paying it and you'll—"

And closer.

"I wouldn't do that for all the world. It's yours and you work hard for it."

And then, the growling started. He had to whisper-scream at the animal approaching him, hoping on hope the people above him were too preoccupied to hear him through the screened window.

"Dog! Stop it, Dog!"

The animal didn't heed his warning. It continued its trek, but Luke's terror shifted when he heard his own name above him.

"...The Martins. We should say yes, then. To the Martin wedding. He just handed me a blank check and I could have—"

"It would ruin a year's harvest and make us late for the next planting season. No amount of money a man's willing to part with could make up for two years of lost revenue. Besides, our reputation would never survive if we missed two years of production."

Harper's voice nearly got lost in the wind; Luke's heart broke for her. "I didn't know it was so bad."

"It wasn't, until I got hurt."

Moonlight caught the dog's wet snout as it sniffed the air, like the glint of an executioner's blade. Lips pulled back to reveal monstrously sharp teeth, but the hammering in Luke's chest only partly owed itself to the approaching threat of the dog revealing his position.

"Please. Please, Dog. You know me. See? You know me."

Luke extended his hand for sniffing, hoping the familiar scent would put the animal at bay. His fingers trembled as he said a silent prayer the dog wouldn't take this as an offer of a snack. It seemed to be working. Nose working overtime, the wet end of the snout ran along his palm, leaving a gross trail of snot and relief in its wake. *I did it. I'm in the clear.*

"Listen, I didn't tell you this so you could worry. I told you so you could focus on finding new contracts, pulling any strings or making any deals you can, okay? I've been doing work on my end, but it's not an old man's game anymore. If something doesn't change—and soon—we're going to have to go back and talk to that buyer."

"You're not old, Dad."

"I need you to—"

Bark! Bark! All at once, the dog went crazy, head snapping left and right with every bark. Shocked out of his stillness, Luke sprinted away from the window just as Harper opened the screen and leaned out to inspect the situation.

"Stella, settle!" With that one command, the dog gave a final, begrudging growl in Luke's direction before sprinting off to the woods, no doubt to sate its bloodlust by eating some helpless woodland creature. "Who's there?"

"It's me! I was just looking for Annie."

He held up his hands in surrender, giving a wave to Mr. Anderson when he peeked out of the window over his daughter's shoulder. Maybe it was psychological, but the older man looked more frail, more fragile than ever before. The man's injuries were unknown to him until now, but it made sense. He'd never seen him running around the fields or doing any of the work Harper did on a daily basis. In fact, he'd never seen him out of his office chair before. No wonder such a young woman worked so hard. Not only was she trying to run a farm she loved, but she was trying to do right by her father, too.

Luke's mind flashed to the emails and phone calls from his business manager he'd been ignoring. Had this been what the man was trying to tell him?

"Luke, my boy!" Mr. Anderson called. "Do you want to come in for some coffee?"

"No," he answered, though he wanted nothing more than to say yes. The new revelations he'd learned tonight piqued his curiosity. "Thank you, sir. I just came to see if Annie was ready to come home."

As if on cue, his sister appeared in the doorway, making a big show of puffing out her belly as she staggered towards the car, waving at her hosts all the while.

"I'm ready, but you may have to roll me home after all the pasta we ate. Bye, Andersons!"

They gracefully—or in Luke's case, less than gracefully, seeing as he tripped over not one, but two loose tree roots on the way to his car—made their exit from the Andersons' company. Annie prattled on about the night and their conversations and the intricacies of making bow-tie pasta—Harper's favorite, apparently—from scratch, but he remained silent, not even doing his normal job of nodding and "mm-hmm"ing in the right places. His mouth remained firmly closed not only because he was so lost in thought that he couldn't be bothered to even perform listening to a thing she had to say, but also because he feared he'd throw up the knot tightly forming in his stomach if he opened his mouth too wide.

His business manager might have known about the Andersons' farm going under. If he'd just answered those emails, he might have been able to help them sooner, before it got this bad. New cords of guilt, thick and heavy, twisted his insides.

"You should have come inside for coffee," Annie finally said, slumping down in the passenger's seat.

"Harper's made it clear she doesn't want to see me anymore."

And he didn't blame her.

"Did she want to see you before?"

"No, but now it's abundantly clear."

"Brother, dear," she said in an overdrawn Italian accent, like something out of a fourth-rate, direct-to-VHS mobster movie. "What*ever* could that tortured expression on your face mean? Do you miss Harper?"

"No."

"Well..." His tone of finality must have worried her. Her fingertips tapped on the screen of her phone, only this time they weren't clicking through an Instagram story or quote-replying to someone's tweet. They drummed across the back of the rose-gold phone case anxiously. "Is something wrong?"

"Don't worry." The lights of the Anderson house glowed in his rearview mirror, illuminating the gears already turning in his head. He'd become accustomed to calling the place The Anderson House, and he didn't want that changing any time soon. Harper had given his sister a friend when she needed one the most. Even if she hated him, he owed her one. In spite of himself, the ends of his lips curled upward in an assured half-smile. "It's nothing I can't fix."

Chapter Nine

In Harper's line of work, Saturdays were for sleeping late. Saturdays were for Big Breakfast plates at Juanita's on the town square. Reading by the creek. Long baths. Trips to the bookstore. Trips to the hardware store (Harper *loved* the hardware store). In short, Saturdays were little gifts at the end of terribly difficult work weeks that offered Harper a little respite from her usual cocktail of bookkeeping, employee managing and what her father called "character-building work outdoors."

Saturdays were *not* for shopping trips to Windsor, the next biggest town over from Hillsboro, and they were *especially* not for wedding dress shopping. Having invited herself for breakfast via text, when Annie arrived at Juanita's this particular Saturday morning—she ordered a "green juice" and, when Julia, Harper's usual waitress, informed her they, like most other greasy spoons, didn't sell green juice, asked for a hot tea and whatever Harper had ordered—began with a hearty greeting of, "Good morning, Harper. Cancel your plans. We're going wedding dress shopping!"

At first, Harper tried to skirt around the issue. After the week she'd had, a week of fighting with Luke and sleepless nights spent wondering if she could pull together enough new contracts to keep her family from losing their entire livelihoods, she didn't necessarily feel like sifting through racks of too-expensive gowns and pretend everything was okay. She offered Annie plenty of explanations or reasons she couldn't go. Wouldn't her brother want to take her dress shopping? What about her friends from L.A.? Wouldn't they get their feelings hurt knowing someone else took her shopping? But, knowing better by now than to fight Annie on most fronts, Harper eventually obliged the request, canceling her only firm plan of the day by asking Rose to check that the chickens had enough feed before she went to bed that night.

And that's how Harper ended up here: La Belle Bride, a cute little wedding boutique tucked into a cozy, out-of-place little colonial house settled onto a corner of Windsor's Main Street. Saturdays were big business for wedding dress shops, it seemed, and Harper immediately felt out of place. Standing in the middle of a sea of pastel sundresses and heels, the only way her jeans and weekend boots could have stuck out more is if she'd elected to top off her ensemble with a 49ers jersey.

"Hi. I'm—"

Annie offered her hand to the immaculately coiffed receptionist behind an antique wooden letter-desk, but the petite blonde woman's blue eyes widened and she shook her head almost as vigorously as she shook the manicured hand extended in her direction.

"I know who you are! Annie Martin! When I saw the name in the books, I thought *it can't possibly be her. Annie Martin . . . that's a name anyone could have. I mean, I know she's staying nearby, but still, I couldn't be so lucky as to meet her*, but here you are! I have followed you since you were doing fashion quick tips on Vine."

"Really? That long?"

"Yes. And you're part of the reason I've been working here. I want to go to fashion school. Start my own lifestyle brand, you know?"

Having never traveled in the company of a celebrity before, Harper hung back in between her friend and the store's front door, ready to make a break for it if Annie gave even the slightest hint of discomfort.

But this new environment fit her friend like a glove, one not even the excitable shop assistant could stretch. From low-key farm sleepovers to high-end fashion houses, Annie knew how to adapt and fit in anywhere. No wonder everyone liked her. Instead of flaunting power she had or the wide-eyed stare and overly bright smile the clerk stretched across her face, Annie returned her gaze warmly and patted her hand.

"Well, then, it's fate that you're here to help me find my wedding dress. I couldn't ask for a better stylist today."

"Oh, I'm not a stylist. Just a receptionist. Priscilla was going to—"

A woman wearing a tailored dress suit in a shade of pink so light it almost appeared white when she stepped under the harsh, photo studio lighting of the store approached them, but before she could even offer her congratulations on the engagement or so much as take a breath in their presence, Annie waved a hand to brush aside any objections.

"Don't be ridiculous. What's your name?"

"Chloe."

"Nice to meet you, Chloe." She turned to the woman in pink, whose name tag read *Priscilla*. "Yes, Priscilla, I think Chloe will be helping me today. I hope you don't mind."

"No, of course, Miss Martin. Whatever you like." By the tightness of the woman's powdered cheeks, she *absolutely* minded losing out on such a high-profile client to the receptionist, but she kept her tone cordial, if a bit clipped. "Shall we open a bottle of champagne for you and your..." Mascaraed eyelashes fluttered and lowered as she scanned Harper's modest, low-key outfit from her dry-shampooed hair to the frayed ends of her weekend blue jeans. For a moment, Harper had felt sort of bad for the woman and considered asking Annie to bring her along for the dress search as well, just as a show of good faith. But now, she realized it was always best to trust her friend's judgment. Chloe hadn't flinched a bit at her outfit. "Guest?"

"Yes, please. Now." She clapped her hands, disturbing the handbag tucked into the crook of her arm as she winked at Chloe, who looked ready to swoon at her good fortune. "Let's get started, shall we?"

"Right. Of course." With that, she shook her head as if to clear it and began walking down the main hallway of the house with confident clicks of her heels against the wood floor. They passed closed rooms with names scribbled on mirrors hanging from them until they reached one labeled, *Executive Suite. Bride Name: Martin,* in swirling cursive too nice to be written in blue dry-erase marker. "Now, I don't want you to think I'm some kind of crazy fan or anything, but I think I have a few things in mind that you'll absolutely go wild over—"

"I can't wait to see them."

"This is your suite." With a turn of a key hanging from a pastel blue lanyard around her neck, she swung the door open and ushered them both inside. The smell struck Harper first. Despite growing flowers, working on a farm meant an almost constant barrage of less-than-lovely smells. This room radiated sweet scents of peony and lime, vanilla and brown sugar. She breathed in deeply as she followed Annie inside. "I'll be right back with some champagne and the first round of candidates. Feel free to have a look around the racks and pull anything you'd like to try on."

The Executive Suite lived up to its name. Like something out of a fairy tale or a movie about modern royalty, she felt like she'd just stepped into a shopping montage. An intricate blue and gold carpet supported two similarly colored and embroidered chaise longues, each bookended by tall end tables covered with bridal magazines. The couches faced a small pedestal in front of a brightly lit, three-way mirror. And, to top it all off, the walls of the room were lined with hundreds of dresses, each more lush and beautiful than the last. The lights and the electrical outlets cleverly hidden and built into the gold-burnished end tables were the only hint they hadn't suddenly been transported to the Palace of Versailles at the height of its glory days.

The beauty didn't distract her from the slight awe she felt at Annie in the moment, and when the door quietly clicked shut behind Chloe, she turned on Annie, who'd made herself comfortable on one of the couches and already relieved herself of her pumps.

"How do you do that?"

"Do what?"

"Make everyone feel like they're special. You didn't have to do that for her, but you did."

Anyone could see Chloe's thrill at the opportunity to work with one of her heroes; she hadn't stopped her face-splitting smile since she'd been offered the post. Annie chuckled as she began to familiarize herself with the selection of wedding dresses lining the walls. Harper knew next to nothing about wedding dresses, current trends or what kind of wedding her friend wanted if she couldn't get married on the farm, but she followed suit, if only to make herself seem busy.

"You're not going to believe this, but I think my brother taught me."

Luke. The one topic of conversation they'd successfully avoided since their sleepover. How anyone could see that man as someone who brought other people joy was beyond her.

"Oh."

"You have so many things you want to ask about him, don't you?"

"No."

Annie snorted, refusing to believe the paper-thin lie. "You've been itching to ask me about him all week."

"Is it that obvious?"

"No, but I have a lot of experience reading people."

As Annie carefully considered a drop-waist tea-length off-white couture nightmare of a dress, Harper rubbed the fabric of a silk sleeve between her fingers. The soft material didn't smooth the rough, choppy waters of her thoughts, but it gave her something to do as she tried to prioritize her confusions and fight the urge to vomit them all up at once in a big stream of *whatisherereallylikewhydoyoulikehimsomuchwhyishesuchasnobwhyisheso-badattalkingwhydoesshethinkhewillchangemymindaboutthefarmwed-dingwhatisshestilldoingintowndoessheliikemeordoesshesecretlyhatemehash-esaidanythingaboutme* ...she chose the most pressing query first, hoping it would clarify some of the other things nagging her. After all, Annie loved to talk. Harper swallowed her pride and hoped one little prompt would be enough to explain everything mysterious about the man she'd been fighting for the last few weeks.

"You said he dropped out of school..."

"High school, yeah. We didn't have the best childhood. Actually, we had a pretty awful childhood. It's one of the reasons I like coming over to your house, really. You've got great folks. They're always so nice to me. It feels like I have a family for the first time."

"Annie..."

Her usual cheeriness muted and muddled until she grew quite unlike Harper had ever seen her before. Solemn. Distant. Trapped in a memory Harper couldn't reach. Even as she held dresses up to her body and inspected them in the mirror, twirling and twisting to judge the movements of the skirt or bell sleeves, her mind wandered away from this room and away from weddings and dresses and joy altogether.

"Don't get me wrong. Our parents weren't bad people. They were just...absent. They didn't really want kids. We were just something on their checklist for being married, I guess. They didn't take care of us. Never checked if we'd done our homework or made sure we got to school on time. We never had enough lunch or shoes that fit right. When we got older, Luke started taking care of me. Packing my lunch and setting the alarm clocks so we made the bus on time. But one day, I was in middle school, and Luke was in... I guess it was tenth grade...and I came home crying because the kids in my class were making fun of me. They caught me trying to find a uniform I could steal from the Lost and Found. All of mine at home were too small and I'd spent the last two months telling our parents I needed a new one, but they never got me one, so..."

Her words trailed off, as if someone lowered the volume dial on an audiobook in the middle of the most riveting passage. Harper cleared her throat.

"What happened then?"

Her next pick was a mermaid gown covered in little beads that caught the blinding light of the fashion mirrors across the room. When she held it against her form, she put Ariel to shame. Tossing it into the ever-growing *keep* pile on the upholstered neck of the chaise longue, she continued, "Luke came home and I told him the entire story. Next thing I knew, he found a job with computers at some company in L.A. He was only supposed to be an office assistant, but Luke kept bugging one of the developers until they taught him how to code." She was so proud of him, and it showed. "Two years later, he was one of their lead guys. And a year after that, he launched AppeX with some of the guys he met while he was working there and now, he's—"

"A millionaire."

"It's actually closer to billionaire." She shrugged, as if *billionaire* wasn't such a big deal, and then cringed at how arrogant it sounded. "He just…you know, made good investments. But, back to your question."

What had that been again? With all of the imagined images of a teenage Luke working fourteen hours at a desk in some dingy office in L.A. to learn computing languages just to try and give his sister a better life than the one they'd been born into, she barely remembered her own name, much less the reason they'd been discussing this.

"He was only getting paid a dollar more than minimum wage when he first started as an assistant, but you know what he did with his entire first check?"

"What?"

"He bought me new uniforms. And new shoes. He walked to work instead of taking the bus so he could give me a little bit of something better. He worked and fought and scrimped and saved and gave everything so I would never have to feel like that hopeless, forgotten little girl again." Her voice thickened. When Harper gathered up the courage to look up, tears puddled in her eyes. "I guess I just want to do the same thing for other people that he did for me. Make them feel important. Special."

Like the last chords of an operatic aria, that sentence hung in the air as both of them were lost on the tides of their own thoughts. Harper stared at a collection of lace and satin in her hands, only now realizing she'd stopped looking through the dresses ages ago. She remembered the way he'd smiled at her when he mysteriously told her he wasn't lonely here in Hillsboro. She'd felt special then. She'd felt like maybe he was talking about her.

Had he been? And did she even want him to make her feel special?

"That. Was. So. Beautiful."

The aria ended with the tearful, overwrought interruption of Chloe, who'd made quick work of the back storerooms and returned with the dresses in enough time to hear at least the tail end of the story. Facing away from their attendant, Annie's tears were hidden from her, but not from Harper. She sniffed and carefully brushed them away, careful not to let the ballooning teardrops disturb her perfectly winged black eyeliner. Then, as if nothing had happened, she slipped a beaming smile onto her face as easily as slipping into a soft pair of slippers and welcomed the host back.

"Chloe, great to see you. What do you have for us?"

Harper was vaguely aware of the room around her and the dress fitting taking place, of a cork popping and champagne being poured, of her nodding and smiling at various dresses presented to them, of snapping pictures with Annie's selfie-lighting-equipped cell phone, but she operated on autopilot, letting instinct and cues prompt her to hum her agreement or laugh or sip champagne at all of the right moments.

Had she been wrong about Luke? He wasn't replacing love or affection with money or material goods. He wasn't living off of a trust fund handed benevolently down to him by distant parents. Everything he'd done was for his sister. Every sacrifice, every long hour, everything was for her.

Were they really so different? Everything she did, she did for her family. Staying up all night to call potential clients overseas? For her family. Driving towards a raging fire to make sure she rescued their prize seedlings and her parents' wedding photos? For her family. Twenty-hour days, manual labor in the hot sun and pay cuts to keep them in the green? For her family.

She wanted to hate him. She wanted an excuse to push him away and hold him at arm's length, to spend so much time despising him she had no room in her schedule for thinking anything else about him. But she couldn't. Not anymore. And she didn't know how to feel about that.

"Earth to Harper?"

"Hmm?"

The slightly annoyed faces of both Annie and Chloe frowned down at her when she finally resurfaced from her puzzling over Luke.

"Were you listening?" Annie asked, one hand on her hip and one making a tight claw around a delicate champagne flute.

"Sorry. I just got distracted. Sorry."

"Well, now that you've finally joined us again, I need your help."

"Sure. What can I do?"

With the help of Chloe, they presented a rippling gown of antiqued satin, an A-line masterpiece of fabric and stitching. Harper spent as much time thinking about her own wedding as she did the state of Idaho or *The Emoji Movie* or the starting lineup for the 1986 Pittsburgh Pirates, so she'd never given much attention to gowns like this, never imagined what she'd look like in one. But, *wow.*

"I love this dress, but they only have it in store in plus sizes. Would you mind, I know this is a lot to ask, but would you mind just slipping into it so I can see what it looks like on someone? I need to see how the fabric falls."

"Me?"

This dress was for a princess. Not for her.

"Of course you! You really can't tell anything about a gown by how it looks on a hanger. Please?"

No. Absolutely not. There's no way I'm trying on a wedding dress. This isn't my wedding. I didn't even want to come here today. On the other hand...she didn't plan on ever getting married. And if the farm kept struggling like this, even if she decided to have one someday, she probably couldn't afford it. Why shouldn't she indulge the fantasy, even for a moment?

"Well...sure. Anything to help."

Relief broke out over Annie's face like an adorable rash, and she handed the gown to Chloe, who led her down the hallway into an equally gorgeous dressing room. As someone familiar with any nook and cranny of the Walmart dressing rooms, the marble flooring, three-way mirrors and viewing pedestal filled her with delight. She'd never changed clothes anywhere this fancy before. Chloe hung the satin dress onto a silver clothing rack.

"Right this way, *madame*. This is our dressing suite. You just give me a shout if there's anything you need help with. I'll be just outside waiting to zip you up."

The door closed behind her and Harper carefully carried the dress into the small anteroom just beside the mirror to change. Annie waited for her in the next room, but she took her time with the fabric, partly to keep from accidentally ripping anything and partly to relish the sensations of a wedding dress against her skin. When she and Chloe managed to safely zip her into the gown, she gazed in the full-length mirror, barely hearing the receptionist when she offered to run out and find a veil to complete the look.

Was that *her*? She didn't look like herself. Or rather, she looked just like herself. If she'd been born a princess instead of a flower farmer. The fabric hugged her body with demure glamor, modestly giving her a shape and definition and beauty that her daily uniform of jeans or overalls never could.

She was beautiful. She'd never felt this beautiful before. Her chest tightened.

A knock at the door made her jump. She cleared the fright from her throat and called out: "Come in, Chloe."

The door handle rattled, then turned. But Chloe hadn't returned with the veil. Instead, Luke Martin stood in the doorway, his jaw slack as he took in the sight of her.

Chapter Ten

He didn't know the human heart was capable of stopping itself. But when the door swung open and he saw Harper Anderson standing under a flood of light, wearing a wedding dress, his heart did just that. The *thump-thump-thump*, his constant companion since before he was born, suddenly ceased, leaving him breathless. Dizzy. Stupefied.

Maybe he hadn't finished high school. He'd never held a diploma or heard his name as he walked across the stage to receive it. Because of that, he'd done more than his fair share of making up for that, reading and studying books and words and theories so no one ever suspected the truth. That studying came in handy now, when the sight of her sent off a flurry of word associations. *Pretty. Fine. Dazzling. Exquisite. Marvelous. Pulchritudinous. Fetching. Angelic. Bewitching. Stunning. Gorgeous. Classy. Lovely. Sexy. Touchable. Magnetic. Magnificent. Regal. Wonderful. Sublime. Beautiful.*

Yes, that was it. Beautiful. Simply beautiful.

Only a few seconds of stunned silence passed between them, yet he fit a lifetime of marveling into it. An impulse to tell her exactly what he thought of her opened his jaw, only to be silenced when she breathlessly called him out.

"What are you doing here?"

"Annie sent me a text! She said she needed to see me."

This wasn't a situation he'd ever been in before. The text from Annie clearly read *I'll be in the last room on the left*, but unless she had concealed herself somewhere in the room of carpet and marble, he sure didn't see her. Harper sighed, brushing a stray lock of hair from her face, a good move, considering Luke's fingers itched to reach up and tuck it behind her ear.

"She's down the hall. Next door on your right."

"What are *you* doing here? And why are you wearing that?"

And do you know how beautiful you look? The confident line of her shoulders and the proud tilt of her chin told him she did.

"Your sister asked me to try this dress on. It was too big and she wanted to see how it would look on someone."

"Really? She hates ball gowns."

"What?"

"Yeah. Says they make her look like an animated character who accidentally came to real life. She's always wanted a mermaid cut."

They both froze. Simultaneous realization struck them both. Harper bit her bottom lip, a terribly cute gesture Luke was just angry enough at his sister to ignore.

"She did this on purpose, didn't she?"

"Almost certainly, yes."

"Rats."

No, actually he wasn't angry. By all accounts, anger should have been his go-to emotion. After all, his sister tricked them into the same room after they'd both made it clear they didn't want to see one another and she did it in the most manipulative way possible, all because, in her bored hours alone at the house, she dreamed up some bogus fantasy about the two of them falling in love. Anger tempted him, but the sight of Harper in a gown fit for some kind of goddess-queen rattled him enough that it no longer mattered. He'd never thank Annie for putting them in this awkward situation, sure. That didn't mean he'd hate her for it, either, especially now, when the most beautiful woman he'd ever laid his eyes on stood there looking like she'd drawn up an ocean's worth of pearl dust and magicked it into some kind of wedding gown.

At some point, his heart started beating again. The dizziness didn't go away. In fact, it only got worse every time he so much as glanced at her. In a room full of mirrors, avoiding her image proved almost impossible.

"Why would she do this?"

Saying *because she's convinced we're going to fall for each other. And for us to do that we have to actually be in the same room and talk to each other instead of ignoring one another's existence entirely* seemed a bit blunt for their current situation, so he settled for a nonchalant shrug.

"She loves chaos, I guess. Don't worry. I'll talk to her. Don't want something like this happening again, do we?" He offered an uncertain laugh, which she echoed as she busied herself with tugging at the waist of the dress, carefully avoiding his eyes.

"No. I guess we don't."

Awkward silence reigned. Was he just imagining her discomfort? Maybe it was wishful thinking that convinced him she didn't believe it, that maybe secretly she *wanted* something else like this to happen again. Just like he did. To think he'd never see anything as beautiful, as confident, as heart-stopping as her ever again...he shoved his hands in his pockets to keep from reaching out to touch her cheek, to see if her skin was as soft and warm as it appeared.

"I'll just get going then."

"Great."

"Harper?"

"Yes?"

The next moment might have happened in slow motion. Or maybe he imagined it. Maybe he imagined the hopeful glint in her eye. But he didn't imagine what he said next. And he couldn't have imagined the brilliant, secret smile she tried to hide once she'd heard it.

"You look absolutely beautiful."

With that, before his stupid mouth could run away any further and say something really stupid and really true, like, for example, *do you want to go on a date with me?* Or, *maybe my sister is right and we should fall in love.*

This was a disaster. He'd left the house this morning to help his sister buy a wedding dress and now he couldn't stop imagining Harper walking down the aisle towards him wearing one. Following Harper's instructions, he found Annie's actual suite, where he found her sipping champagne and comparing no fewer than twelve mermaid-cut gowns with a feigned air of surprise on her pleased face.

"Oh, Luke! There you are! I must have—"

"Spare me the games." He waved her concern away, narrowing his gaze squarely on her and completely ignoring the attendant searching through a rack of veils in the corner of the room. "I know you fixed that whole thing."

"I must be going soft in my old age."

"You weren't subtle."

Pretense—and the dresses she was meant to be inspecting and choosing from—well and truly forgotten, her face blazed with excitement. Back in Los Angeles, he never minded her meddling. It kept her busy, and as far as he understood it, most socialites like Annie spent most of their days organizing charity events and meddling in other people's affairs. If she wanted to raise money for women's shelters and play matchmaker to her friends, who was he to tell her she couldn't? Now, he regretted his lack of intervention. She'd become too good at organizing romance.

"How'd it go? How did she look?" Annie asked, too enthusiastic.

Luke tried to keep his voice calm, level. "I didn't really pay attention, I guess."

"I know when you're lying."

"You picked the dress. I'm sure you knew how she looked."

Becoming something of a social media star with hundreds of thousands of followers didn't just come to someone with no style. His sister curated people and looks, knowing exactly how to present people so that their inner beauty shone to the outside world. It kept her fans clicking her links and liking her photos, but in real life, it worked to devastating effect. He'd only been with Harper for a few minutes at the most, and already he felt pieces of his heart trying to tear in her direction.

Speak of the devil, Harper let herself into the suite. Her face flushed, she didn't even bother to come fully inside the room. She halted in the doorway, hovering there so she could make a quick exit. He knew how she felt. If he could make a quick exit, he'd be halfway home by now. At least there, he'd be far away from sisters with agendas and beautiful women in wedding dresses.

"Annie, what do you think?"

"You know what?" she replied after a moment of stunned silence. "I think I changed my mind. I'm not so sure I want that one. But you look—"

"Save it." Without even knowing she'd copied him almost exactly, she brushed away Annie's lies. "I know you schemed this whole thing."

"Me? I never scheme, Harper."

"Can I take this off now?"

"Of course."

In a huff, she stormed out. The attendant followed behind just at the end of the long train, muttering something about offering her help out of the satin. When the siblings found themselves alone, Annie gaped at him, a perfectly pink manicured hand flying to her chest as if to stop her heart from rocketing out of it.

"Luke."

"What?"

"*I didn't really pay attention.* Are you sick or something? She looked so pretty."

"She doesn't look pretty. She's breathtaking," he said, before he could think better of it.

"Ah-hah!" She clapped with delight. His mouth *never* failed to get him in trouble. "Caught you."

He opened his mouth to scold her for putting Harper in a potentially uncomfortable situation, for manipulating them both, but he sighed and brushed those thoughts away. Changing the subject was a much safer course of action.

"How much champagne have you had?"

"Two glasses. I'm a blushing bride. You can't begrudge me two glasses of champagne!"

"No, but I'm driving you both home, okay? We can get your car tomorrow."

"But—"

"No buts. I want you both to be safe. We'll drop her off at the farm on the way home, but I don't want any funny business, alright?"

Annie saluted. "You got it, boss."

You got it, boss, was not a promise. And, even if she meant it as one, she broke it as soon as they arrived at the Andersons' farm. Instead of hopping in the front seat only just vacated by her friend, she followed said friend to the front door of her house, looping their arms and effectively locking them together. He scrambled to lower his driver's-side window and stick his head out of it, scream-whispering as if Harper wasn't right there, perfectly capable of hearing them both.

"Annie! What are you doing?"

"It was a long drive from Windsor! I'm thirsty!"

Thirsty. The perfect excuse. No one could say no to that. He'd look like a complete jerk if he reminded her their house, and all of its refillable water bottles and perfectly safe tap water, was just fifteen minutes away.

"Fine," he huffed. "But hurry up!"

He considered making up some excuse about a prior engagement they needed to attend. A dinner with Tom Riley, perhaps. But if

Harper and Annie were as close as they seemed to be, she would know by now the happy couple barely saw one another. In fact, he couldn't remember the last time Tom and Annie actually went on a date. If they were so head over heels for each other they didn't even date for a year before getting engaged, shouldn't they want to hang out? Doubts and concerns tugged at his brotherly fears, fears he tried to assuage or ignore. Annie was a grown woman now. She didn't need him butting into her personal life, no matter how high his concerns about this marriage stacked.

Speaking of brotherly worry, he checked the clock. No one took five minutes to drink a glass of water or grab a bottle from a kitchen. Sure enough, after a check of his dashboard display, his worst fears came to life in the form of Mrs. Anderson standing on their front porch, shouting out at him with a smile that could only be described as child-at-Disney-World excited.

"Luke? Is that you out there?"

Just drive off. Pretend you didn't hear her and pretend you thought Annie was staying here for a slumber party. If she's inviting you inside with a smile like that, there can only be one explanation. Your dear sister is meddling. Knuckles tightened around the steering wheel, but he couldn't bring himself to pull the car out of park. Instead, he cut the engine and emerged from the vehicle, completely unprepared and completely terrified of doing so.

"Yes, ma'am. Can I do something for you?"

"Yes. I was wondering if you had any plans for supper. If not, we'd be happy to have you. Annie's already said she'd join us!"

Of course she did.

"Are you sure we wouldn't be an inconvenience?"

"Not at all! We always fix too much to eat anyway. Like to have leftovers to offer people when Stella steals their lunch. Come in! Come in!"

It seemed Mrs. Anderson had the same magical powers of persuasion his sister did, because when she invited him in, he followed without question. Without even thinking about it. It seemed like the most natural thing in the world, to walk into the Anderson home, to be asked to stay for dinner.

And some little part of him, he wasn't sure where it had come from or how it'd gotten so strong, loved that feeling. Feeling like he belonged.

Dinners at the childhood home of the Martin siblings had been sad, quiet events. It usually consisted of their mother throwing a few bananas, slices of bread, and peanut butter on the table and suggesting the children make themselves sandwiches or her leaving less money than they needed for pizza, so ten-year-old Luke would shuffle down the street to the gas station and buy a handful of microwave taquitos or pre-bagged pickles. These meals were eaten in front of the television set or, more frequently, in front of the aging CD player in Luke's room, where they'd either listen obsessively to the Top 20 Countdown on the fuzzy-sounding radio or audiobooks he borrowed from their school library. Their parents had better things to do than cultivate any sort of family connection, much less spend any deal of time with them. Luke remembered dinnertime at the Martin house as stale, as characterized by little more than an emptiness in his chest and the sound of crunching potato chips.

Anderson family dinners... Those were another story.

"Pass me that, will you—"

"Make sure you open the 2013 Pinot, not the 2014—"

"—And today at the shop—"

"—Talked to Juan, and he said—"

"You'll never believe—"

"I'm starved—"

"—The dresses were absolutely gorgeous—"

"Oh, pictures! I want to see pictures!"

"Mom—"

"Can I have—"

"Please pass—"

"Let me see your glass—"

"And how was your day, Luke, dear?"

Until someone called his name, he contented himself with leaning against the hard-carved wooden back of his chair—which, by the way it creaked, had to be over fifty years old and was still finer craftsmanship than anything he'd paid for in his house—while the conversations between everyone else at the table flew by him, too fast for him to catch. It played around him almost like a musical arrangement, with everyone's voices playing different instruments and crescendoing and harmonizing at just the right moments. Even his sister, who'd not known these people before a few weeks ago, fit right into their chorus of trumpeting voices, sharing the table-stage with them as if she were one of their own.

To put it simply, the conversation both awed and intimidated him. He wanted desperately to be a part of it, but couldn't pluck up the courage.

Until Mrs. Anderson spoke, turning the table towards him. He blinked, dumbly, at the assembled parties as he tried to remember the question she'd asked. The three sisters—Rose, Harper, and May—arranged themselves around the table, with Harper sitting carefully between the two siblings. Rose watched them from across the plates as May busied herself with near-constant texting on the phone she stationed beside her glass of Pinot Grigio. Mr. Anderson sat at the head of the table, opposite his wife. The table helped themselves to heaping piles of breaded pork cutlets and mashed potatoes glistening with butter. They filled their bowls with some kind of slaw-salad topped with almonds and avocado. And only then did Luke realize he hadn't even moved to fill his own plate.

"Aren't you hungry, dear?"

"Our food's probably not good enough for him, Mom. He's used to Michelin star dining."

To his shock, the sharply edged accusation didn't come from Harper as he expected. Despite her delicate smile and the lilting cadence of a joke, it cut him. Everyone in town spoke highly of May; her barbed words surprised him.

"I'm sorry." He recovered, trying not to let her see how she'd affected him as he scrambled to pile his plate high with rolls and large portions of the still-warm food before him. "It all looks amazing. We just aren't used to big family dinners like this."

Out of the corner of his peripheral vision, he spotted Harper as she tensed. He hadn't meant to make such a personal admission. The confession surprised even him, but the memories of lonely dinners weighed heavily on his mind now more than ever.

"Well, you're always welcome at our table," Mr. Anderson said, serving himself another glass of wine. Taking a cue, Luke followed suit.

"Yeah. Thanks for sending your sister around here. She's over so often I forget she's not part of the family."

No one missed the less-than-concealed stress May put on the last part of that sentence. Even as she smiled and feigned kindness, the tension in the air tightened. Harper's skin paled slightly. Annie's hand gripped her fork until her knuckles whitened. And Mr. Anderson rushed to fix the mess his child was making.

"Now, Luke. Tell us about what you do."

"I run my own company. Have you ever used the app AppeX?"

"I'm useless with technology."

"It's basically one app that runs all of your other apps. So, you don't have to scroll between screens. I actually made it for accessibility purposes, for someone I knew at an old job who had trouble using his phone because he had tremors in his hands, but eventually, we realized a lot of people would like it. We've expanded the technology now for corporate applications, and—"

"And now you're a billionaire!" Mrs. Anderson practically cheered, immediately flooding the tops of his ears with heat.

"Mom," Harper growled.

"What? It's something to be proud of! Such successful siblings. Absolutely amazing."

May spoke again, purposefully refusing to so much as glance up from the illuminated screen of her phone. "Must be nice. Never having to worry about anything."

"You have such an amazing family. I'd trade everything if we could sit here with you guys every night," Annie said warmly, only a slight, rushing change in her breathing pattern even hinting at her panic.

"Just write us a check. I'm sure we can make a reservation for you."

Almost everyone at the table opened their mouth to say something—anything—but Harper got there first.

"I tried on a wedding dress today!"

"*What?*"

And just like that, Harper threw herself at the mercy of the table, just to cut the tension. Her pained expression showed her discomfort, but she'd blurted out the words to defend him. To save him. When the night ended and the last piece of cobbler disappeared from his plate, he asked her to walk him to the car as Annie collected some leftovers from Mrs. Anderson for later. He needed to know why she'd done what she did, needed her to explain everything, needed to ask her a hundred questions. But she spoke first.

"Listen, I'm sorry."

"What?"

He blinked. As far as he could remember, Harper *never* apologized to him. Not when she'd worked him nearly halfway to losing his legs and not when she snapped at him and not when they verbally sparred. Now, genuine conflict and uncertainty shone in her moon-drenched eyes.

"They're really, I swear, they're not usually like that. Well, my mom usually is. She's a lovable nightmare, but I don't know what got into May—"

"I didn't ask you to come out here so you could apologize."

"Really?"

"I wanted to thank you. I know what you did in there and it was..." *Selfless. Kind of heroic, or as heroic as you can be at a dining room table.* "You didn't have to do that, so thank you."

"They were humiliating. I couldn't just let them make things worse."

"Still."

She smiled, then. A little thing that meant the most to him. A few days ago, when she gave him any attention at all, he couldn't get anything but scowls from her. Now, something changed between them. Maybe they were bonding over Annie's silly, over-the-top attempts to get them together or maybe he'd shown her he wasn't such a bad guy. No matter the cause, he was glad for it. A wind whipped through the farm and she rubbed her arms to keep out the chill.

"You know, I was thinking—"

"Yes?" he asked, too hopeful.

"Your sister told me the other day she still hasn't seen much of Hillsboro. She asked me if I wouldn't mind giving her a tour tomorrow. I was wondering if you'd like to come along?"

Just when he thought she couldn't surprise him any more than she already did.

"Why?"

"I just assumed if she hadn't seen town, neither had you."

"No." He allowed himself a chuckle when really he wanted to laugh and whoop to the heavens and then maybe scoop her up in his arms and kiss her. "I mean, why do you want me there?"

"I..." She bit her lip and stared at him, as if he were a stretch of untouched land she couldn't decide how to plant or a puzzle she hadn't found all of the pieces to solve yet. "I don't know. I just don't understand you. You're a mystery to me."

"So, you want to figure me out after all?"

"I haven't decided yet."

"Will there be pie?" When she didn't seem to catch his meaning, he clarified his query. "Tomorrow. Will there be pie? If romcoms have taught me anything, it's that it's not a small town without pie."

Slowly, she nodded and his pride ballooned when her playful smile returned. "I think we can find a slice somewhere."

"Then count me in."

Chapter Eleven

"Okay, so now we're coming up on Holiday Avenue. No one really knows why it's called that, but it's basically like our Main Street. You can get basically anywhere in Hillsboro by driving this way. I'm sure you've already gone down it millions of times since you got into town."

Harper literally—and yes, she meant literally, not hyperbolically—could not remember the last time she'd talked so much at once. Her throat actually scratched from the effort of trying to keep pace with their moving feet, pointing out landmarks and features of Hillsboro as they walked, waving at family friends and making introductions to the wildly curious, but thankfully polite, people she knew in town.

"Hey, are you thirsty?"

She tripped over her own feet, shocked at the question. Luke offered her a sweating water bottle with a shrug.

"I bought it from the coffee cart a few blocks back on..." He searched for the street name, and when he found it, smiled lopsidedly at his success. "Hayberry Lane."

In his voice, the cutesy street names she loved so fiercely seemed quaint and provincial, but she somehow kept a blush from infecting her cheeks as she took the bottle from his hand. Thankfully, Annie occupied herself at the window of the animal shelter, where she cooed and snapped picture after picture at the rescue dogs pressing their wet noses to the glass.

"Ah, you must have met Beryl, then."

"The lady with the eyepatch and the limp?"

"That's the one. She's my aunt. She doesn't need the eyepatch, but she thought if she was going to have a fake leg, she might as well commit to the pirate aesthetic."

Aunt Beryl wasn't *really* her aunt, but that little fact was irrelevant. Hillsboro was a big, extended family in a lot of ways.

"You know so much about this place. I mean, of course you do. You've lived here your entire life. It doesn't surprise me. It's just... impressive. I've lived in Los Angeles my entire life and I couldn't give you directions from our house to the nearest grocery store or tell you the name of my barista for anything in the world."

Was he...joking with her? Was Luke Martin even capable of joking? He'd made the quip about pie last night, but other than that, he always seemed too nervous, too uncertain, too afraid to ever so much as attempt something as casual and friendly as a joke. Late last night, when she hadn't been able to sleep because she kept asking herself what on earth possessed her to invite him on this little outing around town, she'd countered those thoughts by making a list of everything she liked about him. When she wasn't thinking about how much she hated him and the threat he posed to her way of life, her family, and her friends, she found there were actually *many* things she liked about him. *Smart. Ambitious. Brave. Dedicated to his family. Hard-working. Insightful. Thoughtful. Surpris-*

ingly funny. Quick-witted. Dedicated. Persistent. A little awkward, a little shy, but all man, all masculine grace and devotion. Tall, dark, and handsome. Sometimes he looks at me and I feel like I'm the only woman who's ever walked the earth. Oh . . . and he called me beautiful. But she hadn't been able to admit any of that to herself until her conversation with Annie. The discovery and revelations about his past rocked her. Not enough to like him more than she despised him, not enough to open her heart to anything about him, but enough that her curiosity piqued.

"Was your family okay when we left last night?"

She did *not* want to think about her family right now. After the disastrous dinner, she'd tried to talk to her sisters, but for the first time since they'd fought about which Hogwarts house each of them would fall into, she found herself frozen out. Rose's room was open, but she wasn't in there. It didn't take much investigating to realize she was in May's locked room, comforting her. Harper returned to the present, to Luke, with a shrug.

"I don't know, really."

"I think your sisters might hate me as much as you do."

A tear opened up in her chest. After declaring she hated him, and often, to hear *him* say it with such confidence rattled her.

"I don't hate you."

"Is that so? You could have fooled me."

Again, he didn't say it with any kind of malice, which perhaps hurt even worse than if he'd screamed it at her. It was matter-of-factly heartbreaking.

"Okay, you caught me. I didn't like you in the past, but the jury's still out on whether I'll start liking you now," she teased.

"That's fair. But what about your sisters? You can't say they didn't hate us last night. Or, at least, May seemed to."

She glanced into the adoption center, where Annie had quickly befriended Tony, the eccentric older man who always walked around with an overlong lizard perched on his shoulder. Through the window, Harper watched as Annie stood in the center of the crowded room of pups and juggled two overeager dogs in her hands at once. Overhead, heavy clouds swirled, blocking the sun and casting shadows everywhere. She had checked the forecast earlier though, and the rain should hold off for another hour or so.

"Do you think she's busy?"

Thankfully, Luke laughed, breaking the stoic distance he held as he'd talked about her hating him. "If there are puppies in that store, we could be waiting here for hours."

"Come on." Her fingers twitched to reach out and take his hand in hers, but she gripped the strap of her purse instead. "Let's get you that slice of pie."

The town square of Hillsboro claimed many famous landmarks, but no statue or folly got them as much acclaim as Millie's Pie Joint. During the Great Depression, after a run on the local Savings and Loan, the building closed down and was left abandoned until the start of the Second World War, when Millie Talley bought the building—complete with a working bank vault—and turned it into a diner. The bank, and its recipes, had been in the family for years now, a true local treasure, and even if Harper had had a full seven-course meal and couldn't walk properly because of how stuffed she was, if she happened to pass by, she'd always walk in for a slice. Their peanut butter and chocolate pie couldn't be missed.

It took Luke Martin a full ten minutes to decide which pie he wanted, and when he couldn't decide between lemon chess and caramel dream, he simply ordered both. A man after her own heart. Once he'd paid for their treats—a gesture she tried to refuse several times until she realized that during her protesting he'd slyly handed his card to the cashier—they made their way out to the park in the center of the town square. With the rain coming in during the afternoon, the benches sat empty, so they made themselves comfortable on one just in front of the fountain in the center of the greenery. It hadn't run for years during the drought, but now it flowed freely, the water rolling musically in the background of their conversation.

Harper couldn't remember the last time she'd done something like this. It wasn't a date, obviously, but it was something close. She spent most of her time on the farm, at the grocery, balancing the books or running errands. When had she last just sat down in a park with a friend and a snack?

Friend. Oh, jeez. She was already calling Luke her friend and she hadn't even decided if she wanted to like him or not.

"So," he asked through a bite of whipped cream. "Why do your sisters hate us?"

"Can't a girl finish her pie first?"

"Of course she can. I just hope she isn't using the pie as a distraction to—"

His fork scarcely shoveled a large forkful of lemon chess filling and crust into his mouth before he released a groan and threw himself against the back of the bench.

"Are you okay?" she asked, scanning his person to make sure he hadn't been shot or stabbed, the only two likely reasons she could think why he would ever make such a noise.

"Uh…" Remembering himself, he straightened up. "Yes. It's just so good."

Lemon chess was one of her favorites.

"Can I have a bite?"

"If I can have a bite of yours."

They exchanged forkfuls of dessert in silence. Not awkward silence, either. Calm, companionable silence. The kind where she could actually hear her own thoughts in her head, the kind she heard when she went out to Sae's Place.

She tried not to think of his lips as they wrapped around his fork, or the way his low moan vibrated across the table and straight through her entire body. The task should have been simple enough, but she couldn't help her acute awareness of him…nor could she help that every physical part of him awakened something inside her.

When they were done with that bite, he waited expectantly for her to continue their talk. She took her time before beginning.

"Will you promise not to tell your sister?"

"Don't I look like a man who can keep a secret?"

When she first saw him in a suit, he had reminded her of James Bond. And though James Bond was a spy who, for some *stupid* reason, insisted on using his real name, he could keep a secret.

"Good point." She swallowed, hard. Whenever anyone in town asked about the entire Tom Riley situation, the family would shrug it off with an excuse about teenagers growing apart or some other such platitude in an attempt to save both of their reputations. She'd never discussed it with anybody besides Rose, yet here she was, on a bench in the middle of their town, about to tell the man she considered her enemy just yesterday morning. "May dated Tom Riley for four years. They were best friends since they were kids, and then they started dating right before they went to high school. Everyone thought they were going to get married..."

"Including May," he said, his voice dry.

"Yep. And the night they graduated, he just dumped her. Or that's what everyone thinks happened, anyway. They've never talked about it. So, I think seeing Annie is a little bit difficult for her. I try to keep her out of the way, you know, bring her to the office or the barn or—"

"Sae's Place?"

"No."

"Why not?"

She paused, tripping over the thought and how to express it without seeming like a total sap...or like she cared too much about him. "Sae's Place is kind of special, that's all."

There wasn't any way she could think of to say that without him thinking *he* was special for being brought there, but thankfully, if he caught the distinction, he didn't mention it.

"So, you knew May might get her feelings hurt, and you still chose to take Annie under your wing?"

She swallowed, hard, and stared at her hands. "Yeah."

"Why?"

"I liked her."

"You didn't even know her."

"She's got spirit. I like that."

And now that she *did* know Annie, she adored her, just like everyone else who met her. Tossing his empty pie container in the nearest trashcan, Luke smiled, his lips tilting up halfway in a manner that on other men would have looked arrogant or conceited, but on him, just lit a burning flush along her collarbone. When he returned, he scooped up his second slice and began digging in, offering her a bite she didn't accept.

"And I hear she has a very charismatic, very well-spoken, hilarious older brother."

"Shut up and eat your pie."

He did, for a moment. But then, he spoke up again, seemingly unable to help himself.

"You're a very good tour guide, you know."

"Good to know I'm good at something other than getting dirt under my fingernails."

"I never said—"

"You kind of implied it."

He scoffed, an almost offensive sound that sparked familiar threads of offense in her. "Only because you take such pride in it."

"In what?"

"In being a real, independent, tough woman."

"I *am* a real, independent, tough woman."

"To your detriment."

All along, they'd been playing around the barriers of sincerity, cloaking their words in teasing tones and eye rolls so neither of them could take the other too seriously. This changed that. Harper dropped her voice to dangerous lows.

"What's that supposed to mean?"

This man always dodged left when she predicted he'd swing right. Instead of stooping to her quietly infuriated level, he started to speak, his eyes lighting up as he did. Not a word came across as condescending or rude. It was almost as if he wanted to trade ideas with her, share possibilities. "Have you thought about all the ways that you could revolutionize your entire operation? Bring in modern sprinklers and new, resilient cross-breeds and I was reading about this farm in upstate New York that is able to reuse their water—"

"We do things the way we do them. We can't be something else. Especially not now."

She'd lived by the tenants of her family's history her entire life. Protect your family. Protect the past. Protect the farm with your family by abiding by the ways of the past. It was the only way she knew how to live, the only way she knew how to produce the blooms and the life she loved. Everything else, frankly, scared the daylights out of her. Not that she'd ever tell him that. Trying for the fancy, new technology was *exactly* what she wanted. But they couldn't afford it. Not now.

"I could help you, you know," he said, his voice was so soft it raised goosebumps on the back of her neck. "I'd like to help you."

Defensive walls shot up around her. "Why? So you can then use that against me and make us host your sister's wedding?"

"No. Because no matter what you think about me, the jury's *not* out on whether or not I like you."

"What?"

Her dumbfounded question received no answer as fat, heavy raindrops began to slip out of the sky and down towards them. First, one landed squarely on the last bit of Luke's pie.

"Ah!"

A torrential downpour quickly followed in that solitary drop's tracks, racing down towards them with a chilly ferocity.

"It wasn't supposed to rain until noon," Harper shouted over the grumbling of the shower, as if the sky could hear her and would apologize.

"C'mon." Without pretense or self-awareness, Luke slipped his jacket off and held it over Harper's head until she took it from him, shielding herself from the raindrops. It was still warm, a tiny respite from the icy cold of the rain.

They made quick work of plans to return to the house, but then the digital watch on Luke's wrist buzzed and he swiped the screen to call up the text message, pausing their conversation. When he'd read it, he snorted and displayed the illuminated text to Harper, who spotted that it'd been sent from Annie. *You guys go ahead and go to lunch or something. I'm going to stay and play with the puppies and call a taxi back home. There's some clean clothes at the house that should fit Harper if she wants to change into something dry. Top drawer!*

"Another ploy to get us to fall for each other?" she asked, raising an eyebrow.

Luke laughed, a sound that reverberated over the thunder. "If anyone on Earth would try to change the weather just so she could cause something like this, it'd be her."

*

"*You live here?*"

The devil with her *too-cool-for-school-whatever-I-don't-care-about-your-money-anyway-ripping-up-blank-checks-because-the-sight-of-them-is-insulting* attitude. This place had everything. Intercoms! Real, marble finishes instead of the cheap stuff on their countertops at home! A panel on the wall that controlled the blinds! Those artificial intelligence boxes you can talk to and that'll make dentist appointments for you! Paintings on the wall that had been done by a *real* artist, not just a print bought at a junk sale! Everything sparkled with a fresh-clean shine and practically glowed despite the lack of sun pouring through the oversized windows dominating the front of the house. Without having to be asked, Harper slipped her boots off as soon as she crossed the threshold. She wasn't going to dirty up this house for anything in the world. Luke didn't even attempt to conceal his amusement at her shock.

"Just temporarily. Not that you'd know it from the way Annie's been redecorating. She'll move in with Tom after the wedding and I'll head back to L.A."

Back to L.A. She bit the inside of her lip to keep from focusing on the pain in her chest.

"You're going back, then?"

"I think so, if you think you can get along on the farm without my superior raking skills."

He winked, and he looked so rumpled and handsome that she *almost* forgot about the twinge in her heart at the thought of him leaving. He continued.

"It's only an hour and a half or so by plane to visit. I won't be too far. Can't get rid of me that easy." He moved through the open-concept layout of the first floor into the kitchen. "Are you hungry?"

"No, I think the pie sufficiently stuffed me."

"Are you sure? I have plenty to eat in here. We've got—"

"Let me see." As a farm girl, she could always find at least a *little* room for snacks, even when she was stuffed. So, she dove through the open fridge door, her damp shoulder brushing his. A spark of electricity snapped between them, one that not even the chill of the fridge could dampen.

Let's see what we have here, she thought, trying to give no more attention to his closeness. Tons of to-go boxes, milk, protein powders and eggs filled the icebox, but, more importantly, so did an obnoxious amount of boxes stamped with the *Millie's Pie Joint* logo. "I see you're already acquainted with Millie's pies, then?"

His shrug was noncommittal and it didn't explain anything. Why on earth would he have agreed to go into town with them on the condition that they find a place to get pie if he was already extremely familiar with Millie's? Abandoning the fridge before she could ask him any more about it or get lost in the pinewood scent of him, she shook her head to clear the echo of his words from it. *The jury's not out on whether or not I like you.*

Changing the subject, she asked if he'd show her to Annie's room for a change of clothes, a request he happily obliged. The over-the-top glamor of Annie's room shouldn't have surprised her in the least, but when she pressed the top button of the command panel by the bedroom's door and an army of lights flooded the otherwise dark room, nearly blinding her, she staggered back a step before she could turn them off again. The lights must have been for pictures and videos Annie did for her sponsors or for her personal brand and marketing, but even without them and despite the storm outside, Harper treated herself to the tiniest of snoops. First, she retrieved some oversized pajamas from the top drawer, which must have dwarfed Annie's frame but fit perfectly on hers. Then, as she slipped into the dry clothing, she scanned the room for hints and clues about these people, anything about them to help her understand.

Annie loved pictures. But her room only had one. She and her brother at what appeared to be her high school graduation, both looking so happy and so proud she couldn't help but smile back.

When she emerged from the bedroom, Luke waited outside for her in dry clothes of his own. Having only seen him in suits or work clothes, she liked the sight of him in a pair of perfectly fitting jeans and a faded *Star Trek* T-shirt. A good look on him. He extended his hands to her.

"Can I take those for you?"

"I'm going to need them back," she snarked.

"I was just going to throw them in the dryer, smart aleck."

"Thanks," she said, smiling genuinely up at him as he took her clothes and led her back downstairs.

In the hall he pressed a panel in the wall, revealing a hidden laundry with two *sets* of washers and dryers. He tossed their collection of wet clothes in and set them on a spin cycle before returning to her.

"Now, how about a tour? Annie says you can't invite someone to your house without giving them a tour."

Side by side in the wide hallway, they made their way through the labyrinthine house.

"Is there a dungeon? Or an indoor roller coaster somewhere?"

"No, but we *do* have a movie theatre."

"A movie theatre?"

"Don't get too excited." He pushed open a door and showed off a high-tech media room. "It's just what Annie calls the TV room."

The tour took them through the house's many rooms and features, showing off his house the way she'd shown off her town. About halfway through the second floor, though, a chipper voice cut through the air between them like a whistling meadowlark. The front door slammed.

"I'm home!" Annie cried. "Guys! Guys? Where are you?"

"Up here," they replied, voices overlapping. Her heels clicked up the staircase towards them almost at a jog. The rain outside hadn't stopped, meaning every step was accompanied by the drip-drip of water coming off of her.

"I've got good news."

"What's that?" Luke asked.

She appeared at the end of the hall and the sight of her rendered her thrilled declaration absolutely useless.

"I got a puppy!"

"*Annie!*"

"No! Her name isn't Annie! Her name is...well, I don't have a name for her yet." She rubbed the puppy's snout, only to receive puppy kisses in return. She cooed. "Do I, sweet thing?"

"Annie, you can't have a dog!"

"But Harper has a dog!"

"No, Harper has a monster. She does *not* have a dog."

From the way Annie's face had lit up, someone who hadn't seen the wriggling creature in her arms would have thought she'd just discovered the cure for polio.

"Monster! I love that name! Do you like that name? Huh, Monster? Huh? C'mon. Let's show you to my room."

Ignoring her brother's protestations behind her, she flounced away, muttering to the sweet animal as she went. When a distant door clicked, signifying she'd retired successfully to her own corner of the house, Luke shook his head at her.

"You're a bad influence, Miss Harper Anderson. She hangs out with you and suddenly she's adopting puppies."

"What can I say?" She chuckled and waved for him to continue their tour. "It's a gift."

They moved through the halls while consciously ignoring the *yips* from the dog upstairs. He took such care to explain every little detail that when they turned a corner and he skipped a room, her curiosity got the better of her. She opened it.

"And what's in here?"

"No, don't go in there—"

With a reaction like she'd been about to open a portal to another dimension, she was surprised to find that when she opened the door, there was little more than a piano, a vase, and a desk and chair set in the impeccably plain room.

"A piano?" She snorted at his apparent distress and raised a curious eyebrow as her fingers trailed along the top of the Steinway. No dust came back on her fingerprints, meaning it'd probably been used and cleaned recently. "This is what you were hiding? Or is there a dead body in here or something?"

Rolling his eyes, he rooted himself to the doorway with all of the unmoving determination of a tree. "I'm not going to dignify that with a response."

"And flowers." She brushed her fingers against the petal of one of the peonies. "Annie has good taste. Peonies are my favorite."

"They're from your farm. I bought them from Rose's shop yesterday."

"You did?"

"Don't look so surprised."

"Sorry, I just assumed all of this was Annie's doing."

He shrugged, not even seeming to care that she understood him less and less with every passing moment. "Well, it's my study, so she doesn't come in here much." The gears in her jaw sprung, and she stared at him with unabashed shock. "What? After I came into a little money, I wanted to learn."

"Can you play?"

"No."

This man learned software development by watching over a stranger's shoulder. Not one ounce of her believed he'd take piano lessons not to play at all.

"How many lessons have you taken?"

"Not enough."

She helped herself to one end of the instrument's accompanying bench and patted the empty seat next to her. "C'mon, play a little song."

"No, thank you." A retreating step backwards made the floorboard behind him creak. "Do you want to see the library?"

"I should have known. Just like a rich guy to buy a piano and never play it. Unless, of course, you actually *can* play?"

"I'm not going to embarrass myself in front of you. You can't reverse psychology me into this—"

"Please." The plea reverberated through the room, an unresolved chord of sincerity. When they agreed to come here, she didn't know what she'd gain out of it except some dry clothes and maybe a chance to see Annie again once the rain cleared up and they could go back into town for a more complete tour. Now, she knew why the rain came earlier and she ended up here. She *needed* to hear him play. "I'd like to hear."

Deliberation lasted about a moment before he bowed his head and joined her. She didn't miss the way he did his best to sit on the farthest end of the bench away from her.

"Don't say I didn't warn you." Long fingers, now scarred with calluses from the work he'd done on the farm, lifted the black lid to reveal ebony and ivory keys so perfectly bright their reflection shone in them. "I'm really not very good."

"Then, just play the easiest song you know. Impress me."

His fingers settled into the keys, and before she knew it, she was giggling.

"'Heart and Soul,' really?"

"It's the easiest one I know! Besides, I thought you'd like this song."

"Why?"

"Because it's so old-fashioned."

Their eyes met. He smiled, and then, he started to sing, a tripping, beautiful sound that broke through every wall she'd ever been able to build around herself. *I fell in love with you, heart and soul...*

As she sat there, close enough to touch him but afraid to even breathe in case it knocked them out of this spell, a realization dawned on her. Slowly at first, but with all of the rushing energy of a star bursting within her very heart.

She'd been falling for him this entire time, and she didn't even know it. *Rats.*

Chapter Twelve

"Okay. Just go in there, knock on her door, and tell her what's going on. You have coffee. You have breakfast. You have the confidence. Just ask her. There's no way she could say no."

Luke hadn't hyped himself up like this since the last time he asked a woman out on a date, which was...well, he couldn't remember the last time he asked a woman out on a date. His schedule and the unspoken marriage contract he'd entered into with his work made fun Friday nights out at a bar in The Hills almost impossible, but as he walked up to the door of the Anderson house at four in the morning on a Tuesday, once again in his work clothes, the vague memory of pre-date butterflies transformed into very real butterflies in his stomach.

No, not butterflies. Butterflies daintily flipped their wings on summer breezes. His stomach housed tornadoes.

It wasn't the prospect of seeing Harper that had him all out of sorts. Seeing her always lit a fire in him, but today, he had bigger things on his mind than impressing her or trying to keep himself from smiling at her too often. It wasn't even really a date. It was a business meeting, though she didn't quite know that yet. Over the time they'd spent together on the farm, he'd come to realize that the flowers they grew there were exceptional, the kind of beauty that didn't deserve some kind of corporate hostile takeover or whatever would happen if they lost the place. No, that kind of special deserved celebration, and he was going to make sure the Andersons got it. As time went on, he spent every spare moment he had making calls to friends in L.A., to acquaintances in San Fran, to people he met once at a fundraiser in Portland, talking up the *most amazing flower farm in the entire country.*

And finally, he had a lead. A big lead, in fact. One of his sister's former sorority sisters' brothers managed one of the most important event planning businesses in Los Angeles. Academy events, fundraisers, Betty White's birthday party. He did it all. And a contract with him—with celebrities whose word-of-mouth meant everything—could set up the Andersons for life. They'd never have to worry about money again. All he needed to do was make the "accidental" introduction today at the farmers' market, let Jerome see the amazing flowers the Andersons grew, and everything would fall into place.

Oh, and he had to make sure she never found out he'd done this. That element was key. In his entire life, he'd never met another person who wore their pride like a suit of armor. She wrapped her ability to take care of herself and her family over her shoulders like a royal cloak threaded through with gold and jewels. Deciding to help her meant also deciding to protect her pride, and he'd do it a million times over if he never had to see a stitch of worry in her face or hear doubt in her future ever again.

Juggling a sweating bag of greasy breakfast sandwiches and donuts—he didn't know which she'd prefer—and a tray of four different types of coffee—he'd seen her drink coffee almost every morning on the farm, but he couldn't figure out how much milk she'd want, so he got four with different amounts just to make sure—he elbowed the door three times in an attempt at a knock. When the door opened, May, rather than Harper, opened the door. With the wealth of new knowledge he had about her, he couldn't stop his pulse from going off to the races without him at the sight of her.

"Look what the cat dragged in."

"May. Hi. It's good to see you," he lied, barely able to hear his own words over the hammering of his own heart. If his being around made her uncomfortable, he didn't want to force himself into this situation. But, as he inspected her face, he found no signs of distress. On the contrary, she leaned in the doorway with an arrogant smirk, looking like the snapshot cover of a country music album rather than a still-heartbroken woman shaken by his very presence.

"I heard you kidnapped my sister and took her to your palatial fortress on the other side of the county."

"I didn't—"

"Look, you don't have to explain yourself to me. It may have been a kidnapping, but at least she got out. Harper never gets out of this house. Need a hand?"

She snapped the bag of greasy breakfast sandwiches before he could even open his mouth. This was *not* the lovelorn woman he'd expected after Harper's description. Charming and easy, so different than the last time he saw her, she breezed into the house and waved for him to follow her.

"Harper!" she shouted as she went. "Your boyfriend's here!"

"He's not my—" Like a flash of lightning, Harper appeared, but stopped short when she spotted him in the doorway to the kitchen. "What are you doing here?"

For the first time, that kind of question didn't feel like she was trying to shove him away, didn't feel like he was an unwanted plague trying to encroach upon her family. Instead, it was filled with surprise. Happy surprise, like she'd gotten an Amazon package in the mail she didn't remember ordering.

"I still work here, don't I?" he asked with a lazy smile and an internal cringe at the thought that she might tell him to ditch his plan and go and work a shift outside.

"Well, you haven't been to work in a while. I assumed you'd quit."

"And give you the satisfaction? Not a chance." He offered her the coffee. To his delight, her smile didn't falter as she took it. For the last few days, things between them had been nice, comfortable. He was so glad to see his arrival this morning hadn't changed that. For the last few days, things between them had been nice, comfortable. He didn't want his arrival here to disturb that. "I brought breakfast."

"I can see that...why?"

"I thought I'd help you with the farmers' market today."

"May already agreed—"

"Oh my God." May's entire face brightened. "Would you take my place? I could really use a day off."

"But—"

The youngest of the Anderson clan would hear no *buts*. Without confirmation from either Luke nor Harper, she sprinted up the stairs, her heavy boots thudding against each creaking floorboard.

They sounded as angry as her eyes always looked when they were turned in his direction.

"See you later, lovebirds!"

Alone again. He extended the coffee a second time.

"So, what do you say? I'm a good salesman."

"What've you got in those bags?" she asked, pointing to the brown paper bags turned almost see-through by grease and sugar that May brought in as soon as he arrived.

"Every breakfast sandwich and donut type they offered at Trent's."

"Blueberry Cake donut and a bacon, egg and cheese bagel?"

"I've got both."

"We'll eat them on the way. The truck's already loaded."

The Hillsboro County Market was like something out of a Broadway musical, and as much as he loved delivery food and ordering his groceries online, Luke vowed that when he moved back to Los Angeles, he'd make it a point to find something like this out there. Everywhere he turned, new smells, sights and sounds arrested him until he thought maybe he'd struggle to focus on the task at hand. Butchers, bakers, and yes, even candlestick makers littered the parking lot on Main and Oxford Street which—once a month—turned into the biggest and most renowned farmers' market in the northern half of the state. Back home, the biggest collection of fresh food he ever saw in one place was a weekly food truck roundup near his house, but that little hipster showdown paled in comparison to this.

"How do you like it so far?" Harper asked as they set up a table in front of the truck's bed.

"I'm just glad I left my wallet in the glove compartment."

"Why?"

He nodded to a stall across from them, which sold handmade meat pies and empanadas. Every time the slightest of breezes kicked up, the spicy, sultry scent of red pepper and jalapeño sent shockwaves straight to his already growling stomach.

"Because I would have bought a hundred of those meat pies by now if I could."

"Your lunch break isn't until noon and you just ate breakfast. Trent's isn't exactly light food."

"I'm a growing boy who's been doing more manual labor than sleeping lately, Harper. I need my energy."

Setting up the stand proved easier than Luke had expected. He'd thought there would be more hauling and arranging involved, but no. They simply pulled the car in reverse, dropped the back of the truck bed and opened the lid to reveal the rows and rows of flowers just waiting to be taken home by some lucky patron. Now, they were setting up the accoutrements, a little table and credit card reader for the transactions, a sign hung from the top of the truck declaring their brand and the prices. Most of the flowers weren't arranged in bouquets—according to Harper, Rose got *very* cross anytime someone in the family besides her tried to arrange their product, so she always arranged a few to sell at the farmers' market, just in case any tourists stopped by and wanted some—but these events usually ended up being more for wholesale purchases to local restaurants or event spaces.

Eventually, they settled in behind their table as the clock struck nine, meaning the patrons could filter in through the rest of the day. With his newly acquired knowledge of the flower industry, Luke actually found himself well-equipped to answer questions about shelf life and taking care of the blooms. He'd never tell anyone at the office this, but he felt almost as proud of his first sale of a few cyclamen flowers as he had been when AppeX made their first million. He always kept one eye on the open fairground, though, trying to search for and spot Jerome. The tall Black man who usually shirked convention and wore colorful suits or faded Dolly Parton T-shirts under tailored, equally colorful blazers was hard to miss in a crowd, but Luke wanted to make sure he wasn't caught off guard by the man's arrival. He wanted to be one step ahead.

Which proved almost impossible given how magnetic Harper turned out to be. His knowledge was passable, enough to sell some flowers and impress tourists who wanted a few flowers to spruce up their weekend rental. *She*, on the other hand, could have sold flowers to someone deathly allergic to them. Passion shone through every conversation she had with every potential customer. She got lost in her own explanations of their growing techniques and cultivation habits, of the soft petals of this flower or the especially bold scent of that one. He watched her as one might have watched Baryshnikov, a master at the height of their powers, someone who made art out of their work. During a lull in the customers, when most of them had hurried off to buy armloads of empanadas or specialty cheeseburgers or vegan mac-n-cheese, he spoke.

"What do you like about this job?"

"You don't like this job?" She raised a teasing eyebrow.

"Is there any answer that won't make you hate me just a little bit?"

Either he'd seem like a stuck-up man who couldn't be bothered with something so menial as this job or he'd seem like a tourist who only liked the job because he didn't have to do it forever and had barely come into work since his injury. Harper nodded and smirked her understanding.

"Good point."

"It's just that you clearly care about what you do. What makes it so special?"

She toyed with a snipped piece of twine, discarded when she'd tied up some flowers for their last customer.

"I like to see every flower as a possibility, you know?" Warmth coated her cheeks. He couldn't stop staring. "When I look at them, I know they could go anywhere and be anything. Maybe they're an apology. Maybe they're a declaration of love. Maybe they're for condolences. But they always mean something. I guess I like imagining what that *something* might be."

He marveled at the idea that she could see so much hope in tiny, multicolored plants, but held on to hating him for so long. Not that he'd given her much of a reason to like him. For a brief, fleeting moment, he wondered what it would have been like to give her flowers—for real, this time, not as some kind of apology. What would it be like for him to walk up to her house at the beginning of a date, give her a big bouquet of flowers, and have her look at him like he hung the moon? He spun this around in circles until a voice snapped him out of it.

"Luke Martin, is that you?"

Oh, no. If he was going to pull this off without Harper suspecting his hand was in it all along, he should have first checked to see if Jerome had any acting chops to speak of. His first line delivery was less than promising.

"Jerome? What are you doing here?"

Jerome's life was nothing less than a fascinating one. He'd started out playing professional football, when an injury cost him his job at the height of his career. So, he took his money and his celebrity connections and moved to Los Angeles to plan the parties he'd always loved attending as an athlete. He'd been a wide receiver in The League, so he stood a good foot taller than anyone else around, and carried himself with the careful grace of a man who'd made millions of dollars trying not to get knocked into next Sunday by a defensive end.

"I'm just taking a little sojourn to the country. Big City Life can be exhausting, but, of course, I don't have to tell you that. I haven't seen you or your sister in *ages*. How has she been adjusting to life in a town with only one Starbucks?"

"She's been coping. You should try the Blue Hills Coffee at the end of the market. It's unbelievable."

"Luke, I—"

Harper's interjection forced the full weight of Jerome's stare to land squarely on her.

"I'm so sorry. We've been so rude. I'm Jerome Lemoyne. Luke and I are old friends." The lie came easily to him. So easily, in fact, that it took Luke a whole three seconds before he realized that he'd never *actually* met this guy in person before.

"I'm Harper Anderson. Nice to meet you." They shook hands. "I taught Annie everything she knows about where to get the best pie in Hillsboro County."

"I know! I recognize you from her Instagram. I was so jealous of all the fun she'd been having I had to come out here and visit for my—" As if on cue, he whirled to spot the truck half-full of flowers behind them, his face displaying genuine delight. *Either he's better than I thought or he really does love the flowers as much as I told him he would*, Luke mused. "Oh my goodness. Are these yours?"

"Yes, sir. We're—"

But Jerome had already retrieved his phone and by the time he cut her off, he'd snapped no fewer than twelve pictures of the inventory in the back of the trunk. "I'm absolutely wild about them."

"Thank you so much. We work very hard—"

"How do they hold up?"

"In what conditions?"

"Indoor ballroom, for example."

"They'll last basically forever. I mean, forever in flower years, so, like, a week or two."

It was completely silly, unfounded, and not his place, but his chest puffed out with pride as she put on her businesswoman face and went toe-to-toe with one of the biggest influencers in one of the most influential cities in the country.

"Can you ship to Los Angeles?"

"In big enough quantities, and there is one florists' shop that sells them there in small batches but—"

"What about your entire farm? Is that a big enough quantity?"

She blinked.

"I'm sorry—"

"No, *I'm* sorry. I'm getting ahead of myself. What's your annual production?"

She stumbled over the figure.

"Perfect. Absolutely perfect." His phone stopped acting as a camera and started working as a notepad. His fingers hurried across the screen, taking down everything she said. "And are these all of the varietals you have?"

Voice and breath rising in pitch and speed, she explained the varietals they couldn't harvest yet. These were the early blooms or the flowers they'd been harvesting through the spring. Their summer blooms wouldn't be ready yet for a few weeks.

"Peonies are going to be everywhere this season. Everyone's just going crazy over them. How much of your harvest can I secure today?"

"I—"

This wasn't so much a negotiation as a lay-down. Jerome took one look at the flowers and all negotiation went out of the window. Without so much as putting up a fight or bargaining, Harper was winning. "You know what? You don't have to twist my arm. My suppliers in L.A. are nothing but a big, overpriced, corporate pain and I've been looking to go with someone different. These are... simply breathtaking. Here's my offer. I'm going to write a number down on my card. You go back to your family—this is a family business, right?—and you talk it over with them. I'll give you this number this year for all of the peonies you can give me, and I'll double it next year."

Harper's jaw hung open. Her chest rose and fell with quick, disbelieving breaths. She tried to speak once, then twice, and on the third try, her voice was finally strong enough to get the words out. "You're joking, right? This is a joke."

"Trust me, I'm a lot funnier than this. When I'm joking, you'll know it."

"I'll have to talk to my family."

"Of course. I'm here till the weekend, but if you need more time than that, just give me a ring. Phone number and video messaging contacts are on the card. But, while I'm here, I'll want something for my hotel room. It's so drab and lifeless. I was shocked that such a lively little town would have such *beige* hotel rooms. And I'm going on a date tonight. I'll need some flowers for him..." Soon, he'd cleared out a quarter of their remaining stock, reverently placing flowers into various reusable tote bags he'd brought with him for the market. "Alright, goodbye now! I look forward to hearing from you soon!"

Luke waved him off, muttering through a clenched-jaw smile to Harper, "Wow. What did the card say? Harper? Harper, are you..."

Are you okay sounded insignificant and hollow when he looked down and realized she was crying. Sitting on the edge of the truck bed, legs dangling off the side and face firmly pressed into her palms, oblivious to the noise and joy around her, her body shook with quiet sobs. He knelt down in front of her, placing his hands chastely on her knees with a butterfly-wing touch, afraid any more pressure would spook her or break her.

"Harper?" he prompted again, putting all of his concern into that one word instead of wasting his breath on something as pithy and understated as *are you okay* or *what's wrong*. He tried to think of what he did for his sister when she cried. Glasses of cold water or hot tea usually helped. Hugs usually helped. But he wasn't sure what Harper would want in this situation, so he held his position and simply asked, "Is there anything I can do for you?"

Suddenly remembering his presence, she snapped her head up, revealing the full extent of the damage the tears had done to her face. Hot skin puffed around her eyes and tracks ran down her lightly powdered cheeks.

And she was smiling. A tearful, grateful, over-the-moon smile so contagious Luke immediately returned it, stretching his lips until they actually started causing him pain.

"Luke, we're saved."

"What do you mean?"

"The farm...we were going to lose the farm and now..."

She placed the now crinkled and tear-marked business card in his hands, and when he checked the number, his stomach dropped. He'd been offered ludicrous sums of money for the tech he'd built in his apps, but still, this number sent a thrill of surprise and relief down his spine.

"And now you're going to be okay?"

"We're going to be okay."

Every synapse and neuron in his body and his brain went off at once in a physical sort of fireworks finale, tugging him left and right and filling him with giddy joy and sparks until he couldn't contain himself for another second. Jumping from his place on the ground, he scooped Harper into his arms and swung her around, holding her to his chest as if he were the only thing tethering them both to the earth.

In a moment of freedom, of lightness, of whatever hummed in

the erratic air between them, she giggled, releasing peals of laughter as she held on to him right back.

When the spinning stopped, though, neither of them let go. Not immediately. Not at first. Instead, he found himself holding her even closer and burying his face in her hair, his eyes sliding closed as he drank in the scent of earth and flowers, of the real and the romantic.

"I guess you should go discuss this with your family," he said, whispering so close to her ear she shivered.

"I guess I should."

But she didn't move. Not for a long time. They just stood there, holding on to this moment and each other like their lives depended on it. And Luke held on to something else, too. A secret. *I think I'm falling for you, Harper Anderson.*

Chapter Thirteen

Returning to her family's house so they could share the good news and so she could teach him how to bake a pie seemed, at the time, an innocent enough suggestion. But now that they were there, rushing through the doorway only to be greeted by her family's dumbstruck faces, she couldn't be sure if she'd made the right decision.

Mostly because, once the entire room went silent and stared at them, she reached out and grabbed his hand, an impulse decision she immediately fixed, but couldn't make herself regret. She flexed her hand to rid herself of the tingling.

"Did you guys elope or something?" Rose's teasing voice asked, handing her father the section of the newspaper she'd just finished and picking up one of her own. As May went white and worried-looking, their mother clapped and gasped and made a big fuss that injected red-hot heat into Harper's collarbone.

"That would be simply wonderful! Did you?"

"No! Why would you even say that?"

"Besides the fact that I knew it would drive Mom crazy?"

That response earned Rose a pillow in the face, courtesy of their matriarch. Though they no longer held hands, Luke's and Harper's shoulders brushed, a fact she was reminded of when that particular gesture made him chuckle. She'd forgotten what he'd said the last time he'd been here. And what Annie told her hundreds of times before. They didn't have a big family. Maybe that's why he'd scooped her up in his arms and spun her around. Through her and through Annie, maybe he'd begun to care about her little family, no matter how rude they might have been to him in the past. Perhaps he understood how much this contract would mean to them, what this big business would do to their lives.

She refused to believe it had anything whatsoever to do with her. He didn't like her. He couldn't like her. And she wasn't about to tell herself that he did. Even pretending or wishful thinking could break her heart.

"What happened, then?" Her father licked his thumb and turned the page of his paper, which he peered at with the help of his thin reading spectacles.

"Do you want to tell it?" she asked Luke.

"It was your deal. I don't know why I'd get to tell it."

Her father offered a small smile, though his eyes remained trained on his paper. "Good man."

"Okay, so we're at the farmers' market, right? And Luke happens to see this guy he knows..." Her family hanging on her every word, Harper laid out the story, giving them every detail she could remember in her adrenaline-high fog. Even her father, who generally checked out during wild displays of emotion like this, tuned into the tale, nodding along with the twists and turns. "And..." She dragged the word out for maximum suspense as she fished around in her pocket for the business card that would change their lives. Purposefully, she marched to her father and held it out to him, so he could see the sum contained inside. "This is the fee he threw out for this year's peonies alone."

Her father's face went white as a spring cloud.

"You can't be serious."

"What? What's the figure?"

She turned and showed it to her mother, who immediately went silent.

"Alright, show us, too," Rose demanded.

Then, everyone knew exactly what they were dealing with. They knew the story. They knew the man. They knew the number. And they were speechless.

But only for a moment before the entire family exploded into conversation, some of it whispered between her parents, some of it declared between siblings, but all of it rushed and excitable, full of the promise of things to come.

"This could really change things—"

"If he's big with celebrities, there's no telling—"

"—Could buy more land—"

"—Expand our store in town—"

"—Pay off our debts—"

"—Pay the girls a better wage—"

"Guys!" Harper called for silence, holding the business card in the air. "We can't start spending the money until we decide if we're going to take it or not."

A sea of dropped jaws and wide eyes faced her. Her father spluttered to life first.

"You didn't already agree to take it?"

"No. I'm not the boss around here," she reminded him.

"Give me that." He snapped the card out of her hands and shot her and Luke a secret smile. His lopsided, difficult walk picked up a jolly pace as he looped his arm around his wife's shoulders and started walking her to his office. He leaned heavily against her, abandoning his cane. "Your mother and I have to go make a phone call."

"What about dinner?"

"Hang dinner!" her mother shouted. "We'll go out to a restaurant."

Restaurant. The word was sweet as cream. Had they been their twelve-year-old selves again, they all would have starting losing their minds with joy, considering how rare a treat it was for their parents to be able to afford to take them all out. Tonight, the reaction was only slightly more tame, with May popping up from her position on the loveseat and dodging for her shoes by the door.

"And if we're getting a raise, I'm going into town to get a new dress. Big sale at Water's. Want to come?"

Rose reached for her own pair of shoes and glanced expectantly at her. "I'm in."

Dress shopping. Possibly with Luke. Again. She couldn't risk it.

"I was actually thinking we'd stay in."

"Really? Just the two of us?" Luke asked.

"I told you. It's not a celebration without pie, so I'm going to teach you how to make one."

"We can go to Millie's when we get into town," May retorted.

"I was thinking about using Grandma's pie recipe. Family tradition and all that."

A perfectly tweezed eyebrow raised on May's suspicious face. Their grandmother's recipes were notoriously difficult, notoriously old-fashioned. She even had one that instructed the reader to "milk the cow," prior to beginning the actual baking portion of the instructions. "Are you sure?"

Harper nodded. Literally anything to get out of shopping again. The wedding dress fiasco had put her off the experience for good.

"More power to you."

"C'mon." Rose grabbed her younger sister's arm and nearly dragged her to the door, gliding past Luke and Harper as she went. "I've been dying for some new work clothes." She tossed a pointed glance over her shoulder at the pair of them. "See you two later."

"See you."

May slammed the door behind them before Luke finished his goodbye, leaving them alone again. In all of the hurried excitement, this was the first moment of peace since Jerome showed up at the farmers' market. The two of them had managed to fall into an easy rhythm, a friendly back and forth. Now, she felt awkward. Uncertain.

"So . . ." Luke drawled. "Pie?"

"I just didn't want to go dress shopping. We don't have to do—" The clock above the mantelpiece read six o'clock, and her entire body stiffened. "Oh, my God. I forgot you're on the clock. You need to go home. I've kept you so late—"

She'd forgotten, for a moment, that they weren't friends. Not officially. Officially, she was his acquaintance and his worker. She had no business holding him hostage at her house.

"Go home and miss the celebration?" He feigned hurt, but he injected real hope into Harper's veins.

"You want to celebrate with us?"

"Am I invited?"

"I asked you first."

"Okay, you caught me. Yes, I want to celebrate with you. And get a slice of that amazing pie. I didn't know any of my grandparents, but everyone says something made by a grandma is better than anything from the store. And if you can beat Millie's, then I've got to try it."

Despite the rest of his messy taunting, she didn't miss the way he said *with you* instead of *with you all*.

"Alright. How much do you know about making pie?"

"Absolutely nothing."

"Great." She pulled her hair up into a ponytail, readying herself for a battle with the kitchen. "Then you'll be very good at following directions."

As it turned out, neither of them were very good with directions. The handwritten recipe didn't help. Grandma's curvy, old-school penmanship drove them both to the point of blindness, where neither of them could tell which numbers or letters were which. Not to mention all of the ingredients they'd had to substitute to make the recipe work with their limited pantry. The strawberry glazed pie with ornamental strawberry-shaped crust topping became a peanut butter cup pie with a lattice crust, with the two of them combining their understanding of Grandma's writing and televised cooking shows to throw something together. It took a lot of elbow grease and a lot of guesswork, but eventually they managed to shove something resembling a pie into the oven—at 300 degrees, though it was very possible the pie was meant to go in at 350, something they debated for a full fifteen minutes before pre-heating the machine. With their treasure in the oven, they set about tidying the kitchen of the immense mess they'd made.

"This pie's going to be a disaster."

"No question about it, but at least we made it with our own two hands and I didn't have to go dress shopping."

"Do you think your grandmother's going to come back from the grave and haunt us if it's inedible? Will we be cursed for ruining her memory with an abomination of a pie?"

"Very possible. From what Dad says, she was a very spiteful woman." The disposal roared to life as she dropped the cracked eggshells down into its belly. "Could really hold on to a grudge."

"That sounds like someone else I know."

"Who?" She spun around just in time to spot him tilt his head in a *please-don't-make-me-say-it-when-it's-so-obvious* look, so she responded with an equally sarcastic, "Surely you can't be speaking about *moi*?"

"At least you come by your stubbornness honestly."

Since that day at his house, she'd been unable to stop the growing feelings building for him with every passing day. Constantly finding new things to like about him only added to the sensation. Whenever they spent much time in close company, she spotted something new she hadn't spotted before, another quality to add to her growing list. The ease with which he teased her, now that they were comfortable around one another, proved irresistible. She couldn't help but return it in kind.

"My stubbornness?" She reached for the nearest pile of flour and flicked a bit of it at his fitted, blue flannel button-down. "What about your pride?"

He stared down at the flecks of white powder as if they were blood splatters, then raised a challenging eyebrow in her direction. "Harper Anderson, don't start something you can't finish."

"Who says I can't finish it? I've been having flour fights since I was in a cradle."

This time, she didn't settle for a light spray of flour, she grabbed a handful of the stuff and hurled it in his direction with the force of a pitcher facing down the batter's box in the Bronx.

"That's it. You're on. Come here!"

And just like that, a war broke out. A war of flour and skill and who could slip and slide around the kitchen island or duck behind it the fastest. They exchanged barbs and taunts and soon, their weapon of choice covered the kitchen in a haze of white, leaving them both coated in a thick layer of the stuff.

When the flour finally settled and they called a ceasefire, Harper found herself suddenly close to Luke, looking up at him as he stood over her, carefully searching her eyes. She searched him right back, and she was shocked to find that the deeper she looked, the more magnetic his lips became—

"*What on earth is going on in here?*"

It only took eight words for the CEO of a tech company and the forewoman of a farm to turn into shaking children. Harper's mom stood in the entryway to the kitchen, arms folded and eyes firmly narrowed in her daughter's direction.

"Mom. Hi." Harper nervously brushed a strand of hair behind her ear, only to disturb a cloud of powder, which flew down her throat and caused a coughing fit. "We're just making one of Grandma's pies."

"Mm-hm. And which step of the recipe called for all of this?"

Luke stepped forward. "It was my fault, ma'am. I started throwing flour. Harper was just defending herself."

"Luke, I'd never blame you for something like this." Her sickly sweet tone shifted to pure motherly rage as she turned on her daughter. "Harper, outside. Now. I want you both cleaned up so you don't trek even *more* flour all over my house!"

"How are we supposed to clean up outside?"

"I don't know. I don't care! Hose off if you have to! And of course, Luke, if you need anything, please don't hesitate to ask."

With that, she disappeared again, leaving the two flour-coated adults to their own devices.

"She likes me." Luke beamed, an arrogant show of teeth and that pride she'd accused him of being full of just a few minutes ago.

A few weeks ago—heck, even a few days ago—Harper would have snarked some witty retort like, *no, she likes your money*, or *she likes that you're always around me. It makes her feel like her daughters won't be spinsters after all.* And she would have been right. Today's change in response didn't come from any kind of softening of her heart, but instead from something different in her mother's smile. Her mother had two modes of smiling: the genuine smile she used with her daughters and her husband, the kind she'd give while telling the girls a story before bedtime or while dancing, and another smile she slipped on like a pair of false teeth, shiny and a little too big and perfect. She reserved that smile for strangers or business partners, anyone she wanted to keep at arm's length for inspection and dissection.

Today, Luke had earned her special smile. Her family smile.

"Yeah," she admitted. "I think she does like you."

"What are we going to do about this, then?" Luke asked, gesturing to his entire, flour-drenched person.

Somehow, even coated head-to-toe in flour, he managed to look sinfully handsome.

With a quick peek at her watch, Harper considered their options. Her mom hadn't given them much room for debate or changing the plan, so the only option they had would be following her instructions and using a little bit of creativity. She waved for him to tag along.

"Follow me."

"Where are we going?"

"You don't mind getting wet, do you?"

"What?"

Eye roll. If he couldn't handle getting wet, he shouldn't have engaged in baking combat. Which she had totally won, by the way. "Just follow me."

Edges of daylight crinkled and tugged around the edge of the property, filling the sky with a brilliant arrangement of colors and light, which caught the source of Harper's idea: the arcing crystalline curves of the sprinkler system. Almost as soon as they came into view, Luke dug his heels in and refused to move any further.

"Harper. No."

"What?" she asked, oh-so-innocently.

"I'll bake pies and I'll haul manure, but I'm not going to—"

Another eye roll. Today, they'd saved her family. With the help of Luke's connections, she'd secured their futures and given them a fighting chance. Didn't that call for a little bit of recklessness, a little bit of freedom? She grabbed his hand and dragged him directly into the spray, joining him with a shrill giggle as the cascading water hit them both, washing away the veil of flour covering her skin. His jaw dropped, wide enough to betray his surprise but small enough to keep from drowning under the water.

"Who are you and what have you done with Harper Anderson?" he shouted over the noise.

"What are you talking about?"

"I don't know...you just seem different." He shook his head, and she realized he'd gotten closer than before. Closer than they'd ever been before, in fact. When had her heart started beating so fast? "Different than what I expected you to be."

"Well," she gulped. Her eyes flickered down to his lips, so tempting. When she met his gaze once again, she could hear her own heartbeat hammering in her ears, could feel her fingers burn to reach out and touch him. "Maybe you're not what I expected either."

They were so close. Their lips so near. And she leaned forward, unable to help herself.

Bark! Bark!

Until Stella ruined it with a surprise appearance in their little dance. To characterize the noise she made at the sight of Harper and Luke so close as a bark wasn't really fair. It was more of a guttural, defensive noise from the depths of a small monster, but whatever one decided to call it, the results were the same. The moment was lost, and with a sudden jump, Luke retreated.

"Oh, no," he mumbled as the growling dog advanced.

"Wait," Harper shouted, reaching back to offer her arm as she gazed at Stella's crouched countenance. "Just…hold my hand and wait."

Their hands linked. Of all the relationships she'd had in her life—platonic or otherwise—she hadn't had the opportunity to hold many hands. It was a type of contact she neither understood nor was used to. But when his fingers intertwined with hers, everything felt right. As if she were meant to be there, in that moment, holding on to him. With her free hand, she extended an open palm to the sheepdog and reassured her in calm, friendly tones.

"See? He's okay, Stella. He's okay."

When they'd first gotten Stella two years ago to keep deer and birds away from their flowers, the trainer they'd hired told them about the sheepdog's herd structure, about how they would do anything to protect the people they'd adopted into their care. Each of them learned, in turn, how to introduce people as non-threats, to assuage Stella's fears and show her this person wasn't the enemy. Exercising that protocol now, Harper watched as Stella sniffed her way from her to Luke, for the first time not growling at him. In fact, she drew near and licked his hand, bending her head down to be petted. Luke glanced in Harper's direction, as if waiting for a confirmation this wasn't a trap that would end with him getting his hand bitten off. When she nodded, he threaded his fingers through her fur.

"She likes me," Luke muttered, eyes wide and amazed.

She's not the only one.

Before she could do something blazingly stupid like say something like that out loud, her mother's voice once again broke into the silence. Stella bolted off, and Harper found herself standing there, holding hands with Luke. Even though she wanted nothing more than to hold it forever, she snatched it away and walked away from the water falling overhead to a drier patch of grass.

"Harper! Harper, where are you?"

"Out here, Mom!"

"Good." Her mom huffed out towards them, careful to keep a safe distance from the sprinklers. "I have some news!"

"Good news?"

"The *best* news. Jerome has wired a deposit and your father... Oh, dear, I think he's gone a little mad with excitement! He wants to throw a party. A big dance night in the barn. We'll invite everyone in town and—"

"Wow, a dance! When?"

"Saturday. No time like the present, right? Speaking of which, if I hurry, I can still make the overnight shipping window online."

With her mother's track record with parties, she should have expected this. The only reason they didn't host parties every other weekend was because of their lack of funds, but now that wasn't an issue any longer... they'd probably be holding one *every* weekend now. Running a hand through her wet hair, she shrugged off her mother's eccentricities with a half-smile at Luke, carefully avoiding any mention of the electricity that passed through them all night.

"How are those blisters of yours?"

"Are you going to ask me to dance, then?"

Surely she imagined the hopeful note in his voice.

"I'm an old-fashioned girl. *You* will have to ask to dance with *me*."

Chapter Fourteen

Nothing said small town, country folk like a good, old-fashioned barn dance. And because of that, Luke felt justified in believing he'd never be invited to one. Before his sister started taking trips to Hillsboro, the most rural place he'd ever been was Venice Beach, so not only was he unfamiliar with the concept of barn dances, but he'd never met anyone who would even attend one.

Now that he and The Dog (and The Dog's owner, for that matter) were on friendlier terms, he'd made several offers to arrive early and help Harper and her family set up for the festivities only to be banned by Annie, who insisted she be the one to help the Andersons make the evening picture-perfect. So, he arrived on the nose of eight o'clock to the sound of music already shaking the barn doors and light already pooling out of the few windows.

Annie's expertise was on full display. It was the only explanation for the complex and organized parking system set up at the bottom of the hill, far away from any of the blooms. They'd taken rope and marked off paths for people to walk up the hill, close enough to the flowers to smell their perfume but far enough away that even the most enterprising of mischievous children or the most slovenly of tipsy men couldn't reach out and disturb them. Lanterns hanging from trees and cords of fairy lights strung around the ropes guided the way through the darkening night, giving the entire landscape a hint of the magical, of possibility. Anything could happen here, the lights seemed to whisper.

Carrying his bounty under one arm, he joined the crowd in their march up the illuminated path towards the source of the booming music. Part of him wanted to give Annie full credit for all of the small hints and touches, but he knew better by now. Sure, his sister knew how to plan a party and find everyone's perfect selfie angle, but he had a hunch that the sense of unbridled joy and warmth tinging the air was all down to the Andersons. This certainly wasn't their first party, and telling by the excited, beaming smiles on everyone he passed during his walk, previous parties had been rousing successes. He recognized some of the faces. Phil, the man who worked behind the counter at the drugstore. Amy, who often slung ice cream scoops at Ferrara's. The Cho twins, who ran the running club he often saw sprinting through the center of town or scarfing down beers afterwards.

When had he started thinking of these people as *his* people? Of this town as his town? Or, most importantly, of the Andersons as his family? Of Harper as his...something?

Shaking that thought from his head, he shivered at a cold gust of wind. Summer was coming, but no one told the nighttime, when these hills turned into a landscape of goosebumps and frigid breezes. Looking at the hills, he couldn't stop thinking of that day when they landed the contract with Jerome. Over the handful of nights between then and now, he'd picked apart every look, word and touch that had passed between him and Harper, searching for clarity and finding mud. The electricity could have been one-sided. Perhaps she only felt grateful to him for introducing Jerome. They could be completely wrong for each other. In the face of millions of alternatives, the chances of falling in love seemed infinitesimal, dwarfed by all the ways he could have misread the signs.

But the chill in the air melted away when he saw her. And she saw him. And she smiled. And waved. And somehow captured his heart with just that one, simple gesture.

From across the barn, he watched as she excused herself from the conversation she'd been having with Jones, one of her farmhands, and made her way over to him, an amused expression on her face.

"Luke! What in the world is that? You didn't have to bring anything!"

No, he certainly didn't. They'd cleared out the entire barn floor, turning the space into an open area for dancing and conversation. Instead of old saddles and storage bins lining the walls, long tables covered with food and drink lined the room. Cakes and sandwiches and small bites and alcohol of all variations and descriptions covered the plastic tablecloths. He spotted a fried chicken sandwich with his name on it and silently vowed he'd come back for it as soon as he had a free moment. Half of the town must have showed up tonight. The place was packed nearly to the gills.

With a flourish, he yanked the lid off of his precious cargo and presented it to her. Her face lit up as if she'd opened a case of gold instead of a case of sugar and butter.

"Is this—"

"Your grandma's pie? Made to her exact, exacting specifications? Yes."

The deviled thing took hours upon hours of practice and handwriting analysis and no fewer than seven trips to the grocery store, but he'd finally accomplished the task this morning. Annie had delighted in his efforts, teasing him about his crush, but he paid her no mind. After the disaster that their attempt had ended up as (the chocolate burned but somehow the crust remained uncooked), he wanted to get it right.

"But how did you—"

"I asked your mom for the recipe after dinner the other night. It's not perfect, but I didn't want your relatives to place a curse on us from beyond the grave."

She took the case from his hands with the reverence of a holy relic, lifting it up and moving it around to get perfect angles and perspectives on it. At one point, she even raised it to her nose to smell it.

"Luke, this is amazing. Thank you. But you didn't have to do it—"

"I wanted to. I thought you'd like it."

Please like it. He hadn't even considered the possibility that she wouldn't like it.

"I do. Well, I don't know yet. I haven't tried any. I mean, I like the gesture."

"It's my fourth try, so if it's not perfect, I blame Granny Anderson entirely."

The laughter from her lips was sweeter than honey.

"C'mon. Help me put this down."

Edging her way through the crowd, she headed for one of the snack tables, only to be intercepted by his own sister, who snapped the pie out of her hands.

"No, you don't."

"Excuse me?"

"I'll take this from here, thank you."

"Why?"

"You'll see."

Without another word, she vanished into the crowd.

"Do you know what's going on?" Harper asked.

"No. No idea."

But, if his sister had anything to do with it, whatever she had planned was sure to be painful and potentially humiliating for them both. As his sister stepped up onto the makeshift stage at the end of the hall, taking the microphone in a lull between two songs, he could only pray she wouldn't make them too miserable.

"Ladies and gentlemen, thank you so much for coming to our little celebration. We're so glad that you came to support the wonderful Anderson family." Wild applause from the folks around them, which wasn't a surprise. The Andersons were known around town, at least from what Luke could dig up with his snooping, as the golden family. During his library searches for information about the flower business, he'd found countless articles about May driving through fire-filled valleys to help rescue horses and bee sanctuaries or their father organizing a rebuilding effort when the local public school was damaged during an earthquake. The community's love didn't surprise him, but it did thrill him. With the exception of his sister, no one had ever loved him as much as these people loved this family. And he couldn't help but feel proud of Harper, for winning their love and affection just like she'd won his. "But there are two people who made all of this happen. Harper Anderson made this incredible deal, and my brother, Luke Martin, was there to witness it. And to give them a moment in the spotlight, why don't we ask them up here for a dance? C'mon, folks. What do you say?"

A roar of applause went up, filling the room with cheers and clapping that sounded almost like mockery to Luke's ears as he stormed through the crowd and up to the stage. From his place below her, he couldn't exactly whisper in his sister's ear, so he hissed instead.

"Annie! This is completely inappropriate. You can't just bully us—"

"It's alright."

He hadn't even realized Harper followed him all the way up here. He swallowed hard and spun to face her. When he'd walked in just a few minutes ago, of course he'd noticed how beautiful she'd looked, but that felt almost trivial, like he was seeing her beauty in the way he saw it every day, as an established fact of reality, as one might look at one of the world's natural wonders. Now, with her face made golden by the artificial light flooding the barn and her lined eyes gazing up at him expectantly, he couldn't help but see her as a new creation, a beautiful being who'd been especially crafted for him to love and adore.

"It is?"

For someone who decried dress shopping of any kind, the one she wore tonight flattered her figure and reminded him of those photographs of soldiers returning on V-Day to dance with their best gals. The waist nipped in below her generous bust, before flaring out at her hips. *Old-fashioned. Of course.* But there was nothing old-fashioned about the way his mouth went dry at the sight of her.

"Gotta give the people what they want, right? What do you say?"

"I say…" He considered it, glancing between Harper and his sister and the waiting crowd who'd again taken up their conversations during this little interlude. Dancing was an intimacy, one he knew he couldn't afford without paying the price of his heart. But if he walked away now, he might go through his entire life without experiencing the thrill of spinning her around a dance floor, and he couldn't live with himself if he let that happen. "May I have this dance?"

"Yes, please."

Another round of applause broke up the hushed conversation as he took her hand in his and led her out to the dance floor. When they'd arranged themselves in the center of the room, all eyes on them, the band struck up some romantic song he wasn't sure he recognized. Everything in his mental programming rejected this moment. The romantic music. The attention of the crowd. The dancing. The beautiful woman. It formed a mixture potent enough to fray the ends of his nerves and raise the temperature of his blood.

It combined all of his fears: making a fool of himself in front of strangers, making a fool of himself in front of people he knew, and making a fool of himself in front of someone he cared about very, very deeply.

To make matters worse, he'd sworn to himself he'd stay far, far away from Harper Anderson. But as he wrapped his arms around her and let her do the same, he couldn't remember why. All of a sudden, every argument and reason for denying his feelings were petty and wrong, shackles he'd thrown on himself for no reason at all.

"So," she asked, staring at a button on his shirt, probably to avoid making eye contact with anyone watching them so intently. "Did you put her up to all of that?"

"No, believe me. I couldn't be more embarrassed."

"Oh."

It was like he'd fallen back through time to the first few days they knew each other. His nervous mouth made easy but painful mistakes, mistakes written all over her stung expression.

"Not to be dancing with you, of course. This is— You are—"

"You're doing your talking thing again." A glance up from under her thick, black lashes. The light and something playful danced in the pools of her eyes. She couldn't stop looking at him now, instead of his tailor's handiwork. "I thought we'd gotten past that."

"I'm sorry. I'm . . . nervous," he said, though with every syllable he couldn't believe he was doing something as stupid as admitting it out loud.

"Why? Got stage fright?"

"No." Well, if he'd gone as far as to admit part of his feelings, he might as well go the entire way. His nervous *talking thing*, as she described it, trampled all over his desire to keep his feelings private. With the dancing and the music and the light in her eyes and the feeling of her in his arms being just so right, he couldn't hold it in any longer. "It's that there's nothing I'd rather be doing than dancing with you."

"Really?"

"Yes."

They spun, and the room dissolved around them. Suddenly, they were the only two people in the world, dancing on the edge of something beautiful and possible. His heart slammed against his chest. Could she feel it?

"Well," she said, breathless. "That's quite convenient because there's nothing I'd rather be doing than dancing with you."

There it was. A declaration from her slyly smiling lips. He'd thought that would satisfy him, but now that he knew the sight of him or the light touch of his hands didn't disgust her, he wanted more.

"That's not something I ever thought I'd hear from you."

"Don't gloat." Her fingers lightly brushed the back of his neck, just enough to give him the shivers. "Just dance with me."

How could he deny such a request, especially when she whispered it in his ear, close enough to feel her breath on his skin? As the song climbed towards its climax, he tried to get his own hopes under control before they spun wildly out of control, taking him with them.

"But, be honest," Luke started, "did you ever think we'd be here?"

A snort. Good-natured and wry. "Not unless I'd somehow died and gone to hell."

"And now? What about now?"

Her breath caught. He watched her eyes widen as all of her defenses, all of her jokes and zingers, her casual evasions, crashed down, leaving her vulnerable.

"Now…"

She stretched the word out, hanging it in the air between them. When he knew she couldn't bring herself to finish the thought, he let his impulses run away with him again.

"Take a walk with me?" he asked, nodding to the open barn door over her shoulder.

"We're supposed to be dancing."

Right. He'd forgotten about the people watching them. He'd been too lost in her to think about all of them, too lost in the confession dancing on the end of his tongue. All at once, the room re-materialized around them. There was nothing more he wanted than to escape and talk with her in private, to really be alone with her as he had been just a moment ago in his daydreams.

"I don't think anyone will mind."

After a moment of consideration, she nodded her head. "Yeah. It's a little close in here."

He glanced at Annie with a meaningful furrow of his brow, and she rushed to one of the band's microphones, encouraging everyone to join in dancing for the last verse of the song. As couples flooded the floor, Luke and Harper took their chance to sneak their way off of it and out of the room altogether, until the tight air of the barn gave way to the cool spring night. Once they'd made it to the sanctuary of the outdoors, he rushed out the question popping against the tip of his tongue.

"Now what?"

"What do you mean?" she asked, almost amused.

"You said you used to think you'd die before we danced and now . . . now, what?"

"Now . . ." When she said that word, she re-enacted her reaction from the first time she'd said it, all dewy-eyed and uncertain. "I don't know."

His entire being hummed with what could be, what he wanted to be. After their dance, he couldn't hold it in any longer. His heart wouldn't let him.

"Can I go first, then?"

"Luke—" She tried to finish the thought, but something—curiosity or hope, he couldn't tell—pushed her to say, "Yes. You first."

Falling in love with her hadn't been a snap decision. He hadn't even done it consciously. He couldn't point to the minute he looked at her and said, *oh, you're the one.* Sure, he'd thought her beautiful on first glance, but he hadn't fallen in love with her then.

That made answering the "now" question almost impossible. He knew where he stood now. He just didn't know how he'd gotten there. And he was a man who believed in process, in incremental changes in ones and zeroes and lines of code until the program worked.

"You know, before I met you, I didn't believe in things I couldn't quantify, things I couldn't explain. All of the work I do is about concrete, real things, things I can see and explain. Numbers. Code. Software and digital storage." In the back of his mind, he could almost hear his sister's cringing voice saying, *Stop talking about your work. Get to the romantic stuff.* "And, to be honest, I didn't want to believe in anything else."

"Why not?"

"Because that would have required hope. And trusting my own future to someone else."

"You've always provided for yourself," she said, though he could barely hear her through the hammering in his ears. He'd never told anyone this.

"If I fail, then I get to blame myself. If I trust someone else…"

"Then, they might disappoint you. They might break your heart."

"I never thought I'd meet someone who'd make me want to take that risk."

"And have you?" she asked, breathless.

Yes. Absolutely.

"Even answering that question is a risk."

"Then, maybe it's my turn." He braced himself for the *it's all been in your head and I still think you're a jerk, so please get out of my house.*

She'd traded in her worn boots tonight for low, chunky heels, which crunched the ground beneath her as she marched herself left to right, staring at the ground as if she'd written a script upon it. "I didn't see it when we first met, but you have a good heart. Sure, you're a nervous wreck who gets tongue-tied and stumble over yourself when you shouldn't, but...whenever I thought I had you pinned as rude or arrogant or selfish or cruel or—"

"Or devastatingly handsome?"

A pause as she realized she'd spent more time during this little declaration focusing on his negatives than his positives. A blush colored her cheeks, visible even in the darkness. "Sorry. Whenever I thought I could file you away as a bad person and forget about you, you proved me wrong. And every time you proved me wrong, you showed me what a good man you were." It took her a moment to catch her breath after the flood, but she cut the tension with a tease of her own. "And yes, you're devastatingly handsome."

Footfall halted. Eyes met his. Silly smile slipped into sincerity. "I guess what I'm saying is that I like you, but, I love you, too."

Was this how it felt to get off of a roller coaster? All adrenaline and roaring pulse and shaking hands? Was that what it felt like to look into someone's heart and see love there?

He'd wanted her to love him. But he hadn't dared hope for it.

"...*Love* me?"

"Don't look so surprised. You're very lovable, once you get past that hard shell of yours."

"No." He laughed and closed the space between them, gripping her shoulders and resisting the urge to spin her around like he had that afternoon at the farmers' market. "I love *you*. And I never thought—"

"Someone could love you?"

"No."

Like the confident woman she was, she wasn't content to let his hands sit on her shoulders. She picked one up and guided it to her cheek, placing it there so she might rest against the palm as she looked up at him, a gentle smile pulling at her lips. The butterflies in his stomach rioted.

"I never thought so either. I guess it's lucky we found each other, then."

"So lucky."

His head bent so that his forehead could lean against her, and for a moment he stood there in her presence just breathing her in. He'd come to Hillsboro to find a place for his sister, to make sure she was okay. But now, he realized he'd come to make sure *he* was okay, too. No, better than okay. He discovered that he could be blindingly, unimaginably happy. They swayed back and forth as the band inside strummed their guitars and crooned their sweetheart lyrics, and all of a sudden, holding her in this way wasn't enough any longer. He needed something more.

"Harper?"

"Yes?"

"I have a confession to make."

"What's that?"

"I lied to you earlier. There's something I do want to do more than dance with you."

"And what's that?"

"I'd like to kiss you."

Unconsciously, she tilted her head up to him, presenting herself in all of her beauty to him. "Well, that's convenient. Because there's nothing I'd rather do than kiss you."

Chapter Fifteen

When Harper woke up the next morning, tucked under the comforter in her bedroom that overlooked the remnants of last night's party, she couldn't be entirely sure last night had actually happened. No one ever accused her of having an overactive imagination—jumping to conclusions and rushing to judgment, sure, but never daydreaming—but the memory of Luke's lips against hers, his strong hands cupping her cheeks as if he were handling something precious, proved too unbelievable.

Even her still-tingling lips and the ghost of his warmth against her skin didn't convince her. They'd *hated* each other, despised each other, and then he'd gone and broke his back working on her family's farm, but made her fall head over heels in love with him?

Preposterous.

Except...it did happen. They'd danced. They'd kissed. She'd given him the key to her locked-up heart. When had that happened? Not the kissing. She knew *exactly* when the kissing happened because she wrote everything about it down in her diary that night, and according to her watch—which she checked no less than a minute and a half after that magical, fireworks explosion of a kiss—the event took place at exactly twenty-three minutes after ten o'clock, just as the band in the barn started playing the final song of their set. For the life of her, she couldn't remember the name of the song, but she'd remember the tune for the rest of her life. It reminded her of the afternoon they'd gotten caught in the rain, when he'd been too embarrassed to try anything complicated and ended up serenading her with "Heart and Soul."

"Dum, dum dum dum, bah, bah, dahdah…"

Which is why she walked down the stairs the Sunday morning after their party mumbling the song under her breath, replacing each of the notes with a different nonsensical word, considering she couldn't remember any of the real ones. In the song they'd played last night, she could have sworn there was something about a graceless lady and living after we die, but beyond that, she'd been too lost in swaying back and forth with her head against Luke's hammering heartbeat to hear the words as they flew from the band's speakers.

"Good morning, Harper."

The shock of another voice in the kitchen this early—she'd gotten up at her usual hour of six a.m. out of force of habit, but on Sunday most of her family took the opportunity to sleep as late as humanly possible, which normally meant she had an hour and a half or so before anyone emerged from their caves—spooked her. Bare feet practically flew over her head when she missed the final step while trying to swing her neck to see the intruder on her morning routine, and she landed firmly on her backside.

What a way to come crashing back down to earth after falling in love.

"You can't just sneak up on people like that."

"Are you okay?" May asked, though Harper noticed she didn't move as much as a muscle to get out of her chair to check.

"I guess. Is my butt still there?"

With a wiggle of her hips, she hissed a laugh between her teeth, an attempt to see her sister laugh, something they hadn't done together in so long. To no avail. Sitting at the family table, May sipped her coffee and stared at the wall in front of her, seeing nothing. The hot mug of coffee sent little puffs of fog up every time she brought the drink to her lips. The sight of anyone in the kitchen this early on a Sunday would have caught her off guard, but the fact that it was May of all people was enough to stop her heart in her tracks.

"What's got you up so early this morning?" she asked, trying to keep her voice light and casual and teasing so as not to let her sister hear the suspicion scraping the back of her spine. "Did you just get in from a boy's house?"

"I didn't go to sleep last night."

"What do you mean, you didn't go to sleep? Weren't you tired? I know I was. I was asleep before my head hit the pillow. I'm still pretty tired, matter of fact. I might—"

Her nerves caused the rambling, and they both knew it. May's unsettling quiet ended as she flashed the newspaper in her sister's direction.

"Have you seen the newspaper this morning?"

"No. I just woke up. Anything good?"

Reading her sister came easily to Harper. Even when she was all smiles, Harper knew exactly what muscle twitches and eyelash flutters correlated to which emotion she was hiding. But somewhere between last night and this morning, May must have read the entire Stanislavski and Stella Adler collection, because she put on an impressive acting performance of cold detachment. Nothing—not a hair, not a line in her face—betrayed her thoughts.

It was...unsettling, to say the least, as if her sister, one of her best friends and favorite people in the entire world, had been replaced by a ghost in a horror movie. Sure, she *looked* like May. But she sure wasn't acting like her. Harper made herself busy by pouring herself a cup of lukewarm coffee and microwaving some life into a stale, leftover muffin.

"Hmm."

"Hmm?"

"Do you know why I've been up all night?"

"No, May, I don't know. Are you going to tell me?" The muffin steamed on the plate as she carried it to take her usual seat at the table. Her sister refused to smile. She'd kissed her enemy last night. All things considered, she felt like she'd fallen into a parallel universe. Uncomfortable with the sensation, she again tried to compensate with humor. "What, too many espresso martinis at the party last night?"

The joke fell on deaf ears. With a fact-of-the-matter flourish, May slammed the newspaper onto the table between them, open to the "Society" and "Town Talk" sections.

"I was trying to keep this picture out of the newspaper. They snapped it last night and I saw them."

These pages of the *Gazette* were the ones Harper only read on the weekends, when she had enough time to sit down and read the news from cover to cover rather than just skimming the headlines while she scarfed down a few slices of toast. The pages weren't unfamiliar to her.

Problem was, neither were the people in the blown-up photograph that took up half of the exposed page. Her and Luke. Outside of the barn. Kissing.

"Oh."

Maybe she should have been ashamed. Maybe she should have been angry that someone invaded their privacy like that. Maybe she should have asked May what the big deal was. But she lost herself in the perfect image, and the sudden memory it conjured up of being held by him and kissing him like nothing else in the entire world mattered. Her heart fluttered, then stilled when May snapped the image away and her voice brittled.

"I was tracking down anyone who had anything to do with the paper to get them to pull it. You *kissed him*, Harper. It's bad enough that you brought Annie here all the time! Now you're—"

"I like him. I think... I love him." Her sister gasped. She'd said it out loud now, not just to him, but to her sister. There was no taking it back now, even if she wanted to. Which she absolutely did not. She meant it. With every heartbeat and breath and ounce of strength she had, she meant it. She'd never felt this way about anyone before in her entire life. No one ever looked at her or saw her the way Luke did, challenged her and made her laugh and think the way he could. "And he's done good things for us." Her voice dropped to a harsh whisper. "We were going to lose the house and he helped me land that big contract."

Their family was always in a tenuous financial place, but the certainty with which she declared how close they truly were to losing everything set May back a pace. "You would have gotten it on your own."

"Maybe. I don't know that. But I *do* know he helped. And now we're going to be fine and he had a big part of that. He isn't the guy I thought he was. He's... more than I ever could have imagined."

"This isn't about him. I don't care about him." May pivoted. "I..."

"You what? Need to get over Tom Riley?" Sometimes, in the movies, after a gunshot, the air went quiet and the sound design only played the ringing sound that filled the character's ears. That sentence was like a gunshot, and the regret was instant. It took both of them a moment to recover from it. Her heart bled for her sister. It did. But it was worse because such an amazing woman locked herself away from the rest of her life just because she'd been hurt. "I'm sorry."

There was no sorry big enough for that. No sorry that could survive it. May's hand clenched around a corner of the newspaper, almost as if she were crumpling her own heart in her fist. No tears yet appeared on her cheeks, but they were welling in her eyes. Harper just couldn't tell if they were furious tears or hurt ones. She stretched her hand across the table, reaching to brush her fingertips across her sister's hand, but she recoiled before Harper could manage it. Softening her tone, she tried to make her understand what she'd always known.

"It's been six years, May. You're incredible and you could be in love with anyone. Anyone would be lucky to have you. You don't need to be stuck on Tom Riley forever and Annie Martin isn't your enemy."

"Tom Riley and Annie aren't my only problem, Harper. That's not... that's not the worst thing, you know?"

"It isn't?"

May swallowed hard and placed her coffee mug on the table, giving the inanimate object all of her attention.

"You've been abandoning us for them."

Harper snorted. "That's not true. I'm here every day."

"Working. By the time you get home, you're running around town with the woman who's marrying the man who changed my entire life."

"Oh, please—"

"You're *replacing* us."

No. No, no, no. This wasn't a fight about just May's feelings any longer. Somewhere along the way, this turned into a fight about *her.* The rising, boiling anger rising in Harper's chest popped, leaving only exhaustion behind in its wake. She should have slept in. She should have ignored May's bait. She should have, should have, should have. But now she could only play the cards she'd dealt herself. Shrinking down in her seat, coffee long forgotten and cold, she withered under the weight of that accusation.

"I was just trying to be a friend," Harper muttered. "She needed one."

"And we needed our sister. *I* needed my sister."

Their eyes locked. She'd seen her sister's eyes countless times in their lives. They'd fought and scraped and shouted and tantrumed, but never before did she display such devastation. Like she'd been replaced. Harper ducked her head, shamefully cloaking her now.

"I'm sorry," she choked.

They didn't say anything for a long time. Too long. Harper's mind pulled her twenty-eight different directions and all of them led to a rushing river of guilt she couldn't survive crossing.

"I still love him, you know," her sister said.

"You never talk about him."

"Yeah, because I love him." It would have been less painful if May had ripped out her own heart and tossed it on the table between them. The tears in her eyes now started to fall, and Harper felt heat pooling beneath her own lower lashes. "I love him so much. I miss him. And she...and you...and he..."

The words died in her throat, and all hope for Harper's great love story died with it. She couldn't condemn her sister to a life of misery, of feeling abandoned by one of the people who loved her most in the world.

How could she love a man and welcome his sister into her life if it meant breaking her own sister's heart? How could she live with herself? An unsteady breath rose in her chest.

"What do you want me to do?"

"I don't know." With a rough hand, May rubbed her face, which was now puffy and red from tears. "I just...I can't handle it, Harper. I can't see them around town and...it's breaking my heart."

Her sister, who had always held herself as the neutral too-tough type, was now a broken, small thing, hunched over their kitchen table as tears spilled shamelessly down her face. Harper couldn't remember having ever seen her this way, and it filled her heart with cold resignation.

Annie never talked about Tom. Annie and Tom didn't seem to have a particularly warm relationship, even when they were together. Maybe...maybe they just needed a little push to separate them. And if they were separated, the Martins wouldn't need to live in Hillsboro any longer.

Her heart cracked at the thought. No more Annie and no more Luke…She'd lose them both. God, she didn't want to lose either of them.

"But there's more, Harper," May added, her voice low and deadly serious.

"How much more could there possibly be?"

"Luke tried to buy the farm."

Pulse shuddering, Harper stumbled over the words. Over her very thoughts. Dread puddled in the pit of her stomach.

"He what?"

May stared at her hands.

"I overheard Dad talking to his financial advisor on Friday morning. Apparently, they're willing to offer us more than your little flower contact in L.A. for the place. He must want that wedding real bad. Thankfully it sounded like Dad wasn't going for it. At least someone in this family can say no to the Martins."

Harper tried to piece together what she'd just been told. "No. He wouldn't do that to us."

"Okay. Then go ask Dad if it's true. If you don't believe that Luke Martin would do something like that, then go and get the facts for yourself."

Her hand twitched to shove away from the table, but she stilled when she realized…she didn't need to ask her father if it was true. She *could* believe it. Luke wanted the farm and he was the kind of man who didn't know how to take no for an answer in business. All it took for him to ruin their lives was to distract her with a few warm smiles and easy conversations.

He had made her believe they were falling in love...all to steal her family's farm out from under her nose. Bile rose up in her throat, burning as it went.

A sharp breath from between her teeth signaled how close she was to bursting into tears, but no sooner did they threaten to spill over than Rose appeared at the top of the staircase. Standing there, she looked almost like a queen, with her heavy comforter draped over her shoulders in a most regal fashion and her hair still piled in the intricate style of braids and rhinestone pins she'd worn last night. Not even her wrinkled, woefully mismatched pajamas or her bare feet or the dark bags under her eyes could take away from the look.

"Good morning, guys." She yawned, practically tripping down the stairs with half-open eyes, probably following the scent of coffee instead of using her sight like some kind of millennial badger. "Did my invitation to this little breakfast get lost in the mail?"

May and Harper separated, shuffling and coughing and pretending to go about their normal, everyday morning business. Thankfully, Rose's lack of sleep kept her from scrutinizing them or their behavior too closely. She made a beeline for the coffee pot.

"Don't worry." May slapped on one of those blinding smiles of hers. "You didn't miss much. We were just talking about nothing in particular."

Harper couldn't muster up the energy to do...well, anything. She didn't smile or pretend. The mere idea of trying to zap some life into her face pained her. Instead, she followed her youngest sister's movements, only speaking when she started rifling through the cabinets for something to eat.

"Muffin?"

"Thanks," Rose said, clearly too distracted to notice her sisters' tear-worn faces. "I'm starved. Can I see the paper, too?"

"…Sure."

They watched her as if she were defusing a bomb or about to discover the truth behind Area 51. With her usual attention, Rose flipped through the pages, stopping when something interested her and merely skimming when they didn't. She always said tourists liked to talk, and talking meant more sales. She liked to be up on all of the news.

Then, of course, because it was unavoidable, she landed on the society page, full of snapshots from the party last night.

"Annie sure looked pretty last night."

"Yeah," Harper agreed. "I thought everyone looked great."

Rose didn't say anything for a while, perusing the page at a leisurely pace and scanning the words and pictures with keen interest. She tried to play as if she wasn't invested in anything in particular. "I saw that Tom left after a couple of dances. He used to be such a good dancer. Remember your prom night, May? You couldn't walk for two days because of the blisters."

Laughter from all of the women at the table. Hollow, brittle, breakable laughter just a gentle press away from cracking in a crumpled pile at their feet. Harper noticed something about May she'd never noticed before. It was there in her walk, there in her sitting. She carried herself straight and broken, like she was trying not to disturb an open stab wound right in the center of her back. How had she never noticed before? How had she never taken the time to actually see the pain she'd been carrying around for years now? If Rose noticed any tension between her two sisters, she didn't acknowledge it through her haze of barely-awake fog.

"So, you and Luke, huh?" She perked up slightly. "It looks like you two are getting pretty close."

"No," Harper said, casting a quick glance in May's direction. "I don't think it's going to work out."

"Really?" she asked, sipping her coffee casually, as if her sister weren't just a heartbeat away from losing everything she'd come to love. "Why not?"

Because she knew what she had to do to keep May's heart from being completely shattered. She knew what she had to do to protect her family.

Harper knew there was only one answer she could give.

"We just don't belong together, that's all."

Chapter Sixteen

"I'm so glad you came over. I was just thinking during your party about having another girls' day. This time, with both of your sisters. I found this amazing spa that's by the ocean. It's just two hours away and it's very reasonable—"

Ever since Harper had arrived at Annie's house, the woman she'd come here to see couldn't seem to take a hint. Not when she'd declined the muffins she offered, not when she said basically nothing for the first twenty minutes, and definitely not when she excused herself for the bathroom and found herself retching for five minutes.

She'd never been a meddler. Never. She controlled her business, made her personal judgments and helped the people she loved clean up their messes. Trying to influence someone else's life so directly . . . It frightened her. Even if it was necessary, even if she needed to save May from any more pain, she couldn't find the strength to be confident in any of it. She played with the handle of her coffee mug, noncommittally hmming every once in a while to make it seem like she was paying attention. For a time, her companion seemed content to sit on the back porch of her house and speak and speak and speak with only minimal interjection, but it couldn't last.

"Harper..." Annie trailed off, her head tipping to one side and her curls bouncing. Her fingers curled in the fur of Monster, the puppy who snoozed soundly in her lap. "Are you alright? You don't seem like yourself."

I'm not. That's the problem. For longer than she should have, she took the opportunity to examine her friend, well aware it might be her last chance to do so. Her friendship with Annie was... unexpected, to say the least. She'd always been such a tough person. She abhorred anything frivolous or out of place. Annie barged into her life and taught her the beauty of spur-of-the-moment sleepovers and homemade ice cream. The inevitability of losing that, of losing someone she'd become so close to, of going back to her old life... it made speaking almost impossible.

Almost.

"I actually have an ulterior motive for inviting myself over here, Annie," she confessed, fighting to keep her voice as light and non-confessional as possible.

"I knew it."

Her pulse stutter-stepped. It wouldn't have surprised her if Annie somehow figured out her reason for coming here. She knew everything, was always one step ahead.

"Knew what?" she asked, hedging her bets.

Annie adjusted her designer sunglasses, pressing them down the bridge of her nose to inspect her, unfettered.

"You want me to get my brother to ask you out. For real, this time. None of this smoke and mirrors summer dance stuff."

One mystery solved. Well, not a mystery, more like a Scooby-Doo cartoon where the true culprit was before them all along.

"So, you *did* plan that whole dance thing as an excuse to get us closer?"

"Of course I did. You two would never have done it on your own."

Harper tried to imagine a version of the last few weeks where Luke didn't play a factor, where Annie didn't continually shove them together until they both discovered the real feelings they had for one another. She tried to picture what it would be like to still hate him, to long to never see him and his arrogant face ever again. Part of her wanted to step into that other universe and make herself comfortable there. After all, this man tried to steal her family's home, her legacy, their livelihood, from them. Hating him would be so much easier than loving him right now.

"Maybe that was for the best," she mumbled.

"What'd you say?"

Clearing her throat, she sat up higher in her rocking chair, hoping the strength in her spine would spread to the rest of her body and to her flimsy courage. "I said no. That's not what I'm here to talk about."

"But that's what I want to talk about. Tell me everything. I couldn't get any details out of Luke."

"I didn't come here to talk about Luke."

That came out harsher than she'd expected. But regardless of her intentions, it had the desired effect. Annie shrunk down, the light in her spirit dimming into a concerned flicker. The movement awoke Monster, who slunk off of his owner's lap only to immediately rest near her feet. Harper would have done anything for the cuddly warmth of a puppy right about now. Because what she was about to do wouldn't be easy.

"Oh . . . okay, What's up, then?"

Last night, after ignoring his every text message and call, she stayed up almost until dawn playing out and rewriting how this conversation would go. She'd rehearsed until her mind gave out and the words she'd been tossing back and forth all night lost all of their meaning. She'd hoped the script would make things go smoother, help her direct the conversation instead of being directed as Annie was so fond of doing. Now she put that script into action, putting on the performance of her life.

"How are things going with Tom?"

"Fine."

"Is it *really* fine?"

Annie scoffed and took a long sip of her iced coffee, leaving a bloody lipstick stain on the reusable metal straw. "Why does everyone keep asking me that?"

"Because it's important. Marrying someone is one of the biggest decisions of your life and—"

"Did my brother put you up to this?"

"No. No one put me up to this."

Lie. A lie she'd practiced countless times last night, but a lie all the same. And Annie called out the fib without hesitation. The only problem was that she didn't know the truth either. The speed of her rocking chair picked up to agitated heights as she did everything to avoid looking at her.

"You're lying. He's not been happy with Tom since the day they met. He hates him."

"He wants you to be happy."

"I guess."

"And are you happy?"

That question wasn't exactly integral to the plan, but curiosity got the better of her. The mystery of Annie and Tom's relationship hung over them like a hazy, pregnant rain cloud waiting to burst. For a long time, she bit her lip, smearing more of her lipstick and destroying a bit of her picture-perfect look. A good sign. It meant Harper was getting under her skin.

"You don't understand." She didn't bother to ask what she didn't understand. If Annie wanted her to know, she'd tell her. And the longer Harper waited in silence, the more likely she'd want to. Sure enough, after thirty seconds of silent discomfort, she played with her fingernails, chipping some of the perfect paint. "You don't know what it's like to have someone *always* taking care of you."

"You mean Luke?"

She nodded, miserably, still rocking too fast, still staring out at the middle distance through her mirror-shine sunglasses.

"But I thought you adored Luke. All he does for you—"

"I do. I love him more than anything. He's the best big brother… the best dad, really, anyone could have. He was always more like my dad than a brother." The creaking of the chair slowed finally. She grew quieter, more contemplative, speaking as if Harper weren't even there. "But that's the problem. He's taken care of me his entire life. He's given everything to make sure I have a chance, and because of that, he hasn't done his own living, you know? That's part of the reason I was pushing so hard for the two of you. I wanted him to experience something wonderful. To feel excitement and happiness and want and love. Something real. Something that's not work and business and numbers and making sure I have everything I could possibly want."

Memories of the night of the party flooded back to Harper. He'd told her he was afraid of trusting, afraid of being disappointed. Now that he'd finally opened himself up to living, she was going to prove him exactly right. To distract from the pain dragging itself up her throat, she pivoted.

"And Tom...?"

"He's part of it, too. And I really do love him. Maybe not like *being* in love, but I do love him. I thought that if I moved out on my own, Luke would just worry about me and dote on me like he does now, but in a different house. But if I got married..."

"He'd know you were safe. He wouldn't have to worry anymore."

Annie sniffed, rubbing her cheek self-consciously. "Pretty sexist, right?"

"Yeah. But..." She tried to consider things from her own point of view. If one of her sisters just decided to move out, she'd be worried, too. But if someone loved her and they were partners who lived together...she could see what Annie was thinking. "Maybe you should have tried talking to Luke first? It's not about the man. It's about knowing someone's looking out for you, loves you enough to put your best interests first. A room-mate wouldn't do that, but family would. People who love you, would."

"I'm fine now." She huffed. "I'm a grown woman and I can take care of myself. He's given me every opportunity in life and now... I just want to see him enjoy his own."

The discordant noise in Harper's head reached a fever pitch as the similarities between their two families became so abundantly clear. They really weren't so different after all. Everyone was just trying to look out for everyone. No one wanted their loved ones to be abandoned or miss out or have their hearts broken. Just as her sisters watched over her and she over them, Annie and Luke did their best to protect one another, even when they didn't know it.

Did he know she felt that way? She couldn't imagine Annie would have told him all of this.

The caretaker in her wanted to shake them both and force them to confront this together. Annie felt stifled and a burden on her brother. He carried his responsibility for her like a shield of duty, one he'd never put down until he knew she'd be looked after and made happy forever.

But the big sister in her wanted to do what she could, do what she came here to do. Maybe saving May from the ghosts of her past would also help save Annie from mistakes in the future. Maybe breaking off all ties would keep them from wanting the farm. And maybe...maybe she could protect herself from any more heartbreak.

"Annie." She reached out and touched the top of her friend's soft hand, which rested on the arm of her rocking chair. "You know that's not reason enough to marry someone."

"I'd be happy if I married him. I love it here. Hillsboro is amazing. I love it."

The most painful part of her response was that it was true. Harper could hear it in the warble of her weak voice, in the ripple of her usually unfaltering smile.

"But you don't love *him*."

"I just told you—"

"That's not love. Thinking you could put up with him for a few years until your brother's had some fun is not love." It was then that Annie began to cry. At first, Harper didn't even realize it was happening. She made no noise, broke into no sobs or pealing whimpers. Beneath her oversized sunglasses, one by one, teardrops trickled down her face. They went slowly at first, then faster and faster until she had to dip her head and wipe them away. Harper moved in closer, her voice sympathetic. "You barely see him. You barely know him. You're not going to be happy with him."

"But Luke hasn't been happy for years and now he's finally letting himself open up. I think it's because he knows I'm going to be okay. He's letting himself fall for you because he knows he'll be free again."

No. I didn't come here to talk about Luke. I didn't come here to think about Luke. I didn't come here to listen to a story about how I'd changed Luke's life for the better. Because I don't want to—I can't—think about how he has changed mine. And how it will change again when he's gone.

Now, time for the ace up her sleeve. The last bit of information she had that could end the relationship between Tom and Annie forever.

"I think there's something you need to know about Tom."

"What's that?"

Deep breath. You can do this. Just think of how happy she'll be when she's free.

"My sister was almost engaged to him once. They were together for years, they were inseparable and then one day, he just...broke things off. Left her out in the cold and hasn't spoken a word to her since."

That's when she got into the worst parts of it. All of the promises he'd made through the years. How he was like a member of the family for the Andersons. How May's acceptance to Yale ended up driving a wedge between them that, perhaps, he couldn't handle, despite the fact that he'd been the one to encourage her to apply in the first place. The way he started looking through her whenever they were in the same room. The way he left her with no closure or reason for leaving, just a broken heart and more questions than answers. And when she was done, Annie leaned back in her seat as if someone stole the energy from her entire body.

"Oh my God."

"I don't think he's a good man, Annie. And you deserve to be with a good man. Move out of your brother's house, get a life of your own and let him live his, but don't chain yourself to a guy just because he says he'll help you out now. Tom Riley doesn't keep his promises."

She bit a trembling lip, retiring her half-full, totally melted iced coffee to the table beside her. "Why didn't you tell me sooner?"

"Because I thought you were happy. I thought you loved him. But now, I know better. I can see it in your eyes."

"I don't love him. I just want to do what's best..."

"I know you do. That's what makes me so sure you deserve better."

And she did. She did deserve better. Annie wasn't her sister, but she felt as good as one.

"I need to talk to him. I need to go to him. I need to..." She shot up out of her chair, hand on her head. "Thank you, Harper. I might have made a huge mistake."

Her stomach twisted as she realized this was, perhaps, the last time she'd ever see her friend. Luke would never want to stay once he'd heard about this. She conjured a weak smile, then turned her face away when she realized it felt more like a grimace.

"I'm just glad I could help."

*

The conference call on which Luke had been all morning merci-
fully ended around ten o'clock, when he finally resurfaced from his
bedroom and hopped down the stairs. He'd cleared his to-do list for
remote working responsibilities, so he planned to head over to the
Andersons' house and bother Harper for a few hours, tagging along
at her heels while she worked and maybe taking her out to lunch
if he could convince her to allow him to steal her for a few hours.
The lead weights he'd been carrying on his shoulders his entire life
lifted with their kiss two nights ago—had it only been two nights
ago?—and he couldn't wait to see her again. Thinking about her
made him feel light, airy, as if he'd float away if he didn't tether
himself to the ground properly. Even the memory of her smile, her
kiss, the warm glow she carried with her wherever she went, filled
him with excited giddiness, the kind he'd never thought he'd be
able to feel for another person.

So, when he walked into his kitchen and spotted her outside,
sitting alone on his back porch, the brightness of the world turned
all the way up. Following her silhouette, he leaned out of the back
door and greeted her.

"Harper!"

She shivered at the sound of her own name, jetting up out of
her rocking chair.

"Luke."

"I didn't know you were coming over."

"Surprise visit. Sorry. Annie left a few minutes ago. I just got
caught in my thoughts."

"You don't have to apologize. You're welcome here. Do you want me to—"

He reached for her, not to take her in his arms or anything, but just out of an impulsive desire to touch her. Just as quickly as he made the movement, though, she dodged out of the way and collected her purse, heading for the steps that would lead her off of the porch and towards the garage.

"I've got to go."

"Back to work?"

"Yeah."

Pursuing her quick steps, he tried to puzzle out her sudden attitude. She'd become cold. Distant. Almost allergic to him. A slight stabbing pain blossomed in his chest as he tried to remain positive. Maybe she was just worried about something. Maybe she and Annie had gotten into an argument. Maybe she just wasn't in the mood for company. Anything could explain her prickly detachment…Right? "I could come over and help—"

"I don't think your services are needed any longer."

A laugh. He couldn't help it. "You never needed my services. That wasn't the point."

She threw open the door of her truck, carelessly threw her purse in the back without looking, and turned the key in the ignition. They both had to shout over the noise of the struggling machinery.

"We're coming up on harvest and I need to focus. No distractions."

"Okay, but…" Where was the woman who'd danced and laughed with him just the other night? "Can I see you for dinner? Or take you out on a date? I'd like to see you again."

"I don't know. Just—"

Just what? You can tell me anything. I'll listen. She dropped her head onto the steering wheel for the briefest of moments, a sign of quiet defeat. His fingers itched to wipe the stress lines that drew their way across her forehead, but, remembering the way she shied away from him just a minute ago, he resisted the urge.

"Have I done something wrong?" he asked, hating how vulnerable he suddenly felt, but unable to help himself. Harper picked her head up and checked her mirrors. Careful not to look at him.

"No. I've just got a lot on my mind. And I've got to go." She revved the engine. "Bye, Luke."

"Alright...goodbye."

He waved after her, following her a few steps down the road until she turned out of the property and disappeared from view, all the while trying to shake the feeling that this goodbye would be the last one.

Chapter Seventeen

After Harper disappeared, Luke found himself at a loss for what to do. Since moving to Hillsboro, he'd been consumed by two things: helping Annie plan the perfect wedding, and convincing Harper to give him the farm for the perfect wedding. When he wasn't working on achieving one of those two goals, he had occupied himself with the mounds of work emails and digital conversations flung at him from the L.A. office of AppeX.

Today's lack of anything to do was unprecedented. It took him longer than he would have liked to find something with which to occupy himself.

Eventually, after trying to play the piano and somehow managing to hit every sour note, he landed on playing against himself in a game of chess, moving the pieces in a mock game, playing out the scenarios and working out the angles as he went. He'd always loved mind games like this. They kept him sharp, on his toes.

Deep into his game, the phone rang. Caller ID informed him that it was Seth, his business manager, who had been trying to get hold of him for a few days now and he guiltily realized he had been too distracted by Harper to return any of his calls. He picked up the phone even as he continued to fiddle with the game pieces before him.

"Seth, how's it going?"

"Not great, boss," his aging voice said, tinged with enough disappointment that Luke's heart seized.

"What's wrong?"

"I tried to make a move on that farm like you asked me to, but they're not budging. Apparently, they just got some big floral contract and—"

"What are you talking about?"

"You wanted everything on that flower farm in Hillsboro. The full works. So, after seeing how dire their financials were, I tried to make a move to purchase, but—"

The blood drained from Luke's face; a tidal wave of sickness took hold of him as realization dawned.

"What have you done, Seth? I didn't want to buy the farm!"

"What did you want, then?"

"Not that…Listen, I have to go. Do *not* try to buy that farm. In fact, please rescind the offer now and apologize."

As Seth piped up, Annie ran in through the front door, looking more disheveled and distraught than he'd ever seen her. And was she…Was she *crying*?

"But—"

"Annie?" he called out to her. Something about the sight of her red face contorted in misery sent him hurtling back to tenth grade. "Are you alright?" Stupid, stupid question. What kind of person would sob and be alright? She collapsed against the wall beside the front door, sliding down the neutral grey paint until she was curled into a ball on the floor. He approached carefully. "What's the matter? What happened?"

In an attempt to muffle the tears, she raised a trembling hand to her face. It was then that Luke noticed her ring finger. She wasn't wearing her engagement ring. And she *always* wore her engagement ring. Even when her fiancé was nowhere to be found, she still wore it with pride. When she'd controlled her breathing enough to speak, she managed: "I broke things off with Tom. I just...couldn't be with him anymore."

The words were barely words when filtered through her sobs and slack jaw, so he held out his hands in an attempt to slow her down.

"Okay, slow down. I don't understand—"

"I talked to Harper this morning." She sniffled and ran the sleeve of her trunk-show sweater under her nose. Her makeup ran down her cheeks. He'd never seen her this way, not since she was thirteen and hadn't yet discovered cosmetics. "And she made me see everything."

Maybe he'd misunderstood her through the sobs. Crinkling his brow, he lowered himself to his sister's level. The pieces clicked into place, lining up like the perfect attack on a chessboard.

"Harper?"

She knew it was coming. Every moment he didn't call or text or check in on her, like he usually did, she felt the inevitable approaching her at a deadly crawl. The time bomb ticked, but she didn't know when it would explode.

That didn't make it any easier when the moment did come. In fact, it almost made it worse. Because she'd resigned herself to it.

Since returning from Annie and Luke's house, she inspected the plants on the lowest patch they owned, peeking at each bloom and comparing its progress to the weeks before it. Usually, these inspections filled her with wonder and awe. Such little plants drank water and sunshine and became proud flowers. Today, she did her work mechanically, hoping that acting mechanically would somehow turn her heart to steel, too.

But when Luke's car screeched to a halt at the bottom of the hill, those defenses hadn't yet activated. The quality of the air around her shifted, and the hair on the back of her neck stood on end.

And when he called out to her, erratic and fiery, a chill in her blood joined her goosebumps, manifesting and externalizing the terror she felt inside. This confrontation was inevitable, sure. But she didn't like it or want it. "Hello."

Keep things cold and cordial. Don't let him get to you. Build your walls so high he'll never be able to scale them again.

"Hello? You're *hello*-ing me?"

"Yes. I'm busy." She scribbled something nonsensical on her clipboard, not so much noting the height of a flower as drawing a random shape. "No time for chit-chat."

"Chit-chat? You…" Hissing in a breath, ostensibly trying to gain control over himself, Luke lowered his voice, speaking from just a few steps behind her. She wondered if he was trying to get her to turn around and face him. She wondered if he would be disappointed when he realized she wouldn't. "Do you know what happened this morning?"

A shrug, just enough to frustrate him. Pushing him away wouldn't be an easy task. Even with what she did to his sister, which he would take as an ultimate insult, she'd need to cut her ties even deeper to make sure he never came back. "As far as I can remember, the sun came up. I had breakfast, the usual."

"With Annie."

"No, is she okay?"

Behind her, the ground shifted, but he didn't approach. Temptation begged her to turn around and read his face for any clues about his feelings, but she didn't fall prey to it. Instead, she focused on her work of measuring and notating, even when the numbers on the page blurred and the pen wobbled in her shaking hand.

He cleared his throat. "I could ask you the same thing."

"Why?"

"Because you gave her the idea."

"For what?"

Anger dissolved into desperate exasperation. With her back turned, she couldn't see it, but she could almost hear him close his eyes in frustration, rubbing the bridge of his nose to keep a headache from coming on. At least, that's how he'd dealt with stress in the past. Perhaps now, he'd graduated to clenching and unclenching his jaw or something more extreme for his practiced sensibilities. "Don't play this game. Please don't."

"Why don't you just come out and say it?" she growled. "I know you're dying to."

"You had no right to interfere in her life!"

"Yeah, believe me, I saved her."

"From what? Being in love?"

"No, from giving her life away to some guy—"

"Who broke your sister's heart?"

He didn't sound sympathetic to anyone's plight but Annie's.

"I—"

"I know you only told her about Tom Riley and May to push her away so May could win him back. And, even worse, you did it to get back at me about the farm."

Offense gripped her spine, clenching its hand around and pulling her up from the crouch over her flowers to a full standing position. She still didn't give him the satisfaction of looking at him. Steam started rising up in her chest.

"Excuse me?"

"I really should have seen it. You told me all along who you were. Your family comes first, right?"

Stick to the plan. Don't stray from the script. Don't let him in. It doesn't matter if he thinks you're garbage and betrayed his sister. You know you're trying to do the right thing, even if he can't see it.

"Yes. They do."

"That's why you got close to her. Why you got close to me. You wanted to ruin her life and make sure you had insurance against me in case I ever did anything to cross you. Well, congratulations. Your plan worked brilliantly."

Harper said nothing. Defending herself might only keep him from leaving. And she needed him to leave. She needed them all to leave. Breaking his heart meant defending her own. Breaking his heart meant saving her family. And that had to matter more than anything else. Grinding her jaw to keep herself from saying anything, much less defending herself, she went back to her work.

"You're not even going to say anything?" he asked, incredulously.

"I think you've made up your mind. It doesn't matter what I say. You've already decided what happened and what I did."

As she spoke, she barely opened her mouth. She couldn't trust herself not to crumple in his arms and beg him to forgive her and help her and never leave her.

"So, it was all fake. You were with me...why?"

"...You and Annie are a package deal."

An understatement, but saying anything further carried so many dangers she couldn't face. From there on out, the conversation rose in pitch and volume and emotional intensity, but no one would have ever noticed it by the way she looked. She composed herself, keeping a tight rein on every muscle in her body so as not to betray herself.

"The kiss? What you said that night? That was all fake?"

"What do you think, Luke, it seems like you've already made up your mind."

"You broke my sister's heart. You broke off her engagement. All because you think we're some kind of threat to you. I can barely even want to look at you, but I came here so you could—"

"Then don't look at me. Go back to L.A. and forget all about me."

"That's it, then? You just want me to leave?"

"What else do you want me to say?"

He was almost shouting now. She'd never heard him this upset before. He wasn't commanding her. He was begging her. "Defend yourself. Explain yourself. Tell me it's not true or tell me I'm wrong or give me some reason not to leave. Tell me the truth."

"The truth?" *The truth is that I love you. The truth is that if I dress all of this up as some righteous crusade for my sister's soul, I can pretend*

I'm not pushing you away just to keep myself from getting hurt by you later. The truth is that the longer you're here, the harder it will be to watch you walk away and forget me one day. If you do it now, there's a chance I could still salvage my heart. She turned to face him. Their eyes locked, and she could see him searching for any hint of promise in her, any vague notion that all of this would work out somehow. The fear and longing mixing together in him almost drove her to spit out the truth. But she knew she couldn't. She had to kill his hope. "The truth is that you're right. My family is everything. Just like your family is yours. They'll always come first. *Always.*"

It was a death blow. And they both knew it. She returned to her notation, while he let out a long sigh that carried on the wind. *You have to be strong,* she reminded herself. *You can fall apart later.*

"Well." He gave her one last look, and shook his head in disappointment. "At least no one will be bothering you about using the farm for a wedding. And, you know, I have learned something from you."

"What's that?"

"Don't trust anyone. You'll always end up being disappointed."

"Luke!"

Again, she spun on her heel, turning to face him. She wanted to look at him one last time, wanted to see his face and remember it always. Even if his eyes were filled with hate and disappointment and hurt.

"Yes?" he asked, betraying a hopeful note that almost shattered her.

"Tell your sister I hope she's alright."

A wry laugh. That *did* shatter her. "I won't lie to her, Harper. I'm not like you."

He got into his car and left as she returned to her flowers. Until the sound of his engine disappeared in the distance, she forced her body into a show of doing her job. But once she knew he was gone, knew he was never coming back, she dropped her clipboard and moved. Somehow, she staggered away from her place in the field. Somehow, she staggered to her car, knowing she couldn't hike up the hill looking like this. Somehow, she managed to see up the road through a hazy wall of tears. Somehow, she made it home.

And somehow, she'd managed to do it all without letting those tears slip.

"Harper? Are you alright?"

May. The reason she'd done all of this. Well, part of the reason. The other reason was to protect her own heart. But now…she couldn't imagine when she'd ever thought making him leave would save her pain. In this moment, the pressure on her chest pressed harder and harder down until she thought she might die.

But May couldn't see that. Instead, Harper arranged her face into a smile, praying the movement of her cheeks wouldn't disturb the water hanging at the rim of her eyes.

"Yes. I'm fine. Just got something in my eye at work. I'm going upstairs to flush it out."

From that moment on, she thanked God that their rooms were on opposite ends of the house. She couldn't bear the thought of her sisters hearing all of the sobs she poured into her pillow that afternoon.

Chapter Eighteen

Harper returned to work the next morning with a swollen face and unfocused eyes. And by noon, everyone on the property could tell something wasn't right with her. They whispered about it behind her back and muttered about what they could do about it, but no one dared say anything to her face, not even when she skipped her lunch break to see to some menial labor in one of their storage facilities, hauling empty shipping containers from their original places into a more orderly, packing-line-ready system. Even empty, the containers weighed down in her arms, but the pain was good. Screaming pain in her muscles distracted from all of the rest of it, gave her something else to focus on besides the memory of the look in his eyes when he stared at her for the last time. After about an hour of this, and by the time her arms had almost gone numb from the strain, the radio at her hip crackled to life and gave a shrill ring, which she answered by pressing the *open channel* button and lifting the small device to her face.

"Harper!"

"Yeah, Dad?"

Her father barely used the radio system unless it was absolutely necessary. Her mother was more likely to use it, calling down to her for everything from lunch orders to news that a spider had gotten loose in their house. The sound of his rough, humorless voice spooked some life back into her tired limbs.

"Harper. My office. Five minutes."

"Yes, sir."

Dragging her away from work was not her father's usual game. He preferred to wait until the end of the day to speak to her face-to-face. Fear crept up inside of her, rising with every step towards her father's office perch. When she stepped inside, though, her fear muted. Nothing was wrong with the property or their operations. He was disappointed in *her*, personally. He spun in his chair to face her like some kind of Bond villain, his arms folded firmly across his chest. Clearly, he didn't care about looking intimidating. She composed her face in a cool mask, hoping it would be enough to ward off whatever attacks he flung her way.

"What are you doing?"

"Well, I *was* working, but—"

He tutted.

"You know that's not what I mean. You're not yourself today."

Harper let out a wry laugh. "You called your head of production up here to see if she was *feeling like herself* today?"

Her father leveled his worried gaze at her. "No, I called my *daughter* up here because I'm worried about her."

Harper pursed her lips. "I've just got a lot on my mind."

"Like that Martin boy?"

Yeah. Like him.

"Not really. Just worried about the harvest. Now that we're working for hotshot celebrities, I want everything to be perfect."

Yeah, that's it. Give him a weak smile and a shrug. Joke a little bit about the work and get out of here before he can see past the facade.

He shook his head. "I'm worried about you."

She shook her head, her smile thin but convincing. "I'm fine."

And she would be. She would be.

He didn't know what day it was. Or, more accurately, Luke didn't care what day it was. And was willing to allow the calendar on his phone to order and maintain his life, meaning three small beeps were all he needed to remind him that today was the day he returned back home. Back to his real home. Far away from small towns and flowers and Harper Anderson.

Try as he may to deaden his heart, every time he thought her name, it cracked painfully down the middle all over again. They said time heals all wounds. If that was right, he could only hope time would hurry up. He wasn't sure he knew how to carry around so much pain all at once. He struggled under the weight of it, even as he made a good show for Annie's benefit of being cool and collected, detached from it all. He retired his farmhand clothes in exchange for his suits, and they became a kind of armor for him, a reminder of who he had been before he came out here, before he fell in love. It didn't change anything for real, but it made him feel like pretending was easier.

Leaving Hillsboro behind was, actually, quick work for him. It was all a matter of making a few phone calls and filling up a few suitcases of essentials. His PA would make sure the rest of their things made it to L.A. soon. He was glad for that. A quick getaway.

He didn't want to spend any more time in this town, with these people, than he absolutely had to.

Annie wouldn't talk to him. After he'd broken things off with Harper, he'd gone into her room to inform her they'd be leaving as soon as possible, news he thought would come as a relief to her, but she'd merely nodded her head while looking through him. He thought she'd be grateful. A broken engagement meant she had no reason to stay here and nothing to keep her tethered to this place, and leaving meant a return to reality as they knew it before this chapter of their lives.

She was probably just shell-shocked and embarrassed, sad and disappointed, he told himself. Given time, she'd return to her old self. She had to.

Yet, even when they were buckled into their seats on the tiny jumper plane that would take them from the county airport back to Los Angeles and the plane lifted off of the tarmac towards home, she still wore the same drawn, broken expression she'd worn all week. Not even the puppy in her lap, who panted contentedly as she absent-mindedly scratched his ears and held him close through take-off, made her any happier.

"Are you excited to be going home?" he asked, deciding that six days of respecting her space and quiet was more than enough. Maybe a little friendly conversation would jar her back into her old self. When he glanced in her direction, subtly moving his eyes from his tablet screen so she wouldn't suspect him of checking in on her, he spotted so many things out of place, things he hadn't noticed before now. For one thing, she was wearing leggings as pants, something he'd never seen her do before. Her nails—usually painted to absolute perfection—were not only chipped, but they were *bitten*. She'd stopped biting her nails at twelve when he'd gotten her the first nail kit she ever owned. And she tapped her foot anxiously, though he was well aware she wasn't the least bit afraid of flying. Monster whimpered and snuggled in closer to her lap, as though the animal could sense Luke's scrutiny.

"I don't think we should be leaving," she whispered in a voice she only reserved for airplanes and libraries.

"What?"

"Do you really need me to repeat it or are you incredulous?"

After not speaking to him for six days—choosing instead to hide in her room and only come out when she needed to heat up a frozen pizza or take Monster for a walk—*those* were the first words she said. They were in mid-air above California, seated in the tiny, four-seat first class of a propeller plane, and she chose *then* to tell him they shouldn't have left Hillsboro. Great. Just great.

"Why *wouldn't* we leave?"

"Because she's still in love with you."

Neither of them needed to say who *she* was. Just when he'd managed to go ten minutes without thinking about Harper Anderson, she blazed back to the forefront of his consciousness, burning him in the process. He'd been haunted by the emptiness of her usually overflowing eyes ever since she'd looked at him and basically admitted what she'd done. If she'd betrayed his sister for her own selfish reasons, she couldn't love him. Plain and simple.

"No, she definitely isn't."

"Luke." Annie clicked her tongue, thankfully not loud enough to disturb the sleeping businessman with the row to himself, their only other companion in what amounted to first class on a plane with only forty seats.

"Annie. You have no perspective. You don't understand what she was doing to you."

"And what was she doing, exactly?"

"Manipulating you."

"To what end?"

Telling her that the only friend she'd made during her entire time in Hillsboro was a fraud didn't sit well with him. Sure, Annie needed to know that Harper wasn't someone with whom she should maintain an acquaintance, but she didn't need to know the extent of the damage or the cruelty. He pulled up his work email and focused his attention there, trying hard not to examine his own pale face in the tablet's reflection. "I'm not going to have this conversation with you."

"And why not?"

"Because you shouldn't have to hear it. It's too—"

She narrowed her eyes, shifting to face him as much as she could in the impossibly thin airline seats. From her place in the galley, the flight attendant frowned, but didn't approach them. "You think you're protecting me?"

"I *am* protecting you," he intoned, matter-of-fact. "Just like I always have."

"And that's the problem!"

"Wanting to keep you from suffering is a problem?"

"Yes, because I don't want to end up like you!"

Her whisper didn't falter, but she might as well have screamed it in his face.

"And what, exactly, is that supposed to mean?"

Whispering turned to hissing, and an explosion of long-held resentment stabbed him in the gut. "Because I don't think you're trying to keep me from feeling anything. You're trying to keep *yourself* from feeling anything. If you focus all of your energy on me, then you never have to experience anything for yourself."

Maybe a few weeks ago, he could have taken that insult in his stride. It would have offended him, sure, but now after falling in the deepest love and having it ripped apart like nothing so strong as tissue paper, he wouldn't stand by and let his sister imply he knew nothing about emotion or feeling. He'd done plenty of living in the last few weeks, and not even she could deny it. "I have had my fair share of *experiences* over the last few weeks, thank you."

"Yeah, because you weren't held back by worrying about me all the time."

He had no answer to that.

"Tell me what you think she was trying to do," Annie commanded after a silence stretched between them.

"She was manipulating you."

"Yeah, you said that."

"She was trying to use you to get her sister's fiancé back. She was trying to ruin your life. And when she thought I was trying to buy her farm out from under them, she hurt you to get back at me."

There. He'd said it. Everyone said the truth would set you free, so...why didn't he feel any better? And why was Annie staring at him as if he were the dumbest man walking the face of the earth?

"Is that what you think happened?"

"That's what *you* told *me* happened. I just read between the lines."

"No, I told you that she told me a bunch of horrible stuff about the man I almost married."

"And ripped you away from the love of your life in the process."

Annie choked on a sip of her diet soda so hard she almost flung the tiny cup across the cabin. "My *what?*"

"Tom," he said stupidly, as if she didn't know who he was talking about. He glanced down at her hands and spotted the thin tan line that had developed on her left ring finger. "Wasn't he...?"

Setting aside his tablet, he surveyed his sister, almost reaching for an air sickness bag as the color drained from her face and she raised a shaking palm to cover her mouth. Then, she slammed herself against the back of her seat, staring up at the ceiling. She blinked rapidly. "Oh, Luke. I think I really messed all of this up."

"What'd you mess up? How?"

"I..." Curls waved back and forth as she shook her head. "Harper told me to tell you all of this, but I was too afraid."

"You really shouldn't trust anything she says."

Admitting his mistake in trusting Harper didn't win him any points with his sister, who reached for his hand and squeezed it, forcing him to meet her gaze.

"Tom wasn't the love of my life. He was someone I tried to love because I thought you'd finally leave me alone and live your own life."

It was too much information to obtain in less than ten seconds. Luke tried to break it down, bit by bit. She hadn't really fallen in love with Tom. Okay, people sometimes fell into engagements hastily. He could accept that. She tried to love him. Okay, sure. He could see that. He hadn't been living his own life. Yes. Sure. But she... she was faking her relationship with Tom just to get rid of him?

The last ten years of their lives flooded his senses all at once, from the day he'd withdrawn from high school to now. Every decision, every move and every calculation had been for her.

How had he not realized how stifling that could be? And why did it take until now, when she'd almost jumped off of the deep end into a relationship she didn't know if she wanted or not, for him to open his eyes and see it?

"I don't know what to say."

"I don't know what there is to say." She shrugged and released his hands. "I just needed you to know."

"It doesn't change anything. Harper's motives were clear."

"Were they?"

"Yes."

"She saved me. She was the only one who told me I shouldn't go through with it."

He wanted to believe she'd done it to help Annie, but she'd given him no reason to believe that. *My family will always come first*, she'd said. And he hadn't seen even a flicker of indecision when she'd said it.

"She had ulterior motives. She lied to us both."

"You think she could fake how much she loved you?"

Don't think about the kiss. Don't think about her hand in yours. Don't think about the way her voice broke when she said I love you or the smile she wore when you said it back. None of that matters now. It can't matter now.

"I think it's suspicious that she went from hating my guts to swooning in my arms in just a couple of weeks."

"And *I* think it's suspicious that Rose, her best friend and the person who knows her best, would have helped me get the two of you together just for some twisted game."

"She did?"

Annie shrugged, smiling. "I couldn't have done it without Rose. Even the barn dance was her idea. I don't think Harper was lying because of some grand conspiracy."

"But—"

"And if there *was* some grand conspiracy, then I think it was because Harper was worried that being close to us meant bringing her sister closer to her old pain, you know. You wouldn't want me hanging out with Tom Riley after this, would you?"

No, he wouldn't. Because family meant everything. To him... and to Harper. It was then that all the pieces of the puzzle started to come together and form a coherent picture, one where he'd made a huge mistake, simply by jumping to conclusions. If Annie was right, it meant so much. It meant he didn't have to lose Harper after all. It meant everything could be different.

"And if she *did* want you to leave because she thought you were trying to buy her farm...I mean...Can you blame her?"

"I got it all wrong?" he breathed, mostly to himself.

"Don't worry. It happens to the best of us sometimes."

"I can't believe I didn't see it."

"I think you didn't want to see it."

"Why?"

"Because it's safer, isn't it? To only care about the people who can't leave you?"

He cursed all of the days he'd spent not talking to Annie, not trying to pry her out of her shell. Now...It was too late. He buried his head in his hands.

"I was horrible to her. I said horrible things to her. Accused her of this horrible plot to destroy us..."

"She'd probably do the same thing if she thought her sisters were in trouble."

No. Not too late. It was never too late. He couldn't live with himself if he was too late. Forgoing his tablet, he reached for the laptop stored under his seat, much to Annie's confusion.

"What are you doing?"

"Booking a ticket on the first plane back to her."

The old saying went, "Go to sleep. Everything will look better in the morning." Harper heard it a million times, both as a child and as an adult. No matter what ailed her, whether it was heartbreak or hurt feelings, sleep was meant to be the solution. Or, if not the solution, it was meant to offer perspective, some distance of time and thought from the pain. Sleep made things better, the saying promised.

Well, she'd had seven sleeps since she last saw Luke Martin, and she could say unequivocally that everyone who ever fed her that line was a dirty, rotten, bold-faced liar.

She tried to console herself with small truths. Even if she'd lost him, she'd helped her sister. She'd maybe saved Annie from a doomed marriage. She'd saved herself from later, greater heartbreak. Luke and his sister taught her to curb her snap judgments, to invest in discovering people instead of just deciding who they were. And...

even if for a short while, she'd felt love. For the first time in her life, she truly understood what that word even meant. Sure, she loved her sisters and her parents and her town and the farm, but what Luke did for her, the way he made her feel … that was the kind of love she couldn't have even dreamt of having.

It would just have to be enough. It had to.

And yet, it wasn't. She went through her days just as she had before she met him, but without any of the joy, any of the lightness. In fact, she always seemed to be more tired than the day previous, as the weight she carried with each passing day compounded until she felt she'd crack under its pressure.

Not even her flowers brought her joy.

Thankfully, her father didn't say anything more about her attitude. She threw herself even deeper into the work of getting ready for this harvest, investing herself deeper and deeper into the work until it completely buried her, leaving little time for meals with her family or even seeing much of them at all.

This almost worked to her advantage. The less she saw of her family, the better. Spending too much time with them meant she'd have to spend too much energy trying to prove she was *absolutely, totally fine*, when in reality, she wanted nothing more than to call Luke and hear his voice again.

The only problem with this plan was that everywhere she looked on the farm, she saw Luke. She saw him in the petals of the peonies he had complimented. She saw him in the quiet whisper of the water at Sae's Place. In the barn. In the stars.

She wanted to apologize. She wanted to defend herself. She knew he'd never take her back, but the idea that he would be out there in the world hating her and thinking she was a terrible person who'd never loved him... She hated it. And she hated herself for caring so deeply.

But she pressed on, telling herself another sleep, another day, another hour of punishing work would make her forget about him. And when she did, *then* she could go back to her old self. *Then,* she could live a normal life again.

It couldn't come fast enough. Especially when everything she saw reminded her of him.

That everything included her sisters, who, after days of not speaking to her, suddenly slammed open the barn doors where she was cleaning and sorting tubers. Or, more precisely, Rose slammed the doors open, her face flushed with excitement, as May shuffled in behind her.

"Harper!" Rose bellowed, but Harper wouldn't take the bait.

"Rose," she replied in a cool, even tone, trying her hardest not to let surprise register on her downturned face. "Why aren't you guys at work?"

"I had Su cover for me, and May's got plenty of help. We needed to talk to you."

"Alright. Shoot."

The energy Rose carried into the barn was bold and erratic, exactly the kind of energy Harper fought against for the last six days, not that she was counting or anything, and her attempts to temper her sister's loud, excitable tone with her own flat one didn't seem to do much good. But that energy shifted when Rose shot May a pointed look, a look that sent shivers through the air in the barn.

"I was an idiot," May said, staring down at her boots, unable to pick her ashamed head up.

Harper's stomach clenched at the words, but she focused on the tubers in her hands, barely breezing a glance away from them.

"About what?"

"About Annie. About Luke. About you."

This wasn't a conversation she was interested in having. She'd done everything for her sister, for her family, and she'd lost the man she loved because of it. Talking about it wouldn't help matters; nor would the tears forming in May's eyes. She shook her head once, hoping it would be enough to dismiss them, but knowing they were here for a fight. If they were both here, it meant they were trying to present a unified front. This wasn't going to be a discussion so much as it was the opening campaign of a war.

"It's fine."

Rose nearly choked. "What in the world is wrong with you?"

"I don't know what you're talking about." Harper practically yawned, though her pulse quickened worriedly.

"Don't play that game with me. You may be able to play it with Dad, but I'm your sister, remember?"

Since her father made his concern known, she'd gone out of her way to avoid talking too much to anyone, much less her sisters. Even if she had talked to them, she certainly wouldn't have talked about his worry for her.

"How did you know about Dad?"

"Because he's worried about you. He's telling anyone who will listen that you're not yourself and you know what? I agree with him. This"—she gestured to the morose expression on Harper's face—"is pathetic."

Pathetic? Harper looked up at Rose with a dangerous growl. "Excuse me?"

"The Martins leave town and all of a sudden you're working even more overtime than usual and not speaking to any of us? You've never done this over a boy."

"This isn't about a boy. I'm worried about the summer harvest."

That's it. Repeat the lie enough times and it'll become the truth. Focus all of your feelings about Luke onto the harvest and maybe one day you'll believe it, too.

"You've *never* worried about harvest. Half of our crop got destroyed by a fire one year and you still weren't worried. Not like this."

"I don't want to talk about it."

"Too bad." Rose grabbed a chair and sunk deep into the seat, clearly preparing to stay for as long as it took, something Harper couldn't abide. Both of her sisters were, in their own way, great listeners and sounding boards. For the last few days, she'd wanted nothing more than to tell them everything and beg for their advice, something she obviously couldn't do. She wasn't sure she could stand the temptation. She'd never kept anything like this from them before. "Because May has something to say and we're not leaving until she says it."

This got Harper's full attention. May's small form was shivering and she hugged herself so tight Harper worried she was going to cut off circulation. Though she always wore thick socks and sweaters once the weather started to turn, it was as if she were afraid she'd freeze on the spot if she relaxed for even a second.

"Harper, I was wrong. About everything. I...yes, it hurts to see them here, and yes, I'm terrified of losing you like I lost..." She didn't finish the sentence. She didn't have to. Ever since Tom, she was terrified of being abandoned. Running her sleeve under her nose, she sucked in a deep breath and pressed forward. "But I thought you wouldn't care as much about losing Luke. I thought it was a fling."

"It was."

"*No.*" May's voice was a rebuke, harsh and cutting. "It wasn't. You're how I was after I lost Tom. You're here, but you're not here. You're heartbroken, aren't you?"

Heartbroken. Even in the quiet hours she spent alone, she didn't admit to herself that she was heartbroken, no matter how true it actually was.

"I was just trying to do the right thing," she replied quietly.

"For me or for you?"

No. No one was going to play that card on her.

"For all of us."

"You gave him up, you let him go, but you didn't have to. You love him, you idiot."

"No, I don't."

Yes, I do.

"Yes, you do. And everyone can see it," Rose interjected, her smile slight and a little bit sad, as if watching her sisters reconcile was a perfect episode of her favorite television show.

"And that's why you have to listen to me," May said, sinking into one of the assembled chairs. "I'm so sorry. I was selfish and I messed things up for you and the man you love. But . . . I think you can still have your happiness."

"No, I can't. It's too late. Way too late. He hates me."

"Hates you? Are you crazy? He's in love with you."

"Absolutely." Rose nodded emphatically.

But they didn't know the entire truth. They wouldn't be so certain of his love if they knew everything. She swallowed hard, pushing the emotion rioting inside of her deep, deep down.

"He thinks I did something terrible, that I broke up Annie and Tom on purpose. That I was doing it to hurt him after he tried to buy our farm."

"But that's the thing!" Rose said, her face shining with intensity. "He wasn't the one who wanted to buy the farm. His business manager went rogue, Annie told me—"

"And you have to go talk to him. He has to know how you feel! You need to explain," May said, the words a rush.

All fear of crying vanished as she choked on her own incredulity. "Go to L.A.?"

"Yes!" May agreed. "Romantic style. End-of-the-romcom style. You need him. And he needs you."

She wanted to. She wanted to *so badly*.

"I thought I was the big sister here," she teasingly scolded May.

"Well." Nudging Harper's shoulder, May winked and shot a warm glance at Rose, who beamed back. "You two have been looking after me for too long. It's my time to return the favor." She checked the watch on her wrist, a hand-me-down from their mother's collection. "And if we hurry, I bet we can get you on the next flight out of Santa Rosa."

They rushed into the house and started the dizzying work of preparing her for her trip, the first trip she'd ever taken on an airplane and the first she'd ever taken out of Northern California. They threw a bag of clothes together and sprinted around the house for any last-minute essentials.

When Harper reached the car, a yell behind her made her turn to see May running up from the back of the house, carrying something small and delicate in her cupped hands.

"Wait!" she cried.

Harper and Rose did as they were instructed, and when May arrived, panting, Harper realized that the small thing in her hand was a magnolia flower. Memories flooded her, memories of their childhood playing under those trees. Memories of the day she'd tucked one of those flowers in May's hair before sending her off to her first day of school. *For bravery*, she'd said back then. *And so you always remember that your sisters love you.*

Carefully, May lifted the flower by the stem and tucked it behind Harper's ear.

"For bravery," May said with a watery smile. "And so you always remember that your sisters love you."

This time, Harper didn't hesitate to throw her arms around her sister. And they piled into the car before taking off at a breakneck speed for the airport. As the house retreated in the rearview window, and her future unfurled before her on the open highway, for the first time since Luke drove away, Harper felt okay.

No, better than okay. She felt brave. She felt the love of her family carrying her. She felt like anything could happen.

And even if nothing good *did* happen, she knew that she would be okay.

Chapter Nineteen

From the moment the plane touched down in Los Angeles, everything was a rush of activity, all planned through the garbage Wi-Fi Luke had purchased on the plane. His secretary met Annie at the airport to drive her and Monster and their heaps of bags back to their Los Angeles house, while Luke stayed at the airport to meet Jerome, who was delivering him an arrangement of Harper's flowers—kept fresh in a TSA-approved three-ounce container of water, of course—at which point he went back through the hassle of checking in for his next flight and returning directly to the Santa Rosa Airport, where he would rent a car and drive straight to her house. A simple plan that would get him at least as far as her doorstep.

From there? Who knew. Every time he tried to imagine what he would do when he saw her again, he just imagined sweeping her into his arms as romantic music played, kissing her until they were both breathless, and asking her to forgive him because he'd never loved anyone the way he loved her. He considered contacting some of Annie's screenwriter friends to help him draw up something coherent to say, but decided against it. This needed to come from the heart. No one could help him.

"Sir?"

He'd just have to do this on his own. He'd just have to—

"*Sir?*"

The southern-twanged voice of an older, maternal-looking flight attendant smiled down at him as he returned to reality. They'd just taken off from L.A. and the captain turned off the fasten seatbelt sign when she'd approached him and broken up his daydreaming. Running a hand through his hair, he glanced up at her, repentant.

"Yes? Sorry."

Practiced and poised, she offered him a smile, bending down to come closer to his eye level. "My name's Susan. I'm your flight attendant this afternoon. I was just asking if you're alright, sir. You're making a few of the other passengers a little nervous, what with the leg shaking and constant looking out of the window and all."

"Yeah. I'm just..." *Don't tell this stranger your life story*, one half of his mind argued, while the other screamed, *you're going to explode if you don't share your nerves with someone else.* Placing a hand on his knee to steady its rapid shaking, he agreed with the latter. "When we land, I'm going to try and win back the love of my life. We had a horrible fight and..." A sigh he couldn't control washed between his lips. "It's just a lot of pressure."

Susan considered him for a moment before snapping back into professional mode. "That is a lot of pressure. Well, here's what we'll do. I'll put these"—she took the flowers he'd been clutching in tight hands from him and tucked them in her arms—"somewhere safe for you. And then I'll get you a glass of wine to calm your nerves and a couple of mints to freshen your breath. How does that sound?"

A few moments later, she returned to his seat and extended the glass of white wine and the individually wrapped breath mints to him. He thanked her and downed the tiny glass in two gulps, praying the altitude would speed the liquor's effects. He didn't want to show up to Harper's house drunk, of course, and he'd now have to call a car instead of renting one, but she was right. His nerves were shot, and he needed something to soothe them. Once the wine was gone, she graciously took the empty cup from him as he stuffed his mouth with a handful of mints.

"Is there anything else I can help you with, sir?"

"No. That's fine. Thank you so much."

"Great. Just let me know—"

Something compelled him to whisper-shout her name again, and when she turned around, he realized it had been so long since someone else helped him with a problem like this. He never shared personal burdens with anyone, much less strangers, and he didn't want to let the moment go, especially not when he needed her help.

"Wait, Susan?"

"Yes, honey?"

"Do you have any advice?"

"For air sickness, or love?"

He hadn't considered that question, but now that she mentioned it...

"Both, actually."

"For air sickness, we recommend leaning back and closing your eyes while holding tight onto one of these." She pulled an air sickness bag from the pocket of her red apron and handed it to him, which he took just in case. "And for love..." A moment of deliberation. "How much do you love her?"

"More than anything."

"And how badly did you mess up?"

"Monumentally."

"Then, you just have to be honest. And hope she's got a heart big enough to fit you in."

"I think she does."

She's opened her heart up to me once. Maybe she can do it again. Maybe I can earn her love again.

"Then you don't have anything to worry about, young man. Unless you throw up in my plane. Then you'll have more than an angry girlfriend to contend with."

When they pulled up to the Santa Rosa Airport—a small collection of buildings and airstrips they'd had to put into their navigation system, seeing as none of them had ever been there before—the reality of her situation finally hit Harper square in the nose. The furthest she'd ever been from home was the quick two-hour drive to San Francisco. She'd never gone anywhere for anyone. Everyone she knew, she could find in the phone book of the town where she grew up and spent her adult years. She'd never been on a plane and had no idea what to expect beyond what she saw in the movies. When May slid the car's stick into park, she immediately moved to get out and help her sister with her bag, but Harper grabbed her hand to hold her in place, eyes wide and unseeing out of the front window. Beyond the glass, there was a meager fence, a few hangars and the stretch of airstrip beyond, all promising flight and escape into a future Harper couldn't see. Her stomach lifted and fell as it did when she was next in line to step onto a terrifying, looping roller coaster.

"I don't know if I can do this."

"Why?" Rose asked, breathy.

"It's just..." When she'd left the house, she'd thought anything could happen today. And that was true. But *anything* didn't just mean anything good. It also meant anything disastrous and frightening. A million worst-case scenarios started bouncing around in her head, taunting her with everything she hadn't considered until now. "It's just so scary."

"Oh, please." May rolled her eyes and leaned awkwardly into the back seat, accepting Rose's help in pulling Harper's hastily packed bag into her lap in anticipation of her exit from the car. The green letters of the digital clock on the dashboard clicked closer and closer to the departure time on Harper's ticket—a ticket she'd bought from her phone with her rainy-day fund—but she didn't make any movement that even resembled preparing herself to leave. "You've done scarier things in your sleep. You and Stella ward off beasts every other weekend. I think she taunts them to the fence line just so you'll have an excuse."

"That's not what I mean. I mean..." *He could already have a girlfriend back in L.A. He could hate me. I could get to his house and he could release the hounds on me or something. He could look me in the eye and tell me I don't matter and never did.* "What if he doesn't want me?"

She whispered that last part, almost ashamed to say it out loud. She'd never had a confidence problem in the past and admitting the one currently chipping at her shoulder almost broke her. But May, as usual, didn't bat an eyelash at Harper's sudden uncertainty.

"Then he didn't deserve you and you can go out in Los Angeles on a very well-earned vacation and find someone who does."

Harper took a long look at her younger sister, sitting there with an oversized backpack in her lap and a determined, settled expression on her face. For years now, she'd almost been frozen in her mind as a teenager, her *kid* sister who needed protecting and coddling. But while she was so busy forgetting that May had to grow up, May had gone and done it without anyone noticing.

"You think it's that simple?"

May threw her arms around her neck, squeezing her so tight that Harper feared tears would come out of her any second. The touch was comforting, a reminder she always had love to return home to, even if everything went wrong where Luke was concerned. "You're my big sister. Someone has to love you as much as I do."

"Thank you, May. For everything. You too, Rose," Harper muttered into her shoulder, meaning every word.

"Don't get soft on me." Pushing her back, May handed over the backpack and gave a playful shove towards the passenger car door. "You're going to be late. Go, go!"

"Yeah, hurry!" Rose said. "And make sure to take one of those Vitamin C pills! Don't get sick and don't be late!"

Late. That word and all of its finality sprung Harper into high gear. Almost throwing the backpack over her shoulders, she ran through the doors of the Santa Rosa Airport and towards the check-in area. Only three or four airlines flew out of this airport at any given time, but when Harper turned to survey the line of meager desks, she saw only one attendant standing behind them.

And he was leaving.

She increased her pace to a sprint, not giving the slightest care to the few strange looks she got as she waved an arm over her head and shouted to get his attention.

"Hey! Wait! Wait!" Of course, the desk for her airline was at the opposite end of the terminal building, but she managed to catch the uniformed clerk before he disappeared behind a staff door. Slamming her license onto the counter, she huffed, "I'm here to check in for the—"

"I'm sorry, ma'am," he intoned, returning to the desk with a sigh. "They're de-planing the incoming flight now, so we're closed for check-in. It will all have been outlined on your ticket."

"But you don't understand," she begged, pulse racing loudly in her ears like an Indy 500 car. "I need to get on that plane."

"Then I'm afraid you *needed* to be here five minutes earlier."

"But this is for love!"

"Listen, lady." His lips drew into a thin, hard, no-nonsense line. "I'm on my lunch break now. I don't want to hear about love and, frankly, now that I'm off the clock, I don't have to."

With that, he disappeared behind the door, taking her chance to reconcile with Luke with him as he went. She fought the tears welling in her eyes. *Don't you dare. Don't you dare cry. You'll just figure something else out.*

"But…but…"

A voice behind her disturbed her sad calls after the air attendant, sending a shockwave through her entire system.

"I'd like to hear about love."

That voice. Her heart stopped. It couldn't be. It just *couldn't* be…

"Luke?"

When she turned around, there he was, wearing a rumpled suit and carrying a bouquet of peonies—*her* peonies—gazing at her with all of the universe's hope swimming in his eyes. "Harper."

"What're you—"

Extending the bouquet, he swallowed sheepishly. "I wanted to bring you some flowers."

"My flowers." She took them in her arms, inhaling the scent of the familiar blooms. She'd planted these herself, packed them and shipped them to Jerome in L.A. herself. She'd watched them grow and blossom into something beautiful. Now, they'd come full circle back to her, carried by a strange, beautiful man who wouldn't stop looking at her as if she carried every answer to every unanswered question he'd ever had.

"Only the best."

Fruitlessly, she tried to piece together an understanding of what was going on here. May told her he'd been flying back to L.A. this afternoon. Why was he still here?

"Am I hallucinating? Is this a stress-induced dream?"

"If you're hallucinating, then so am I. And I hope I'm not."

"I don't understand what you're doing here. This doesn't make any sense."

"What are *you* doing here?" he asked, conjuring up a ghost of a smile from her.

"I asked you first."

Hands now free of the flowers, he ran his fingers through his hair, tugging at the ends as he tried to lay bare his soul. She remembered all of the times he'd shoved his foot in his mouth and said the wrong thing out of nerves. Today, he spoke with a clarity that pierced her chest, giving him a direct path to finding a place inside her heart.

"Annie told me everything. And I realized that...I was on a plane leaving the one person I don't think I can live without anymore."

He loves me. I wasn't wrong. He loves me. At that realization, a spray of words and defenses and explanations poured out of her. "I didn't deceive you. I wasn't lying. I was just trying to push you away—"

"I know. I *knew*." Warm palms rested on either of her cheeks, framing her in his grasp. "In my heart, I knew. But I was trying to push you away, too. And I'm sorry. I'm sorry for everything I said and the way I treated you. I was just terrified of..."

"Trusting someone."

"Yeah."

She smiled as memories of the barn dance welled to the forefront of her mind. It was her turn to ask the question that changed everything for them, her chance to hear him say it. "And now?"

"And now..." He returned her smile, broader and brighter than she'd ever seen it before. He wasn't ashamed to show her—or anyone else in this very public terminal—how he felt about her. A fire crackled to life in her ribs. "What's life without a little bit of risk?"

After everything that happened, everything she'd put him through, all of the lies she let him believe...The fact that he was standing here, holding her face in his hands as if it were her heart, didn't make any sense. She could only thank the heavens this wasn't a dream. And if it was, she didn't want to wake up any time soon.

"I can't believe you're here."

"With the way I spoke to *you*, I can't believe you're here. Were you going to fly to L.A. to see me?"

She refused to blush, especially considering that *he'd* either flown back to Hillsboro or remained here so he could talk to her. Either way, they were equally matched for romantic gestures. "I had to talk to you in person."

"You've got me now. What do you want to say?"

She'd thought she would have an entire plane ride to figure all of this out, what she would say when she finally showed up at his front door to spill her guts. Now, without that time, she would just have to wing it. "When we met, I hated you. And then, when I loved you, I wanted to hate you even more because you'd changed me. You made me feel like I'd never felt before and I was terrified of what that could bring."

"You changed me too, you know," he said, rubbing his thumb over her cheek, as if reminding himself that she was real, that she was present and in his touch.

"Maybe we were both cowards," she replied, leaning into his touch.

"I think that's accurate."

"And maybe... It's time to be brave. For real, this time."

They were just a breath away from each other, just a kiss apart. Her heart beat. Her grip on his shoulders tightened. Her eyes closed. And the moment was ruined by a familiar, feminine voice over Luke's shoulder.

"They're gonna kiss!"

"See? I told you it would work."

Breaking apart, the pair of them spotted Annie and Rose, who each strolled up with oversized gas station fountain sodas and superior, smug smirks on their faces.

"What are you two doing here?" Harper practically screeched in surprise at the same time as Luke asked, "Annie, how did you get here?"

Annie shrugged, unfazed by their shock. "I called in a few favors and hopped on a charter with some folks from that vineyard we like so much. No security lines and no baggage claim. I got here almost an hour before you."

"We had to see all of our handiwork," Rose supplied, reaching her hand out so her partner in crime could give her a low high-five.

"And I think it worked out pretty nicely, don't you?"

Harper wanted to shout at both of them for meddling in their lives and playing secret matchmaker all of this time. She wanted to know how deeply they coordinated this, if *everything* that happened was part of their plan, but ultimately, she set all of that aside and gazed up at Luke.

"I think it worked out pretty nicely, too," she said, reaching down to hold his hand.

"Well, it wouldn't be very gentlemanly of me to disagree."

"Then don't."

Pulling her back into him, mischief in his eyes, he asked, "What do you propose I do instead?"

"I could think of something."

And, for one uninterrupted moment of perfection, they kissed.

Epilogue

One Year Later

Sunset. Harper's favorite time of day for many reasons. For one thing, it was beautiful. But more importantly, sunset meant quitting time, an especially promising prospect now that she was deep in the throes of the harvest, which meant weeks of back-breaking work. Despite what most people thought, including her boyfriend, she wasn't made of steel. Work *did* affect her, and right about now, she wanted to draw the hot water to the top of her bathtub, pour a glass of white wine bigger than her head and soak until the water evaporated and the glass was empty. Her muscles cried out for a long rest, but as she waved goodbye to the workers driving home to meet their families for their own well-deserved weekend, the walkie in her pocket crackled.

"Harper, there's a sprinkler bust on the north rim! The entire patch of peonies is going to flood! I need you to head up there now!"

Of course. She just couldn't catch a break, could she?

"Rats," she cursed, taking off at a sprint for the northern ridge, the farthest point of their property from the bottom of the hill. The peony patch came through for them every year as one of the most profitable portions of the farm. If the whole thing flooded . . . She didn't know what they'd do. Pushing herself faster and faster, she kicked up dirt and grass as she propelled herself further and further up the hill, higher and higher until she spotted the peony patch.

A disaster for her favorite flowers didn't greet her there. Luke did.

"I never knew I made you *this* breathless."

"You . . . *jerk*!" she shouted, bending over her knees to catch her runaway breath. The relief at discovering the peonies were safe didn't stop her racing heart. In fact, seeing him only made matters worse. "You made me sprint all the way up here . . . I could have had a heart attack!"

The way he laughed at her misfortune and teasing frustration only rose the hammering of her heart to dangerous levels. Closing the rest of the gap between them, she took her time walking up to him. After a year and some months together, she'd never gotten used to how good he looked in a suit, and this silver one with the tailored jacket was her favorite. James Bond had nothing on Luke Martin.

"Let me guess. You were on your way inside for a bath and a glass of wine."

"How'd you know that?"

Maybe her father told him about her post-harvest ritual when they'd clearly fallen into cahoots together on this plan, she thought as she met Luke in the space between two rows of peonies. He bent to give her a playful kiss.

"I guessed about the wine part, but you look like you spent the day rolling around in a mud pit, so the bath was a pretty sure thing."

"I was joking about you being a jerk when I walked up here, but now, I really mean it."

"C'mere." He opened his arms to her, and she nestled herself into his side, breathing in the mixed scent of him and her favorite blooms. His woodsy, masculine scent paired well with the soft scent of the flowers. "Watch the sunset with me."

Thankfully, Harper and her sisters lived a safe life. With the exception of that one time when they watched *The Ring*, they'd never feared anything or had anything to fear. Yet, she'd never felt true safety until she found herself tucked into Luke's arms. Today was no different. Like her missing puzzle piece had just been pressed into place. She closed her eyes to relish the sensation.

"Is this your idea of a date?" she asked, her lips quirking up. "Because I can think of about eighteen things we could be doing that would be more fun than this..."

"Hush." He squeezed her playfully. "Just look."

"It *is* beautiful."

A lifetime on this farm and she never bored of the sunrises and sunsets here. Every one painted the sky with new brushstrokes. Every evening sky was a new painting, a new work of art. A hillside on the farm around seven o'clock in the evening was better than any museum or art gallery in a big city.

"Do you remember what you said to me that day at the airport?" he asked, after a stretch of silent sky-watching.

"How could I forget? Everyone in California probably heard me. It was the most embarrassing moment of my life."

Heat colored her cheeks just thinking about it. It wasn't like there was so much to remember. She'd just screamed, "I love you." Three words weren't hard to remember, even a year or so later.

"And do you remember what I told you?"

"Like I said. I couldn't ever forget something like that."

She hadn't been nearly as eloquent as he'd been. His speech was Shakespeare compared to the declaration of love she'd shouted through the tiny, crowded airport terminal. Somehow, though, through the adrenaline of that moment, she'd managed to write his words on the tablet of her heart, pressing them there permanently. On her hardest days, she mentally reread them. They never failed to make her feel better.

"Well, my feelings haven't changed." He released her and turned her to face him. His hands were shaking. "Have yours?"

"No, of course not."

"Then I was wondering…" The sunset froze in place. The birdsong quieted. Even the wind bowed to the moment as he sunk to one knee, smiling at her all the way. A forest of flowers blossomed in her heart. "Would you do me the incredible honor of being my wife?"

"Really?"

"It would be pretty cruel to joke about something like this."

"Yes. Yes, yes! Oh, goodness, yes!"

She probably went on stammering and yammering like that for way longer, but she tuned herself out after the fourth yes, instead letting him slide the ring on her finger and swing her in his arms for a long, sun-soaked kiss. When he finally put her down, she couldn't decide if the dizziness was from the elation or the spinning. She didn't care. She just never wanted it to go away.

"I'm the luckiest, happiest man…" He pressed his forehead to hers. "But there is one problem."

"What?"

Her stomach dropped. No, not a problem. Not now of all times.

"We're going to have to find somewhere to have the wedding."

"What do you mean?"

But no sooner had she started freaking out about the mystery than he dropped his faux-concern act and broke out into a grin.

"Well, I proposed to you here because I knew you wouldn't want to have the ceremony here. Rules are rules. You said no one would ever have a wedding on the farm."

"That's true," she breathed, her eyes slipping closed as she pressed her cheek into his chest and listened to the steady thrumming of his heart. "But what do you think about Sae's Place? That would be nice for a wedding."

"Actually, I think it would be *perfect*."

"Why?" she asked, almost surprised by the sudden ease and agreement.

He held her tighter. "Because that's the place where I first fell in love with you."

"Really?"

"Yes. And I'm going to keep falling in love with you wherever we go."

Acknowledgements

Writing the first book in a new series is always a terrifying and thrilling experience, and writing *The Magnolia Sisters* was no different. I would be remiss if I didn't acknowledge the people who helped make my dream of this book into a reality.

Emily Gowers, my editor at Bookouture, has loved this book from the start, and her tireless support made this entire process a dream. I'm so grateful for all of her work and all of her friendship. My agent, Rebecca Angus, who has been there for every panicked 3 a.m. Google Chat message and every excited email, made this book possible. Jane Eastgate, my copyeditor, Shirley, my proofreader, and all of the folks at Bookouture have my eternal love and gratitude, too.

I also have to thank my husband, Adam. (*This is the first book acknowledgment where you're my husband! How cool is that?*) You've been there for every single book I've written, and I wouldn't be here without your support and your love.

Of course, no Jane Austen writer would be complete without the women who gave her Jane's work, so thank you to Mere, Mom, and Aunt Patty, who introduced me to British period dramas and let me watch as many versions of *Pride and Prejudice* as I could get my hands on.

I also have to acknowledge the brave and deeply wonderful people of Sonoma County, whose zest for life and loving kindness inspired the town of Hillsboro. Sonoma Strong forever.

But perhaps most of all, this book wouldn't have been here without my dad. He gave up so much to move to California and pursue his dreams, and, in doing so, he taught me the power of following my own. That is a lesson I'll always carry, and I'm beyond grateful for it.

And to you, if you've read and loved your time with the Anderson sisters, thank you so much! Getting to share this story with you is an honor, and I thank you for welcoming me, the Andersons, and the entire town of Hillsboro into your heart!

Reading Group Guide for
The Magnolia Sisters

A Letter from the Author

Dear Reader,

Thank you so much for reading *The Magnolia Sisters* and for spending time in Hillsboro with the Anderson and Martin families. I wrote this story when I was separated from my own family by oceans and continents; every time I sat down to type, I felt like my heart was going back home. I hope Hillsboro welcomed you the way it welcomed me and that you enjoyed your time there!

As a writer, I'm always looking for fun ways to harness my creativity away from my laptop, and I've discovered that pie making is almost as good for the soul as a good book. So with every story I write, I create an original pie recipe to go alongside it. As you know, the Anderson sisters love pies from Millie's Pie Vault, so for *The Magnolia Sisters*, I created an easy, no-bake, no-fuss lime and gingersnap pie inspired by the sour and sweet notes of Luke and Harper's love story!

Enjoy!
Alys

"I Lime Him and I Love Him" Pie

For the crust:

    8 ounces gingersnap cookies (about 12 cookies)

    3 tablespoons butter, melted

    3 tablespoons brown sugar

For the filling:

    ¾ cup lime juice (about six limes)

    Zest from two limes

    1 12-ounce can evaporated milk

    1 14-ounce can condensed milk

    ½ teaspoon vanilla extract

To assemble your crust, first blitz the gingersnap cookies in a blender or food processor. If you don't have a food processor (or if you had a rough day and want to take it out on some cookies), place the gingersnaps into a gallon-sized ziplock bag and crush with a rolling pin until the cookies resemble the texture of sand.

In a bowl, combine the cookie-sand, butter, and brown sugar. Then press the mixture into the bottom of a 9-inch pie tin.

For the filling, combine the lime juice and zest, evaporated and condensed milk, and vanilla extract. Then pour the mixture into the assembled crust and leave in the refrigerator to set for at least 4 hours or overnight.

To serve, simply slice and (if you're sugar obsessed like me) finish with a generous dollop of whipped topping!

Discussion Questions

1. The characters of *The Magnolia Sisters* often highlight the differences between small town and big-city living. If given the choice, where would you prefer to live? Why?

2. The current economy often pushes children to live with their parents well into adulthood. This reality is reflected in the Anderson sisters' story. Their situation is not generally considered the cultural norm in the United States, but it is commonplace in many other countries around the world. Would you be able to live with your family for that long? What difficulties do you think you would face? Would your difficulties be the same or different from the ones faced by the Anderson sisters?

3. Despite their disinterest, Mrs. Anderson pushes her daughters toward relationships. Do you think she had their best (romantic) interests at heart, or was she more concerned about the family's financial situation?

4. *The Magnolia Sisters* deals with some heavy social themes, particularly that of rural gentrification. Harper is resistant to wealthy outsiders like Luke coming into Hillsboro and making

their already difficult lives even *more* difficult by, for example, driving up prices and urbanizing their agricultural area. Did you sympathize with her feelings? Why or why not?

5. This book tells the story of four very different women—Harper, May, Rose, and Annie. As you read, which of the sisters did you find yourself identifying with most? Why?

6. Luke and Harper are two characters focused on duty—Harper's duty to her family and their business, Luke's duty to his sister. In your own life, what duties do you feel to others? How has that duty shaped you and the way you live your life?

7. As the middle child, Harper feels trapped between her "perfect" sister, Rose, and her "problem" sister, May. What, then, do you think pushes her to befriend Annie?

8. One way *The Magnolia Sisters* is inspired by *Pride and Prejudice* is how Harper begins the story hating Luke only to understand and ultimately love him by the end. What do you think caused her change in perspective? With what qualities of Luke did she fall in love?

9. Despite a difficult past, Annie does her best to present a friendly, warm facade. Where do you think her strength comes from? Would you behave the same way in her position?

10. Annie jumps into a relationship with a man she just met because she feels her brother is burdened with looking after her. Do you sympathize with her choices? Why do you think her relationship with Tom does not work out?

11. Hillsboro is a tight-knit community. In what ways was the closeness of the town a frustration for the characters? In what ways was it an asset?

12. With the end of Luke and Harper's story, what do you think will happen to the rest of the Anderson sisters and Annie?

YOUR
BOOK
CLUB
RESOURCE

VISIT
GCPClubCar.com

to sign up for the **GCP Club Car** newsletter, featuring exclusive promotions, info on other **Club Car** titles, and more.

 @grandcentralpub

 @grandcentralpub

 @grandcentralpub

About the Author

Alys Murray writes novels for the romantic in all of us. Born and raised in New Orleans, she received her BFA from NYU's Tisch School of the Arts and her master's in film studies from King's College London. She loves black-and-white movies, baseball games that go into extra innings, and reminding people that Michael Bay has two films in the Criterion Collection.